Acclaim for the Marko Zorn Series

BLACK SUN RISING

"Robert B. Parker meets David Baldacci as the irresistible and brilliant Marko Zorn navigates this political noir, where individual determination and bravery battle the dark powers of destruction—and readers will gasp with the hairbreadth distance from reality. This is total immersion storytelling—revealing what happens when the stakes are impossibly high, and the only weapons available are loyalty, honor, and justice."

—Hank Phillippi Ryan, *USA Today* bestselling author

"A scorching tale [and] breathless non-stop thrill ride.... Forget about the old cliché 'ripped from the headlines.'... Here is a brilliant, bracing and blistering book that may predict them instead."

—Jon Land, *New York Times* and *USA Today* bestselling author

"Has all the elements: mystery, chills and characters [that] completely engross ... [Eskin] tells his story with a unique voice that's equally seductive. I loved it!"

—Heather Graham, *New York Times* and *USA Today* bestselling author

"A terrorist attack of an LGBTQ headquarters in DC sends Detective Marko Zorn fleeing danger at every turn as he hunts for an international crime syndicate threatening another attack. Kudos to Otho Eskin for keeping the reader on the edge of the seat until the last bloody page. Zorn gives Jack Reacher a run for the money in *Black Sun Rising*."
—Jodé Millman, award-winning author of the Queen City Crimes series

"Detective Marko Zorn is at his eccentric best ... exactly the kind of anti-hero readers can't help but cheer for."
—Amy Pease, acclaimed author of *Northwoods*

"A fast-moving thriller by a master of intelligence secrets. You will not be able to put it down unfinished."
—Mike Bond, author of *Crude: Ukraine, Oil, and Nuclear War*

"A web of intrigue that feels all too real in today's political climate.... Smart, relentless, and full of edge-of-your-seat suspense."
—Ed Fuller, co-author of the Red Hotel series

FIRETRAP

"*Firetrap* has everything a reader could want in a great mystery—police forensics, action, and a thoroughly compelling protagonist. Otho Eskin is the real deal!"
—Ward Larsen, *USA Today* bestselling author

"High-energy game of cat-and-mouse ... that offers plenty of thrills."
—*Publishers Weekly*

"Zorn gets it done, legally or otherwise. . . . Eskin keeps this plot moving with his foot slammed to the accelerator."
—*Men Reading Books*

HEAD SHOT

"This chilling political thriller is wonderfully textured with a high-stakes emotional drama—and I could not turn the pages fast enough. *Head Shot* is instantly cinematic—and completely entertaining!"
—Hank Phillippi Ryan, *USA Today* bestselling author

"This is a thinking man's thriller that would make David Baldacci or Brad Meltzer proud. And Zorn is one of the most unique and colorful voices in thriller fiction today."
—Jon Land, *New York Times* and *USA Today* bestselling author

THE REFLECTING POOL

"Rough and ragged as the world it so vividly creates, *The Reflecting Pool* crackles with twists and turns, making for a fun and heady combination of suspense and intrigue."
—Steve Berry, *New York Times* bestselling author

"First-person action mixes with hardboiled political noir in Eskin's debut novel [*The Reflecting Pool*] ... Urban warfare, assassination plots, and political intrigue converge in one bombastic climax."
—*Suspense Magazine*

BLACK SUN RISING

Also by Otho Eskin

OTHO ESKIN

BLACK SUN RISING

A MARKO ZORN NOVEL

MERIDIAN EDITIONS
WESTPORT, CONNECTICUT

MERIDIAN | EDITIONS

Published by Meridian Editions
Westport, Connecticut

ISBN (paperback): 978-1-959170-23-5
ISBN (hardcover): 978-1-959170-24-2
ISBN (ebook): 978-1-959170-25-9

Cover and book design by John Lotte

Manufactured in the United States of America

FOR
CHARLOTTE, RAPHI, FIONA, CHRISTOPHER,
MEGAN, JOSHUA, JACOB

BLACK SUN RISING

PART ONE

Chapter One

THE BOMB EXPLODES AT 8:42 A.M.

Windows rattle. The Homicide Branch bullpen shivers. Two detectives across the room look up from their coffees and Danish. Latasha Powell, my new partner, rises to her feet. The Style section from today's *Washington Post* lies open on her desk, the crossword puzzle partially filled in.

Latasha's cool. Nothing rattles her or dampens her sunny disposition, but for the moment, she's tense. She looks at me as if I have an answer.

I've experienced explosions before. I know the sound. I know the feel under my feet. The feel in the air. My heart sinks. "That came from far away." I keep my voice calm, reassuring. No point in panicking people. Not yet.

We're in no immediate danger, but this brings back *that* memory: The burning of the Pentagon, the horrific destruction of the Twin Towers in New York, and how close we came to the destruction of the United States Capitol Building just a few blocks from where we are right now. Everyone who was in Washington that day knows the feeling. If there's an explosion somewhere, the sound of a low-flying plane, or sirens wailing over the city, we stop whatever we're doing, and we wonder: *Is this it? Is the city under attack?*

There's no need to evacuate our building. We are, for the

moment, safe. But I know others somewhere in the city aren't. This was a massive explosion. There will be casualties.

We wait, breathless.

The building alarm goes off, shattering the silence. Red emergency lights pulse throughout the bullpen. There's a citywide emergency now. Outside, sirens shriek over the city.

"Let's go!" I yell to the detectives. "Collect your gear. Coats, hats. It's cold out there. Bring your weapons."

"What's happening, Marko?" Latasha says, securing her police-service Glock 26 in her belt holster.

Latasha knows I never carry a gun. But she doesn't question me. She knows that refusing to use a gun is personal for me. It's complicated.

"Something bad. Something very bad," I say.

"We'll get through this," she says. "We're a team, Marko. Right?"

The corridors are filling with people, mostly in uniform, mostly armed, shrugging into their heavy winter coats, putting on gloves and hats. Latasha and I take the stairs. The elevators are too slow and crowded. When we reach the ground floor, Frank Townsend, commander of the Homicide Branch and our boss, is organizing the troops, getting police officers onto waiting buses. There's no time to ask what happened or where we're going. Nobody knows anything. We're all operating on adrenaline and years of training.

The sky is gunmetal gray, promising more snow, and we button up our coats tightly. The air is filling with acrid smoke, and flecks of ash burn our eyes. Alarm sirens throughout the city deafen us, and Latasha puts her hands over her ears to muffle the sound.

And then the sirens stop.

Chapter Two

A BUS FILLED with armed SWAT units pulls away. Latasha and I board a second bus—green, with DC Metropolitan Police painted on the side. We sit in the front as we leave headquarters.

Latasha is tense but in control. She's a young Black woman, usually calm and upbeat. Before joining the Metropolitan Police, Latasha served in the Army military police and has been my partner for less than three months. She's been a full-time homicide detective for only two years, but what she lacks in experience, she more than makes up in smarts and determination. I can see worry in her eyes. She's scared. We all are.

The bus takes us into the southwest part of the city not far from the waterfront on the Potomac River. We're stopped at a police checkpoint several blocks from the site of the emergency, and a senior sergeant checks our credentials.

"Marko Zorn. Homicide." I show him my police ID, and he waves me through.

Latasha follows, and we go the rest of the way on foot, trudging through the snow from last night's storm. A police captain organizes us into groups. Because we're from Homicide, Latasha and I are sent directly to the site.

We're frozen in horror. Before us, a large building is partially collapsing in black smoke and flames. The front of the building is a gaping, smoking hole. Whole floors are exposed.

"God in heaven," Latasha whispers. She has a hard time speaking. Her eyes glisten with tears.

Until a short while ago, this was Friendship House, a sanctuary for the poor and desperate. At the beginning, it was mostly used by African Americans in need of food and shelter and medical help, but is now used by immigrants, too. More recently, it's become a temporary home for runaway kids and for members of the LGBTQ+ community—for any desperate or marginalized person in need of help.

I've visited this place before and twice met with Dolores Pine, the founder and director of Friendship House. She's a tall, imposing Black woman and the only person I've ever met whom I'd describe as a saint. Of course, in my line of work, I don't get to meet many saints.

I think about those who were inside the building when the bomb went off and I feel like I'm going to be sick. But I've got work to do. I'll throw up on my own time.

Firefighters are pouring water from coiling black hoses onto the flaming ruins while emergency medical workers remove the dead and injured. Those who managed to escape the inferno lie crumpled and broken on the sidewalk and street. As we near the bomb site, another part of the building collapses in flames.

Latasha briefly squeezes my hand. To reassure herself that we would be okay? To reassure me? Then she's gone, rushing into the crowd to help the medics and injured.

More police and firefighters are arriving from other parts of the city and from surrounding jurisdictions. Helicopters appear in the sky to patrol the area and to medevac the wounded. My eyes sting from the smoke.

Surrounding me are people yelling, some screaming in pain, some asking for help. Some weeping. Many lie stiffly on the ground, in the snow, silent. Their bodies are smeared with soot and smoke and blood.

I stop for a moment near the wreck of what must have been a truck. The panels and windows have been blown out. All that's left is the twisted steel frame and the bent driveshaft.

I move through the scene in front of the destroyed building, helping where I can. I join an EMS group taking bodies across the street into a temporary shelter. Many victims are dressed in street clothes. One dead woman is still clutching her handbag. A young man, who looks Hispanic, is holding a brown paper bag in his fist. His lunch? He'll never get to eat it.

I trip over a scorched and twisted wheelchair. More ambulances arrive. People in scrubs rush through the crowd. Dr. Celia Moore, the police department's assistant medical officer, hurries by. We nod to each other but don't stop. There's no time for words.

I spot Latasha standing near a temporary emergency shelter, her face and arms smeared with black soot and spattered with dark-brown stains. Over her shoulder, I see the United States Capitol Building, with its reviewing stands under construction for the presidential inauguration only weeks away. Above, the sky is dark and foreboding. Snow is coming. An icy wind picks up.

More helicopters are arriving. Police. Media. Medical emergency vehicles. Several military craft circle at a distance.

One large chopper lands in a vacant lot a few hundred yards away. The hatch is flung open, steps lowered, and six heavily armed uniformed men and women leap out, forming a phalanx around the ramp. They're followed by a man in a three-piece suit; he's wearing glasses and carrying an umbrella. Finally, a tall, gaunt woman emerges and is helped down the steps by the guy in glasses. She's immediately joined by DC Police Chief Kelly Flynn and, a moment later, by Carla Lowry, the head of the FBI's National Security Branch. They stand close to one another and talk urgently among themselves.

The press corps, their trucks and vans encrusted with TV antennas, is pressed behind temporary wooden barriers.

Snow begins to fall. Big flakes, white and wet, and, for a moment, the carnage at Friendship House lies hidden beneath a blanket of snow. The ground soon becomes a sea of mud and ash.

The air is shattered by the sound of squawking feedback from a public address system a few hundred feet away from me. The mayor is about to give a press briefing. I can't see her from where I stand, but I can hear her clearly. Her voice is full of rage and grief. She speaks of the horrific event that has just happened and she extends thoughts and prayers for the victims and their families. "I promise, my administration will use every resource to bring those responsible to justice. Chief of Police Flynn has committed the full resources of the Metropolitan Police Department to investigate this crime. I spoke by phone with the president just a few moments ago, and he has promised the full support of the federal government to investigate this tragic event. Agents of the FBI and the Bureau of Alcohol, Tobacco, Firearms and Explosives are already on the scene. Secretary Fletcher of the Department of Homeland Security is here and has committed the full cooperation of her agency."

The mayor turns the press conference over to Police Chief Flynn.

"At approximately 8:45 this morning, a bomb exploded in front of Friendship House. It has basically destroyed the building and caused multiple deaths and injuries. We do not yet have the number of injured or the fatalities, but our initial estimate is that there will be several hundred. Many of the wounded are in critical condition and they are being taken to local hospitals. More information about the number and names of those killed or wounded will be provided as soon as available."

Flynn's voice is measured, intended to reassure the people here in Washington, around the nation, and around the world. Her job is to convince them that everything is under control and that there's no need to panic.

"We have no information about who the perpetrators of this horrendous act are and no information about their motivation, but we are certain this was an act of domestic terror. It is clear that this tragedy was carefully planned and intended to inflict the maximum damage possible. This was not just an attack on property. This was an attack on people."

Flynn turns to one of the men standing behind her. "Leonard Silver from the ATF will provide what details there are."

He describes the explosives and the truck they were packed in. An FBI agent whose name I don't catch says his agency is devoting full resources to the investigation. There have been no known threats against Friendship House.

Bottom line: No one knows anything—or, if they do they're not saying.

Other speakers take the microphone, but I miss what they say. I'm distracted by something else.

Carla Lowry, from the FBI, and Chief of Police Kelly Flynn are in deep conversation with the tall woman who arrived on the white helicopter. The three women turn and stare. But not at the mayor. Not at Friendship House. They're staring at me. Carla Lowry seems to be pointing at me while she speaks urgently to the tall woman. This can't be good. Then they're lost among the surging crowd of medical personnel and police. It's snowing heavily now.

I know there's nothing I can do here to help the dead and dying. But there is one thing I can do. I don't know who did this horror, but my instincts tell me there's someone in the crowd connected to the bomb, someone watching this minute. I know what they're feeling. What they're thinking. This bomb attack took weeks of careful planning. You don't just walk away from the scene you've been dreaming of. You need to see it up close. How many people did you kill today? How many have you wounded and maimed? Of course, you can learn the details later on the news or online. But that's not the same as seeing the carnage with your own eyes. Feeling the heat from the flames. Hearing the screams of the wounded. The TV isn't enough. People who do this need immediate gratification.

I'm certain that at least one of the people who planted the bomb is somewhere nearby, in the crowd, watching. Listening. Maybe they're only a few feet from where I'm standing. They'll be just behind the yellow police tape, close enough to see the horror. Close enough to hear the announcements from the mayor and public officials. Maybe close enough to see the dead and wounded loaded into ambulances. With any luck, they're close enough to hear the cries of their victims. Maybe even get some good pictures.

I walk along the yellow police tape, staring into the crowd. What am I looking for? I'm not sure, but I'll know when I see it. I study the faces of dozens of onlookers. Clusters of people are gathered to watch—to experience—the horror, many taking pictures with their smartphones. Probably most are from the neighborhood. Maybe some are ghouls who monitor the police band radio and are here for the thrill. They always show up.

At least one of them is here with a mission.

At first, I see nothing unusual. There's a group of high-school kids, two elderly couples looking dazed. Some middle-aged men in business suits, maybe on their way to a meeting, clutching expensive briefcases. Three Black ladies staring in shock. One seems to be praying silently. A woman with white hair. A small crowd of teenage boys holding skateboards. A couple of men pressing against the yellow tape, glancing quickly at their cell phones. All of them are watching Friendship House collapse into a fiery heap.

Then I spot him. I know in my bones I've got my man.

A single white male, wearing a blue hoodie pulled over his head, is speaking into a cell phone. Every moment or so, he points the phone camera toward the burning ruins, medics, and police. He takes a picture, then quickly resumes speaking. He's talking urgently. I know absolutely the man in the hoodie is the one I'm looking for.

He's young, in his twenties. A little chunky with a round baby face and full lips. He's wearing large headphones.

I duck under the yellow police tape and walk up close. His eyes are pale gray and bright with excitement. He looks like a hundred other losers I see on the streets every day. There's a sour expression on his face. He's wearing mustard-colored

Air Jordan high-top sneakers. I've seen them before. On dead bodies at the police morgue. The sneakers are the kind of footwear you kill for. Or die for. They're kind of unforgettable.

The man talks intensely but softly into his phone and pays no attention to me as I approach. I know the fucker is reporting the carnage to somebody. Maybe others higher up in his group are listening, celebrating their triumph.

"Did you get a good look?" I say.

He doesn't hear me because of the headphones.

I pull them from his head. "Are you happy now?"

Rage and fear distort his face. He drops his smartphone into the snow. "Fuck off, asshole," he says, whining.

"Now that's rude." I grab him by the lapels of his coat. He struggles to escape, but I have a firm grip. I look into his pale, dead eyes. "I'm the police. Talk to me."

"You can't make me."

"Wanna bet?"

There's a look of feral terror in his eyes. He glances over my shoulder as if searching for help. Who's he looking for?

"I'm arresting you on suspicion of multiple murders."

"You can't do that." He struggles to twist out of my grasp. "You'll be sorry if you do."

"Who's going to make me sorry, you piece of shit?"

"Black Sun," he says in a gasp, almost inaudible. "Black Sun will smite you.

Smite?

"Black Sun is watching you right now." He's almost breathless. With excitement? Terror? "Cyclone has come. Our time has come."

Next thing I know, I'm on the ground, my face in the cold, wet snow. I struggle to my feet. I can't seem to focus.

"You okay, mister?" a woman asks. I think it may be the lady with the white hair. She offers her hand to help me stand. The man in the mustard-colored high-tops is gone. I touch the back of my head. It's sticky with blood.

There's no point in going after him. I'm seeing double and I'd just stumble and fall and embarrass myself. I search for the dropped phone, but it's gone. Someone has already taken it. I gather snow and rub it on the back of my head. That doesn't help.

I found the man I was looking for. And now I've lost him. Not my finest hour.

There's nothing more for me to do here. Now it's up to ATF, the medics, and mortuary personnel to do their jobs and the bomb experts to complete the investigation. The press is leaving with their trucks and vans. Another news day. The helicopter that brought the tall woman has gone.

"We're going to find out who did this," Latasha says when we meet. "We're going to see they're brought to justice."

Some of her optimistic enthusiasm is rubbing off on me, softening my standard cynicism. Maybe a bit. "Sure," I say. "We'll find them."

Someone calls my name. I tell Latasha to go on ahead and meet me at the office.

Carla Lowry, the head of the FBI's National Security Branch, is waiting for me a few yards away, standing next to a black SUV guarded by two big men, obviously FBI security. Carla steps away from the SUV so we can speak in private and pulls her coat tightly around her shoulders.

"Carla, have you seen the casualty list? Dolores Pine, the Director. I was wondering ..."

Carla's face clouds over. "Dolores didn't make it."

"Shit. I didn't think it could get any worse."

"I'm afraid it's going to get even worse. I hear you tried to arrest someone, and you let him get away. That was careless." Her two bodyguards watch us from a distance.

"Do you know what's going on here?"

She shakes her head.

"Did you get any warning?"

"Nothing. Liz Fletcher may know something. But I don't."

"Who's Liz Fletcher?"

"The Secretary of Homeland Security. Don't you read the papers?"

"Is she the lady with the helicopter?"

"Yes. And she wants to see you in her office this afternoon."

"Why?"

"She wouldn't tell me. Only that it was important she speak to you in person. A word of warning, Marko. Don't mess with her. She's a major player in this town. Everybody's afraid of her."

"I can take care of myself."

"It's that attitude that always gets you in trouble. And she's already taken a personal dislike to you."

"We've never met. How can she already dislike me?"

"For the same reason so many powerful people in Washington dislike you, Marko. Be nice when you meet her. I know that's hard for you, but please try. And no jokes. She doesn't have a sense of humor. For once, don't be a dick."

"What's really going on?"

"I'm sorry, Marko, I can't explain. There've been some developments I'm not free to talk to you about."

Carla reaches out and briefly squeezes my arm. "Marko, be careful. Don't do anything stupid, please."

Chapter Three

WHEN I RETURN to police headquarters, Latasha is waiting for me at her desk in the Homicide bullpen. I'm relieved to see she's in full control of her emotions. She's strong, but I worry about her. She's a straight arrow—a person with strong principles. Sometimes those are the ones who break when they experience something as devastating as we did this morning at Friendship House. People with no principles can take these experiences in stride. They bend easier. I should know.

"What you saw today was a terrible shock, Latasha," I say. "Don't let it get to you. If you need time to process what happened, take a few days off. Spend time with your family. Talk to your friends. Take care of your cats. I'll cover for you here."

Latasha looks at me as if I were speaking Chinese. "I can't take time off. You and I have a major crime to investigate."

Latasha wears a hairstyle that first upset some of the older detectives. Me, too, if I'm being honest. I guess that makes me an older detective. She shaves her head so she's totally bald. At first sight, it's a shock. The other detectives said it was unprofessional. They meant it was too ethnic. But she's so charming and smart and has such a winning smile the other detectives don't make comments anymore. At least not in my presence. Most of them came around when she proved herself a good cop, and I've grown to like her appearance—or, at least, I hardly notice it.

"You know what the bastards did?" she says. "Friendship House had a daycare center. The terrorists parked their fucking van with the bomb just outside the center, meaning the center took the full force of the blast. There's nothing left. Nothing! Those were little kids, Marko. What kind of person could do that? I'll never be able to unsee it." She takes a deep, ragged breath.

"We'll get them. I promise you." I wish I was as certain as I sound.

"You've got ash in your hair, Marko."

"You would, too, if you had any hair. It's all over both of us." I run my hand over my head to get rid of some of the ash.

"It makes you look quite distinguished." She leans in for a closer look. "And you're bleeding." Latasha examines the back of my head. "What happened to you?"

"I tried to interview a man I think was involved in the bombing. He took offense when I questioned him, and I was coldcocked before I could get any answers."

"Did he say anything?"

"He made no sense. Said Black Sun would smite me."

"That's it?"

"He said Cyclone has come. Our time has come."

"What did you just say?"

"I said I tried to question a man—"

"I mean the word you just said. 'Cyclone.' Are you sure he said 'Cyclone'?"

"I'm sure. 'Black Sun will smite me.' Does that mean anything to you? It makes no sense to me. Sounds almost biblical."

Latasha picks up the copy of the *Washington Post* Style

section lying open on her desk. "Look at this. At the cross-word puzzle."

I know Latasha is a crossword puzzle fanatic. In fact, she's a fanatic about every kind of word game. I've spent enough time with her on stakeouts to know. She's good at these things. So good she does the crosswords in ink, which I find annoying. I do crosswords in pencil, usually with lots of erasures and incomplete boxes.

"What's special about this puzzle?"

"Look at the clue for sixteen across."

I hesitate before I put on my reading glasses. I'm vain and don't like to wear glasses in the bullpen. It invites ridicule. But if I'm going to read the damn clue, I must.

The clue reads, "Winds rotating counterclockwise in the South China Sea."

"Okay, how is this relevant?"

"It's obvious," Latasha says. "It has to be 'cyclone.' That's the word the man you tried to arrest used, isn't it?"

"All right."

"It has to be 'cyclone'—although there are too few spaces. You need seven spaces. There are only six spaces in today's puzzle. I was working on the damn thing when the bomb went off. I've solved most of the puzzle, but I'm stuck on sixteen across."

"What's your point?"

"Do you think there could be a connection between what that man said to you and the clue in today's puzzle?"

"I don't see how. Maybe you read too many detective novels. Killers don't often leave hidden clues. This is not an Agatha Christie mystery."

"We'll see." Latasha puts the puzzle page back on her desk. I can see she's not convinced. She's young and enthusiastic and she thinks I'm jaded. Maybe I am. Maybe I've been in the business too long.

"You should see a doctor," she says.

"I'm busy."

"You may have a concussion. You should look after yourself."

"I need to get the description of my suspect into the system." I sit at my desk and type up the incident report on my desk computer. I'm slow. I use only two fingers when I type. I was the despair of Mrs. Coleman's typing class in grade school. And my computer makes lots of typos.

Maybe the man in the mustard-colored sneakers was on drugs and simply didn't want to get busted. Maybe he was just a guy who doesn't like cops. There are a lot of those around. Looking back on the incident, I can see it all seems speculative, maybe even implausible. I didn't see the man do anything illegal. He was just looking at the effects of an explosion. Like hundreds of others. It is all guesswork and intuition.

But right now, that's all I have to go on, and I trust my intuition. I type out a description of the man I tried to arrest in as much detail as I can, not forgetting the Air Jordan sneakers. I include the words the man said to me—"Black Sun will smite you," "Black Sun is watching you," and, finally, "Cyclone has come," and "Our time has come." I decide not to include the word "cyclone" in today's crossword puzzle. That's too speculative for a police report.

While I type, Latasha wipes the back of my head with a cloth. "This is going to hurt," she says as she rubs alcohol into the wound. She's right. It does hurt. "You really ought to see a doctor. Can I get you an aspirin?"

The door to the squad room opens and Frank Townsend, chief of the Homicide Branch, looks in. "Come with me, Marko. You're needed upstairs."

I follow Frank to an upper floor of police headquarters, and we enter one of the department's conference rooms, already full, mostly with department chiefs and senior sergeants. At one end of the room is a long table and sitting at the table is Chief Kelly Flynn. Frank takes a seat next to her. I find an empty seat at the back of the room. The ache in my head has settled into a steady throbbing, and I wish I'd accepted Latasha's offer of an aspirin.

"This was clearly a deliberate act of terror," Chief Flynn is saying. "Carefully planned and executed. ATF's preliminary examination indicates the explosion was caused by ammonium nitrate mixed with aviation fuel packed in metal containers. Small pieces of metal, including screws and bolts, were mixed into the explosive. It was designed to do as much damage as possible to human targets. This was not the act of some disgruntled amateur. ATF is confident it was professional."

"Has anyone claimed responsibility?" someone in the audience asks.

Flynn nods to Frank Townsend.

"No. We're monitoring every crazy site on the web. The right-wing sites are going bonkers over this incident, but no one has taken credit for it. There isn't even any speculation as to who actually made and detonated the bomb, which is unusual. We've picked up internet chatter about the bombing that suggests it was connected to a group known as 'werewolves.' They're part of an anti-government extremist movement calling for the overthrow of the United

States Government. But so far, they've made no claim of responsibility."

The police officers in the room scribble into their notebooks.

Flynn looks out over the assembled troops. "Does the name 'werewolf' mean anything to anyone here?"

Several members of the crowd nod and say they've heard the name.

"Have your men ask about anyone known as 'werewolf,'" Flynn says. "I want all of you and your staff to search for that name. Talk to your contacts, to your snitches. Anybody who may have connections with extremist political groups. We've got to find out who or what 'werewolf' means before they act again."

This is followed by several moments of desultory exchange of comments and questions, leading nowhere.

"While I have you all here," Flynn says, "I have a further announcement. As you know, the next president of the United States will be sworn in on the steps of the Capitol in less than three weeks. This, as usual, will involve massive security headaches here in Washington. The Secret Service is the lead agency in this operation, and the Metropolitan Police will have a major support role. You've already been instructed on your responsibilities for that day—for you personally and for your divisions. I've been informed just this morning by the Secretary of Homeland Security that certain new developments of a very sensitive nature have increased the threat level to the president-elect. I want each of you to review your threat plans. Look for weaknesses. Look for gaps. I want daily reports on what you're doing."

"Has anybody thought to cancel the inauguration ceremonies?" Townsend says. "The ceremony could be held indoors instead, in a secure area. Holding it outdoors on the reviewing stand in front of thousands of people is just plain crazy. And can we cancel the damn parade?"

"God, I wish they'd change the venue," Flynn says. "The Secret Service is consulting with the president-elect. From what I hear, he's adamant about not changing the plans. He says he will not be bullied by some right-wing bozos. He insists on having an outdoor inauguration. And he wants the parade."

A hand is raised. It's a senior sergeant from street patrol. "Does this increased threat relate to the Friendship House incident?"

"There's no reason to think so. Friendship House is totally nonpolitical."

My gut tells me Flynn is wrong.

The conference breaks up, and participants return to their offices to carry out the chief's instructions. I stay behind.

"Marko, I need a word." Flynn stops where I'm sitting. "I want you to take the lead in investigating the bombing. Ignore any other cases you're working on right now. Friendship House has priority over everything else."

"Got it."

"What about your partner?"

"What about her?"

"I know Latasha's turning into a good cop. She shows great promise but she's young and inexperienced. You need a senior detective to work with you on this case."

"I want to keep Latasha. She's learned to adjust to my eccentricities. I don't want to have to break in a new partner."

"We're dealing with domestic terrorists. Dangerous people. We need to use the best talent in the department. I know you're loyal to your partners, but this bombing is a special case."

"I want to keep Latasha as my partner. If she doesn't get experience she'll never learn. I want Latasha for this case."

What I don't say is that I sometimes need Latasha's positive optimism to keep me going.

Flynn sighs, admitting defeat. "If you insist."

"I insist."

"Marko, do you have anything to add to what I was telling the troops? I'm assuming the bombing was a warning."

"Not a warning. A signal."

"A signal? For what?"

"I don't know yet, but I'm certain the terror bombing was meant to be a signal for something that's going to happen."

"What makes you think so?"

"I know it in my bones."

Flynn winces. She's always uncomfortable when I mention trusting my gut instincts. Although she's reluctantly grown to trust my instincts, she's uncomfortable when I talk about them. She's afraid they reveal something about me—something she doesn't really want to know. And probably something I don't want to know either.

"We haven't heard the last of this terrorist group," I say. "No group is taking credit for the bombing. No one is making demands. There's no manifesto on the internet. That makes no sense. That's not the way terrorist groups operate. There's a reason for the bombing and we better find out what that reason is. It's a signal for something much worse to come."

"God, I hope you're wrong."

I shut up. There's no point in overthinking. "It's just a guess," I say. "And I'm probably wrong." I want to reassure her. It's a little late for that.

I return to the squad room and check to see if there's anything about my missing witness with the mustard high-tops. Nothing. I'll have to do it the hard way and find the bastard myself. For a second, I wonder whether the crossword puzzle clue could have anything to do with my missing guy. *Nah*.

Latasha settles into her desk. "I just spoke with Chief Flynn," I say. "She wants you and me to take the lead in the bombing investigation."

Latasha breaks into a broad smile. "That's great! That means she has confidence in us as a team. We'll do it. We'll prove to her that her confidence in us isn't misplaced." Latasha studies my face, trying to read my thoughts. She senses my doubts. "Isn't it great?"

I don't want to discourage Latasha's enthusiasm. I have a feeling I'm going to need all the positive vibes I can get.

"Sure, Latasha. We'll do it. You and me, we can do it."

She smiles, relieved. "I have a new idea. The perpetrators of the Friendship House bombing made a serious mistake. I'm sure of it. That clue in the crossword puzzle. Cyclone. I know you don't believe there's a connection, but I'd like to check it out. I want to find out who placed that clue in the paper."

"Go for it. We don't have many leads."

A uniformed cop stops at my desk. "Are you Detective Zorn?" he asks. "There was a telephone call for you. We tried to hand it off to Public Affairs, but the caller insisted on talking to you personally. Considering who it was, we decided to give you the message in person." The cop passes me a standard telephone message form with the name of the caller, Cosmo Hunter, and a phone number. Plus two words.

"Who's Cosmo Hunter?"

Latasha turns and stares at me. "Jesus, Marko. You don't know who Cosmo Hunter is?"

"Should I?"

"He's a gazillionaire. One of the richest men in the world. A titan of Big Tech."

"I don't mix with that crowd."

"Honestly, Marko … He's world-famous—a mover and shaker in Silicon Valley and has developed most of today's cutting-edge computer technology."

"Never heard of him."

"He owns and operates half the communications satellites in space."

"How do you know all this?"

"I read *People* magazine. This man owns a global high-tech empire. Computer stuff. Talk to the man."

"I'm not in the market for a new cell phone."

"The man designed most of the electronic devices on your desk."

"Can he tell me how to block junk mail?"

"He's dating Joni Ludlow, the most famous pop singer on earth. You must have seen their pictures at the Met Gala. He's a world-class celebrity. Marko, call the man!" Latasha is losing patience with me.

I know I must make the call. The message, in addition to the telephone number, includes two words: "Friendship House."

When I call, the phone rings twice and a gentle voice says, "Detective Zorn?"

"Yes."

"I'm Cosmo Hunter. You don't know me," he says, "but I know you, and I know we have much in common. We have to talk."

For a moment, I'm disoriented. I expected some assistant or flunky to answer. Instead, I'm speaking to the man himself.

"If you say so."

"I must speak with you in person. Just the two of us."

"I'm busy just now. I don't have the time to fly to wherever it is you are."

"Of course not. I wouldn't dream of asking you to take time away from your investigation. Can we meet this afternoon?"

"I have another appointment."

"The one with Liz Fletcher?"

How in hell does he know about that?

"My driver will pick you up at the Department of Homeland Security at 2:45. Liz will be finished with you by then. My driver will bring you to my home. Will that be satisfactory, Detective Zorn?"

"How do you know my appointment with Secretary Fletcher will be over by 2:45?"

"Trust me."

Chapter Four

THE OFFICE of the Secretary of Homeland Security is large and airy, with expensive furniture and pictures on the walls, all pastel landscapes—nothing abstract or threatening. Windows look out over the campus of what were once the grounds of Washington's St. Elizabeths mental hospital. A fake fire burns in a fake fireplace. The dominant piece of furniture in the room is a carved, polished oak desk. I'm disappointed to see no top-secret documents lying on the desktop. No red phone with a direct connection to the White House or the Joint Chiefs of Staff. There's nothing on the desktop except a copy of today's *Washington Post* crossword puzzle.

Waiting for me in the room are two people. One is a slender man wearing glasses, his hair parted in the middle—never a good sign. He's the one I saw yesterday holding an umbrella in the snow.

The other is a tall, gaunt woman who's half sitting, half leaning in front of the oak desk with her arms crossed. She studies me intently. And not in a friendly way. She's the lady I saw at the scene of the bombing. The one with the contingent of armed guards and the white helicopter.

The young man with the eyeglasses whispers something into the lady's ear, doubtless to tell her who the hell I am and why she should waste her valuable time talking to me. No introductions are made. I'm left to assume I'm in the presence of the formidable Liz Fletcher, Secretary of Homeland Security.

"You're Marko Zorn," she announces. It's not a question. She makes it sound like an accusation. I'm tempted to say, "Guilty," but I remember in time. No jokes. No sarcasm. Don't be a smart-ass.

"You're a police detective."

"I'm a cop. In the Homicide Branch of the Metropolitan Police Department."

"Are you any good at your job?"

"I haven't been fired recently."

She rolls her eyes. "My staff tells me ..." She looks at the man with glasses. "... you abhor violence. That makes you useless as a policeman."

"I faint at the sight of blood."

She makes a disgusted grimace. "I'm told you're insubordinate and a troublemaker. You play by your own rules. You don't respect authority. 'You don't play well with others' is the way you've been described to me. I don't know why Police Chief Flynn puts up with you."

"Neither do I."

"I know all about you," Fletcher says. "And what I know does not impress me. Chief Flynn tells me you're a star of Washington's Metropolitan Police Department. Or was it the dark star? I can't seem to remember which. You're a badass, and you associate with notorious criminals. You're engaged in numerous side hustles. You're a hustler. I don't like hustlers. I think you have a criminal mind."

"It's one theory," I say. "It's true I sometimes steal food

from the common refrigerator in the police squad room, and I've been known to fudge on my income tax returns."

"During some of your police investigations, you make deals with known criminals. Instead of arresting them, you let them go."

"I do whatever serves the interests of justice."

"Do you think you have the right to make that decision?"

"Yes, ma'am. I do."

"Don't be impertinent. You're here to get your orders. Is that understood? When you were at the scene of the terrorist attack, you arrested a man. Is that correct?"

"I tried. He escaped."

"Did this suspect speak to you?"

How in hell does she know about that?

"He warned me not to arrest him."

"Did he threaten you?"

"He said I'd be sorry if I made the arrest."

"That's it? That's all he said?" She smiles an arctic smile.

"That's all he said." I don't know why I don't give her a straight answer. But my instincts kick in—lie whenever possible.

"Do you know why you're here?"

"You invited me."

"Don't be a smart-ass," she says.

"Are you a friend of Cosmo Hunter's?"

Her face flushes. "That's irrelevant."

"But you do what he says. Am I right?"

"He owns much of the technology on which modern society depends. He operates half the fucking communications satellites in space. He could shut us all down if he wanted to."

"Good to know."

"Cosmo has nothing to do with our meeting this afternoon."

"If you say so. Then why are we meeting?"

"Our country is facing a major national crisis. The IDCC has even been convened."

She shuts her mouth abruptly; a pained expression crosses her face. She's just made a serious mistake. That IDCC acronym was not supposed to be heard by innocent ears such as mine. I usually get lost in the thicket of government bureaucratic acronyms, but even I've heard of the IDCC. It's a secret committee that appears nowhere on any government organization chart. A committee that doesn't exist, chaired by the president of the United States, except he never attends (he's too busy) and sends the vice president instead. Which is the same as sending nobody.

The Chairman of the Joint Chiefs sends a colonel. The Secretary of State sends an Assistant Secretary of State for Intelligence and Research. The FBI Director sends the head of the Bureau's National Security Branch—which turns out to be Carla Lowry. That's the only reason I know of the existence of the IDCC. Other Cabinet secretaries send whatever free bodies are around. Fletcher attends regularly in person, rather than sending Mr. Peepers here to keep an eye on other departments and to intervene if the hobbits get out of line.

The IDCC was established by an Act of Congress soon after the 9/11 terrorist attack. Its purpose was to prevent another intelligence failure and to ensure a coordinated response to any threat to national security. Since the time it was established, there have been several catastrophic intelligence failures which jeopardized national security. None appeared on the agenda of the IDCC. The committee has a generous budget, a dedicated professional staff, and agreeable digs in a secure office building in Arlington, Virginia. Like so many government committees established long ago, it does nothing and serves no useful function, and few people can remember its purpose.

Ms. Fletcher swallows hard, hoping I didn't hear what she just said about a committee that doesn't exist, has no members, and never meets. "The US government was informed two days ago by the German Federal Intelligence Service that a neo-Nazi organization is engaged in a plot to assassinate the president of the United States on Inauguration Day. Britain's MI6 and the French General Directorate for External Security have picked up similar reports. This appears to be a coordinated international operation. This information is strictly close hold. You are not to share what you have just heard here with anybody. Is that clear?"

"Then why are you telling me?"

"Do you think you can manage not to tell anybody what I have just told you? Because if you do screw up, I will hear about it, and I'll see to it you are charged with a felony. No gossip with your drinking buddies at the bar this evening. Do you understand what I'm saying? Or am I talking too fast for you?"

"I understand you perfectly. I still don't know why I'm here."

"Because it's essential that we find out who is behind this assassination plot."

"Why ask me?"

"Do you know Robert Grant?"

"I served under General Grant many years ago."

"I've read your military file. Impressive. Except for the parts DOD decided I shouldn't read. You know that your friend, General Grant, is vice president–elect of the United States. He, along with the new president, Emmanuel Lawrence, will be sworn into office in a few weeks."

"For the record, General Grant was my commanding officer. Not my friend. We haven't seen one another in years."

"If you're not his friend, why does General Grant insist you be attached to his security detail?"

"I have no idea. Ask him."

"I have," Fletcher says. "Don't you think it strange he wants you on his security detail when he once wanted to have you court-martialed?"

"I think it's very strange," I say. "But I long ago gave up trying to understand the minds of general officers."

"My staff warned me about people like you."

"Maybe you misunderstood the general."

"Don't be obnoxious, Zorn. Remember to whom you're speaking. I never misunderstand anybody. Why have you and General Grant not seen one another in years?"

"We parted on bad terms. He wanted to have me shot by firing squad."

"General Grant also recommended you for a medal of valor for outstanding bravery in combat. But then he decided to court-martial you instead. And now he insists you be involved in protecting him. Why?"

"Beats me."

"Grant has the full protection of the Secret Service. He doesn't need amateurs around him. Least of all people like you. I have personally tried to talk him out of this lunatic idea, but he insists it must be you. I am ordering you to join General Grant's security detail."

"I don't work for you, ma'am. I'm an employee of the DC Police Department."

"Then I may have to assign you to work for me on a temporary basis as a Secret Service agent."

"Does that mean I get to be a junior G-man?"

"Certainly not!"

"Not even a pair of aviator sunglasses?"

"This is serious. Grant is in real danger."

"Not my problem."

"I'm making it your problem. General Grant and I have a common purpose just now. Bobby Grant will explain it you."

"Why me?"

"You seem to have special ways of seeing into the minds of criminals. Ferreting them out and anticipating their moves. You identify with psychopaths and murderers."

"Thank you."

"That was not meant as a compliment." She nods at her assistant with the glasses, who passes me a piece of paper.

"Go to this address. Don't tell anyone where you're going—including your snippy chief of police."

I resent this woman casting aspersions about Kelly Flynn, my boss. Though Kelly *is* a bit snippy, this woman has no right to say so. I'm tempted to defend her but decide to say nothing. She can take care of herself. And I might be asked what my relationship with her is, and this could lead us down a path where I'd prefer not to go. So I bite my tongue.

"There are serious threats against the president-elect and General Grant," she says. "Take your responsibility seriously. I'll be keeping an eye on you, so don't screw up. Which, I understand, is your normal modus operandi."

She takes a seat and studies the crossword puzzle on her desk. Interview over.

"Thank you for your time, Madam Secretary. I'm honored

to visit the offices of the Department of Homeland Security," I say. "I understand your agency occupies the grounds of Washington's former hospital for the criminally insane."

You must feel right at home here, I'm tempted to add, but I have sense enough to shut up.

By now, Mr. Peepers has me firmly by the arm and marches me out of the office before I can commit bureaucratic ritual suicide. I take some satisfaction in having the last word. But it's just as well I'm out of there before somebody gets hurt.

Chapter Five

ACHAUFFEUR wearing a beautifully tailored white uniform is waiting for me at the front entrance to the Department of Homeland Security. He stands next to a cream-colored Rolls-Royce Phantom, which almost matches the color of his uniform. He opens the rear passenger door.

"I prefer to sit in front," I say.

The chauffeur nods and opens the front passenger door. "Very good, sir. As you wish."

"I find I get a better class of company in the front seat," I say. As we leave the grounds, I ask, "Did you know this was once the location of a lunatic asylum?"

"I prefer to use the term 'psychiatric hospital.'"

"I believe the poet Ezra Pound was incarcerated here for twelve years."

"I'm aware of the history. I did some of my residency here. That was long after Mr. Pound was released, of course."

I puzzle over what kind of residency a chauffeur was doing at Saint Elizabeths Hospital for the Criminally Insane.

"What's your name?"

"You may address me as Doctor," he says.

"That's a little formal for me. What's your actual name?"

"Escher."

"I mean your other name. Like, your first name."

He hesitates. "Drago. The name is Drago."

"Do you like working for Mr. Hunter?"

The driver is silent. For whatever reason, Drago's not going to answer me.

"I have a word of advice for you, sir," Drago says as he pulls up in front of a Tudor Revival mansion set well back from the street. We're in the Foxhall section, an upscale and exclusive neighborhood of Washington. It's winter and getting late, so it's already beginning to get dark.

"When you meet with Mr. Hunter, never look him directly in the eye."

"Why?"

"Because it makes him nervous."

"Well, it makes me nervous when I'm talking to someone and can't look him in the eye. Places me in an inferior position. I don't accept an inferior position to anyone. I'm sure Mr. Hunter will understand."

"Let's hope so. Be warned, though—Mr. Hunter's behavior can be unpredictable. Even violent."

"I'm warned."

The house is surrounded by gardens which I imagine must be pretty in the spring. But right now, the trees are leafless and the plants dead. It's beginning to snow as we arrive.

Drago opens the car door for me, and I follow him up a flight of steps, through the front door of the house, and into a foyer with a marble floor and a spiral staircase. "Mr. Hunter is waiting for you in the Winter Garden," Drago says.

I follow him through a spartan sitting room and a dining room. There is no art on the walls or decoration of any kind. We step through a low stone arch and into a large room completely enclosed in glass—walls and ceiling—which makes it look like a hothouse.

Sitting in the center of the room is a man in his sixties. He's a bit overweight and has a round face with small eyes.

"I am Cosmo Hunter," the man says. "Thank you for coming, Detective Zorn. Please, take a seat."

We face each other, sitting on two black leather Mies van der Rohe Barcelona chairs. There's a small side table next to us. Drago seems to have disappeared.

Cosmo Hunter is dressed in blue jeans and a short-sleeve sports shirt. He wears Birkenstock sandals on bare feet. He has long gray hair tied in a bun at the back of his head and intense blue eyes. I look directly into those eyes.

Outside, it's snowing heavily. I feel as if I were inside a snow globe.

"I've been looking forward to meeting you, Mr. Zorn."

"You know who I am?"

"I know you very well. I think you and I are very much alike. At heart, we're both outlaws. I don't mean outlaws as in one of your cowboy movies. I mean men who live outside the law. Better to say, beyond human law. I needed to meet you face-to-face to make sure."

"Have you made sure?"

"I have."

I don't like where this is going, so I change the subject. "You have a lovely home."

"It's not my home. I keep it as a *pied à terre* for my rare visits to Washington. I despise this town and spend as little time here as possible. Washington is full of phonies."

I feel the need to defend my town, although I agree with him. "Isn't that true of most places?"

"Not as bad as it is here. The public institutions here are criminal. They call Congress the world's greatest deliberative body. What Congress does is a cage fight. The government bureaucracy is no better. It's supposed to serve the people, but all the public service employees are interested in are their paychecks and promotions and parking spaces. And backstabbing their rivals. They're all too stupid or too lazy to get a job in the private sector. Give me a break! And don't even mention the courts.

"I was born and grew up on a small farm in Oklahoma. My dad was a dirt farmer. My mom taught high-school civics. They were honest, hardworking people, and they raised me and my brother to observe a strict code of honor, and I've always lived by that code. That's why I cannot stomach Washington and its corrupt culture. That's why there must be a revolutionary change in this country."

I don't know what I'm supposed to say to that. After all, I'm a government employee, one of those people he despises.

"Would you care for tea, Detective? Or would you prefer something stronger? I never drink alcohol myself, but I'm sure Dr. Escher can find something."

"Tea would be fine."

Cosmo Hunter must make some kind of signal because almost immediately, Drago Escher is standing at our side.

"Two teas, Doctor. And perhaps some biscuits."

Drago nods and disappears silently.

"You're a police officer." Hunter settles back in his chair. "A very effective one, I'm told. That must be stressful. I don't know how you deal with the pressure."

"I handle it. As you must know, I have just been meeting with Secretary Fletcher. Are you friends?"

"Liz? 'The old bitch gone in the teeth for a botched civilization.'"

"Are you an admirer of the poet Ezra Pound?" I ask.

"Why do you ask?"

"You just quoted a line of his poetry. 'An old bitch gone in the teeth for a botched civilization.' Is that what you believe? That Liz Fletcher is trying to save a 'botched civilization'?"

"Don't you?"

"What do you think of Ezra Pound's ideas?"

"I admire his world understanding."

"I mean, do you subscribe to his politics? He was a Fascist sympathizer during the Second World War. He made pro-Fascist propaganda radio broadcasts aimed at US troops. He would have been charged with treason, except that he was found mentally unfit to stand trial and was sent to St. Elizabeths Hospital for the Criminally Insane instead."

"In the end, he was weak. He failed."

Drago appears, bearing a silver tray on which rest a teapot and two porcelain cups. He fills the cups with tea and places a bowl with two cookies on a side table.

We sip the tea, which is lapsang souchong, strong and smoky.

"Why did you send for me, Mr. Hunter? You mentioned 'Friendship House' in your message to me."

"I want you to find the man responsible for the bombing. A man known as Black Sun."

"What is Black Sun?"

"It's an organization, Detective. But it's also a man. And a demon. Black Sun planned and paid for the bombing of Friendship House. I have reason to believe you've recently heard the name Black Sun."

"What makes you think so?" I ask.

"You tried to arrest a man who whispered the words 'Black Sun is watching you' into your ear."

"I have no idea what Black Sun means."

"Black Sun is an instrument of the Devil. Your mission is to find him. Before it's too late."

"Do you mean Black Sun or the Devil?"

"I mean both."

"I'm not an exorcist."

"Don't patronize me, Mr. Zorn. I know all about you. I know what you really are. You have talents and skills others don't have. You have insight into evil. The man I'm searching for—Black Sun—is a demon. I suspect your mind works in much the same way as his. That gives you an advantage that others don't have. You have a special gift, Detective. Or is it a curse? Either way, use it." Cosmo takes a sip of his tea. "I'm told you are something of a chess player."

"Just an amateur."

"Don't underestimate yourself."

"Why do you ask about chess? It's just a game. A pastime."

"You are wrong. Chess teaches how to plan ahead. Most people live one moment at a time. In chess, you must see the entire board and calculate what your opponent will do many moves in advance. You must anticipate in order to win the game that you and I are just now playing. Chess teaches an essential critical skill. Especially if your enemy is a madman."

Who has this man been talking to? I wonder. Kelly Flynn once said during one of our more intimate moments, "You have an instinct for evil. Your instincts are your curse."

I know it is best if I don't examine too carefully who I am. I might find myself in a dark place. And I certainly don't want to explore the dark place with this man.

"You must be able to anticipate Black Sun's actions," Cosmo says. "He's insane, and you understand madness. Use your special skills, find him, and destroy him. But be warned, he's dangerous. Respect him as an equal. Otherwise, he'll destroy you first. And me."

"Is Black Sun your enemy, Mr. Hunter?"

"He's been my enemy all my life." Cosmo gets to his feet. "It was a pleasure meeting you, Detective. You have my private number. Use it."

And with that, he's gone.

A few minutes later, I'm once again sitting in the front passenger seat of the Rolls next to Drago.

"How was his mood today?" Drago glances at me, worried. "Sometimes he has episodes. He has to be watched carefully."

"I looked directly into Mr. Hunter's eyes. It didn't seem to bother him."

"I assure you, it did. He won't forget you. Or forgive you. You will someday understand that. When he no longer needs you."

"You're not a real chauffeur, are you?"

"Do you find my driving inadequate?"

"I find it strange you're employed as a chauffeur. But he calls you 'doctor.' I suspect you are, in fact, a medical doctor of some kind. Maybe even a psychiatrist."

"Board-certified. One of my responsibilities is to see to Mr. Hunter's meds."

"And in between Mr. Hunter's episodes, you drive his car."

"I am also Mr. Hunter's spiritual adviser."

"I think you're Mr. Hunter's bodyguard as well."

"I do what I can to serve."

"Who do you protect him from?"

"Mr. Hunter has many enemies."

"I'm supposed to find one of them. It would help me to know who Mr. Hunter's enemies are."

"Mr. Hunter's most feared enemy is Cosmo Hunter."

Chapter Six

WHEN I GET BACK to police headquarters, I find an envelope among the litter of urgent, unreturned phone messages on my desk. The envelope paper is thick and expensive. My name has been written on it by hand in elegant copperplate script. There's no postage and no return address. Who writes letters these days?

Inside, there's a single sheet of paper on which a message has been typed. I take out my glasses and read:

LASCIATE OGNI SPERANZA, VOI CH'ENTRATE.
YOU WILL FIND ME HERE,
BUT YOU WILL NEVER ESCAPE.

There's no signature. No date.

I show Latasha the letter. It's a puzzle, and she's good at puzzles. She reads detective novels.

"Do you know who left it on my desk?" I ask.

"It was here when I arrived."

"There's a clue here somewhere. See if you can figure it out."

"Half of it isn't even in English."

"It's not in the message. It's in the typeface."

She looks at me as if I've lost my mind.

"Please make copies of the letter. I need one copy for

myself. Check if there are fingerprints on the envelope and the paper the message was typed on. I have an appointment across town to meet an old friend."

I park my MG roadster in the basement parking garage of the Watergate complex at 2700 Virginia Avenue in Washington, DC. An MG is a ridiculous car for a city like Washington, but I love it, even though it spends half the time in a repair shop. Every week or so, some widget goes out of whack and has to be replaced. Invariably, it turns out that said widget can only be found in some obscure dealer's inventory in North Dakota. My MG has put my mechanic's daughter through college.

I make my way to one of the upper floors and to the apartment I've been instructed to visit. It's a building I've been to before—sometimes on police business, sometimes for strictly personal reasons. Many of the apartments have spectacular views of the city of Washington or Virginia across the Potomac River, but the view is probably less important to the residents than the discretion and privacy the building offers.

The Watergate is occupied by the rich and powerful, or would-be powerful, and by celebrities, who demand privacy and security. It's been the site of many plots and conspiracies over the years, notably the 1972 break-in of the Democratic National Committee headquarters, leading to the eventual fall of Richard Nixon.

A young woman with short auburn hair, dressed in discreet business attire, waits outside the door—obviously a Secret Service agent on security detail. She wears flats. She is kitted out with the usual earbuds with squiggly wires attached to a transmitter hidden on her body somewhere. Although I can't actually see anything, I know she's armed.

The agent asks me, "Are you carrying a weapon, sir?"

"I'm unarmed. Except for my cigarette lighter."

She looks at me as if sarcasm is a misdemeanor, then examines my lighter.

"There are words written on this lighter."

"It's an inscription."

"How do I know it's not some kind of code?"

"You don't."

"Who is Carla?"

"Gentlemen never say."

Satisfied my lighter isn't really a bomb, she tells me to deposit the lighter, wallet, Rolex, and cell phone in a plastic tray, promising to return them to me when I leave. She checks me out with a security wand and knocks discreetly at the apartment door, obviously using some prearranged code, which I make a point to memorize. Three short raps. Pause. A louder rap. The agent opens the door and gestures for me to enter. Two more agents wait just inside the apartment. Behind them is a rack holding three shotguns.

I'm in a large living room that's obviously been designed by an expensive interior decorator. There's a couch, several armchairs, a writing desk, and what looks like a fully stocked bar. The floor is covered by a fluffy, thick-pile carpet. On the walls are photographs of the city of Washington, featuring the Lincoln Memorial and the tidal basin with the cherry blossom trees in full bloom. Large picture windows are covered by heavy curtains, so I can't see what vista has been hidden. So much for the million-dollar views. The pretty photographs on the walls will have to do.

"Marko, you son of a bitch," a man yells cheerfully at me from across the room. "How the fuck are you?" He strides toward me and clasps my hand in a crushing grip.

He's six feet, three inches tall. His crew cut is turning

gray, something I hadn't noticed when I watched him on TV during the debates. He's put on some weight since I last saw him. Age catches up with us all, even the redoubtable General Bobby Grant.

It's been years since we've been in the same room together, probably in some shithole military outpost somewhere. Grant then stood across the room dressed in US Army fatigues, a .45 in a holster at his waist. At least he still had a waist back then.

"You may all leave," Grant barks at the Secret Service detail. "You too, Susan. This reprobate"—Grant points at me—"and I must speak in private. I have to warn you, my dear, keep your eye on this man. He's not to be trusted near a beautiful woman. Sometime I must tell you about when Marko and I were on R and R in Bangkok. We were on Patpong Street ... on second thought, I don't think our misadventures are appropriate for innocent ears."

"Yes, sir."

"Just be alert."

"If the gentleman makes any inappropriate moves, I'll shoot him, sir."

The agents slip out of the room, closing the door silently behind them.

"Susan's a great kidder." The general crosses to the bar. "They make them prettier every year."

"Liz Fletcher told me you wanted to see me," I say.

"What did you make of old Liz? She's strange, don't you agree? Do you think she's gay?" He snatches a bottle of Jack Daniel's from the bar. "What's your poison, old man?" He pours whiskey into two glasses, without waiting for an answer, and adds a hint of soda from a siphon. "You staying out of trouble? I hope not. You haven't gone weird, have you? Like giving up booze?" He passes a glass to me. "A number of your former buddies claim they experienced stress in the zone. They're all in rehab now. I shit you not. Real men don't do rehab. What do they call it these days? PTSD? What the fuck is PTSD? Jesus, give me a fucking break! We're becoming a nation of pussies. You haven't gone over to the dark side, have you, and gotten married?"

"Still single, General."

"Outstanding. I hear you're a policeman these days. Can you drink while you're on duty?"

"Am I on duty?"

"Affirmative."

"Should I address you as Mr. Vice President?"

"I'm not vice president. Not yet. Not until the twentieth of the month. That's when Manny and I take our oaths of office. Assuming we live that long." He gestures at the apartment. "These are just temporary digs until they prepare my permanent quarters at Admiral's House. Have you met Manny? He has that marvelous, charismatic smile that everyone loves. I never really managed the smile thing myself."

"I don't much like politicians."

"Me neither. I hope you voted for me."

"How could you expect me to vote for you?" I say. "You tried to have me court-martialed and shot."

"Nothing personal."

"I took it personally."

"Marko, believe me, you were never cut out for an Army career. You could never obey orders. You never showed respect for rank or authority. I don't think you like senior officers."

"I don't."

"If you'd fought like a real man, you could've made captain."

"Except for that thing that happened."

"You fucked up your career is what happened. I ordered you to kill some people. You refused. That's what you were paid to do. You can be a serious pain in the ass, you know. But that was all a long time ago. Let's not let old disagreements prevent our cooperation now. I need you."

Grant sits on the couch and takes a deep swallow of his whiskey. "Since I left the service," he says, making himself comfortable, his arms spread wide over the back of the couch, "I've been masquerading as an expert on national security. Can you fucking believe that? I appear regularly on TV for interviews. You've probably seen me on the Sunday morning talk shows. I've written three books. I shit you not. I bet you didn't even know I could read. I'm told the books are quite insightful."

"Why do you need my help?"

"Because you're one of the few people in Washington I trust."

"You must know hundreds of people here. Many are your loyal political supporters."

"There's no such thing as loyalty in Washington. To paraphrase Harry Truman: If you want a friend in Washington, get a dog. I lost half of my people when I failed to get nominated for president. They deserted me and went over to Manny's camp, looking for a handout. The rest still hang around, hoping I'll find them a job. I don't trust a single one of those fuckers."

"Why do you need my help?" I ask again.

"Okay, I'll be square with you. CIA and the State Department were informed two days ago by the foreign intelligence services of Germany, France, and the UK that there's an international neo-Nazi organization planning to assassinate the president of the United States on Inauguration Day.

Not to mention yours truly. That's why I need you. I want you to find and kill the son of a bitch who runs this neo-Nazi organization."

"I'm not a gun for hire. Or have you forgotten?"

"Let me nuance my request. If you refuse, you're fucked. End of story. This man wants to kill me. Your mission: Find him and kill him first."

"Would my mission be off the books?"

"Damn straight. Grow some balls, Scout. You can handle this."

"You have Liz Fletcher's Department of Homeland Security to protect you. That's what they do. They have the training and the resources."

"Not good enough."

"You have Secret Service protection."

"You mean people like Susan. She's a great kid, but I don't trust anybody in Washington, old buddy. I need more than just protection. I need to know the name of the fucker who plans to take me out."

"How am I supposed to identify this man?"

"Give me a fucking break, Zorn. Yesterday you were at the scene of that terrorist bombing. The place that took care of queers and freaks. You spoke to a man involved in the bombing."

"What's that got to do with the threat against you?"

"It's got everything to do with it. The man you spoke to … he said something to you. What was it?"

"Nothing that made any sense."

"What did he say?" Grant's voice is loud and demanding. I expect the Secret Service agents just outside the apartment door can hear him. They're doubtlessly listening carefully, although they're not supposed to do that. The Secret Service is part of the Department of Homeland Security; therefore, they work for Liz Fletcher. They're doing their jobs.

"The man I tried to question said Black Sun was watching me." Grant closes his eyes and leans back into the couch.

"He used the words 'Black Sun'? Are you sure about that? It's vitally important that you remember his words exactly."

"Those are the words he used."

"The man said something else to you."

How the hell does Grant know that? Everybody in the city of Washington seems to have been listening in on that exchange. There's only one way Grant could know. Someone has hacked the internal communications of the Metropolitan Police Department and read my incident report. I must remember to tell Chief Flynn to review the department's communications security.

"He said 'Cyclone has come,'" I say. No point in being coy. Grant must have seen my entire report. There are no secrets in Washington.

Grant grimaces. "What the fuck is 'Cyclone'?"

"Cyclone is a large air mass that rotates counterclockwise in the northern hemisphere and clockwise in the southern hemisphere."

"I don't want a fucking lecture on meteorology. Now I remember why I wanted to have you shot, Zorn. You're annoying. Find out who runs Black Sun and what Cyclone is. That's an order."

"Why should I?"

"Because my life depends on it, is why. Because I'm telling you to, is why."

"What if I don't want to?"

"Then you're shit out of luck, Zorn. Do as you're told. Didn't Liz explain that to you? I don't want to go through that unpleasant business with you once again and have you shot."

"I don't take orders from you. We're not at war."

"That's where you're wrong, sonny boy. We are at war. And our enemy is more savage and dangerous than the Taliban and al-Qaeda. If you refuse, I'll be obliged to sic Liz Fletcher on you. You don't want that, believe me."

I decide I probably do need that whiskey, and I take a sip. "Why are you worrying? The president-elect has plenty of protection."

"It isn't just the president. It's me. I know you're thinking, why waste a perfectly good bullet on a vice president? Or a nice bomb? You know what they say, 'The vice presidency isn't worth a pitcher of warm piss.'" Grant gulps his Jack Daniel's. "Find out who's behind this plot. When you do, report back to me. If you're squeamish about killing the man, I'll take care of that detail myself. Don't bring anybody else into the loop. Particularly not that bitch Liz Fletcher." He raises his glass. "Cheers, old buddy. And watch your step. They're predicting bad weather in the coming days. I wouldn't want to see you catch a cold. While you're on your way out, ask Susan to come in and see me."

Chapter Seven

I COLLECT MY LIGHTER, wallet, Rolex, and cell phone from the lovely Susan, who does not return my warm smile, and head to the garage where I parked my MG among the Audis, BMWs, Porsches, Lexuses, and the occasional Bentley. Many of the cars have low-numbered license plates and all have been carefully cleaned and polished. My vintage MG roadster is here somewhere among them, not cleaned and polished. It's a distinctive car—racing green—but it sits low to the ground, lost among these behemoths, and is hard to find. I hope it starts.

Maybe I'm distracted by seeing General Grant again. It brings back old memories. Not good ones. Or maybe I'm just getting careless. A man passes behind me, a golf bag slung over his shoulder. I pause next to a black Chrysler limousine to search for my MG.

It's dark here in the underground garage. Darker than it should be. That's when I realize someone has turned off some of the ceiling light fixtures. My skin prickles. I'm getting a bad feeling about this.

In the faint reflection on the black limousine's polished side door, I see the man carrying the golf bag. This time, he's walking directly toward me. It suddenly strikes me—golf clubs in the middle of winter? A blizzard is predicted. Who plays golf in a blizzard? In an underground garage? And why are the lights out?

Where's my damn car!

My instincts tell me there's something wrong here, and I always pay attention to my instincts. I wouldn't be alive today if I didn't.

And the man in the reflection is no longer carrying a golf bag—he's now holding a machine pistol. I drop to the ground and roll under the black limousine as two rounds shatter the car's windows and side door just above my head, spraying splinters of glass and metal onto the concrete floor.

I'm on the ground, crawling under the Chrysler through melting slush and old motor oil. I hear voices yelling. There are two of these fuckers after me. They're double-teaming me and I'm caught in the middle. I see a moving light beneath a nearby car. One of them has a flashlight and is coming toward me, sweeping the flashlight beam beneath the parked cars where he knows I'm hiding. He just doesn't know which car yet. They're being cautious. They don't know I'm not armed.

I have minutes, maybe seconds, before they find me. As I crawl out from beneath the Chrysler, I make out the form of one man moving among the cars. He's crouched low to the ground so he can peer beneath the parked cars. I quickly climb onto the roof of a Land Rover parked nearby and lie flat on top where I'm close to being invisible in the dim light. I can't see either man, but I hear their voices. They seem to be getting closer to me. Then they fade away as they search.

A figure appears next to the Land Rover. The gunman stoops to study the mix of snow and slush, then he kneels and focuses the beam of the flashlight beneath the Land Rover, sweeping the beam back and forth, holding an automatic pistol in his free hand.

I roll off the top of the Land Rover and drop onto him. He collapses under my weight, flat on the ground, struggling to free himself. I hope I didn't break my reading glasses.

The man grunts. Or maybe curses as I slam his face onto the concrete floor. He's strong and agile and almost pulls away from me. I grab the flashlight that lies next to us and smash it into his head. He jerks and lies still.

From a distance, the second voice is yelling. "Marty! Where are you? Fucking say something!"

I'm on my hands and knees, groping in the dark, searching for the man's pistol, but the damn thing's disappeared in the dark. Probably slid under a car, lying in the melting snow and slush somewhere.

"Marty?" the second man calls out. "You there?"

No time left to search for the pistol. I dart through the parked cars, putting distance between me and the second gunman.

I begin to breathe normally when I'm suddenly caught in the beam of a powerful flashlight. I turn, and the second man is charging me. He stops and takes aim. I'm in open space with nowhere to hide. No cars I can dive under.

The man with the gun makes a funny sound, something like a cough, and drops to the ground. He lies motionless a few feet from me. Even in the dark, I can see there's a red hole in the middle of his chest.

Standing just behind me now is man holding a worn leather briefcase in one hand. In the other hand, he holds a Ruger pistol. "Let's get out of here, Detective Zorn," the man says, slipping his gun into the side pocket of his topcoat.

"You just committed murder. I'm a police officer. I should arrest you."

"I just saved your life, so you owe me. The men who were after you are not alone. Their friends will join us at any moment. I have one gun. You, I understand, have none. I suggest we both leave before they get here."

"I can't just walk away from a murdered man lying on the ground."

"Right now, you have something more urgent to worry about. Do you have a car?"

"It's around here somewhere."

"Can you give me a lift? I came here by taxi."

I find my MG a few yards away, partially hidden behind a minivan, and we climb in. My passenger carefully places his briefcase on his lap and fastens his seat belt. To my relief, the car starts.

"Do you spend much time in parking lots helping innocent victims of muggers?" I ask.

"I don't think you're innocent. And those men were certainly not muggers. They're werewolves."

"What brings you here, then?" I ask as I pull the MG out of the parking lot and onto the snow-covered street.

"I was looking for you, Detective Zorn."

We ride in silence while I concentrate on not skidding into a snowbank. "Where do you want me to take you?" I ask.

"Would you care to join me for a drink?"

"I could certainly use one. If you promise not to shoot me."

"I know a small place in Chinatown that has a quiet bar. We won't be disturbed there. I'll explain to you what happened over drinks."

Chapter Eight

"WHO DID YOU JUST SHOOT?" I ask the man sitting next to me in my MG.

"I have no idea. All I can tell you is he was a werewolf."

"I don't believe in werewolves. They're figures in fairy stories made up to scare children."

"You should be scared, too."

"Why would a werewolf attack me?"

"That's what werewolves do." The man takes a cell phone from his jacket pocket and speaks softly to someone in German. I can't understand the dialect.

It takes me almost half an hour to drive across town from the Watergate apartment complex to Chinatown. Driving is slow and treacherous. Although the streets have been plowed, they're narrow. Drifts of snow have been piled along the curbs, and patches of black ice make driving dangerous. Some idiots have abandoned their cars in the streets. My vintage MG is not the ideal vehicle in these conditions. It would be more at home on the Grand Corniche on the way to an apéritif in the hotel Le Negresco in Nice. So would I.

The man sitting next to me looks to be in his fifties. His hair is gray and close-cropped. He wears glasses with thick lenses and unstylish black frames. I think about the object he's carrying in his coat pocket but figure if he meant to do me harm, he'd have done so in the garage or let the other guys do it. I shouldn't worry. But I do.

We drive in silence while I keep an eye out for police cars and clueless drivers. And stray werewolves. Or somebody following us. And the armed man sitting next to me.

Chinatown is a nondescript part of downtown Washington. Once a thriving Chinese community, with many shops selling exotic products, today it's essentially one block long. At one end of the block is an elaborate Chinese arch used these days as a backdrop for the Chinese New Year celebrations. What's left of Chinatown is now mostly mediocre Chinese restaurants, a few stores, and a Chinese church. A few elderly Chinese residents remain, but the area has suffered from gentrification. I suppose most of the original inhabitants have died or moved away and are now living in the suburbs. Apart from some street signs using Chinese characters, this could be any place.

I park my car, and my passenger and I walk half a block, passing several restaurants and small shops—all closed— before we reach a weather-beaten sign: Peking Palace. We descend steep stairs and enter a small, dimly lit restaurant. A garish green and red plastic dragon hangs over the bar. The place is empty, and my companion leads me to a small table in the corner. An elderly man appears to take our order.

I ask for a dry vodka martini with a lemon peel twist. It's been one of those days. My companion orders an apple schnapps.

"Who are you?" I ask when the waiter leaves. "Why are you following me?"

My companion reaches into his inside breast pocket,

removes a leather card holder, and passes me a business card that reads,

Walter Brückner
030 996 2592

There's no address or identification.

"That's a Berlin telephone area code," I say.

"You can contact me on that number at any time." He speaks English fluently but with a slight accent. "I'm only in your country for a few days, so there's no point in my getting a local number."

"You think I'll be contacting you?"

"I know you will."

"You called the people who attacked me 'werewolves.' What are werewolves?"

"You know, people who turn into vicious animals from time to time. In this case, they're thugs belonging to a neo-Nazi organization. The man you tried to arrest yesterday at the scene of the bombing was a werewolf. Perhaps only a junior-grade werewolf, but a werewolf all the same."

"Why are you looking for me?"

"For the same reason the werewolves are looking for you," he says. "You're dangerous."

"How?"

"Because of something you know."

"I don't know anything."

"You know more than you know."

The waiter serves our drinks. The martini is excellent, and I relax just a little.

"What organization do you work for?" I ask. "Or are you a freelancer?"

"The *Bundesnachrichtendienst*. Usually known as the BND. The German intelligence service."

"You work for the BND?"

"To be entirely candid, I'm the director of the *Bundesnachrichtendienst*."

"Why is the head of German intelligence interested in killer thugs hanging around in parking garages here in Washington? I imagine you have plenty of killer thugs of your own in Germany to keep you busy."

"More than enough, thank you. But I had to be sure you weren't killed."

"Don't you guys believe in delegating? I'll bet you have plenty of local talent."

"Of course we do. But the situation we face is extremely sensitive. Only a few people in my government—or in yours—know about cyclone." Brückner pronounces the word with a "Z" sound at the beginning, not with an "S" sound. *Zyklon.*

"You know," I say, "I should arrest you. We have laws in this country against murdering people."

"So do we. I had to improvise to keep you alive."

"We've left the scene of a crime. When the police find the body of the man you shot, they'll undertake an all-points investigation."

"My people will have cleaned up the mess. I made the necessary arrangements when I was on the phone in the car. By the time your police arrived, there would have been nothing left to investigate. And even if there are questions, your people will understand once I've explained the circumstances."

"My people?"

"Carla Lowry will straighten things out, I'm sure."

"You know Carla?"

"We go way back."

"I should arrest you, just the same. She's FBI. This is a police matter."

"I'm afraid I can't allow you to do that. It would draw attention to my presence in your country, which would be awkward. We're keeping this operation below the radar. Only a few people are cleared for Zyklon. Let's just leave it to Carla."

Brückner reaches into his jacket pocket. I have a moment of anxiety, but all he does is take out a briar pipe and a leather tobacco pouch. "Do you mind?" He gestures with the pipe.

"Go right ahead," I say. "You've already committed murder. I'll overlook violating our 'no smoking' regulations."

Brückner knocks loose tobacco ashes from his pipe onto the floor. "I'm sorry to tell you this, Detective, but I'm afraid you're in danger. If I recall your record correctly, this will not be the first time you've been in serious trouble. But you have nothing to fear from me, and you're safe here in Peking Palace. If you ever get in trouble, and I'm not around, remember, you can always find refuge here."

"What's to prevent the waiter from putting poison in my noodles?"

"Zhang works for me." Brückner packs fresh tobacco into his pipe bowl. "I need your help, Detective. You're already deeply involved with Zyklon, whether you like it or not. Welcome to the team."

"I'm not a team person. Why am I involved? None of this concerns me."

"I'm afraid it does concern you. You spoke to a man at the site of the terrorist attack on Friendship House."

"What of it?"

"What did he say?"

"The man said, 'Black Sun has arrived and is watching me now.'"

"He said those exact words? He used the words 'Black Sun'? You're sure?"

"I'm sure."

He takes a small, worn notebook and a stubby pencil from his pocket and makes a few brief notes. "He also said something more, I believe. What was it?"

"He told me 'Cyclone has come. Our time has come.' What is Cyclone?" I ask.

"You don't know?"

"All I know is that people seem to be taking a particular interest in the word 'Cyclone.' And now you're asking, whoever you are. The police are searching for the man I tried to arrest who said those words to me. When we find him, I'll learn what Cyclone means."

"Good luck with that, Detective Zorn. My guess is you're already too late. Your suspect is almost certainly dead by now." Brückner leans across the table and looks intently into my eyes. "Did he tell you who Black Sun is?"

"I don't know what you're talking about."

"Black Sun! Who is he?"

"He didn't tell me any name."

Brückner grimaces, disappointed, then slumps back into his chair. Defeated. "Then I'm going to need your help."

"What kind of help are we talking about?" I ask with caution. People keep asking for my help. That makes me anxious.

"Your government and mine are facing an unprecedented crisis. We need your help to prevent a monstrous weapon from being deployed."

"What weapon?"

"It's called Zyklon."

"What in hell is Zyklon?"

"It's definitely a weapon from hell. It is an extremely dangerous weapon that has fallen into the hands of a neo-Nazi organization called Black Sun. Black Sun plans to use it in an act of terror against your government."

"What's Black Sun?" I ask.

"That's the wrong question. Better to ask, 'Who is Black Sun?'"

"Okay, who is Black Sun?"

He shrugs. "I have no idea. I was hoping you could tell me. Black Sun finances and runs a vast neo-Nazi organization. We've been searching for him for a long time. Our operatives, and those of other friendly intelligence services, including yours, have penetrated the organization, but only at a low level. We've sometimes been able to track the movements of Black Sun. He doesn't have a fixed location. He moves all around the globe, constantly—one day in Paris, a few days later, he's in Odessa, then in Caracas."

"I think it's time you tell me about Zyklon."

"It's a long story. One that begins in April 1945."

"I've got the time."

Brückner reaches into his briefcase and removes a sheaf of papers. "Do you read German?"

"Well enough."

"This is a report filed many years ago. Read it."

He pushes the papers across the table to me. I put on my glasses and begin to read. The paper is brown and mottled with age. The text is in German and typed, but not by a professional typist. Even at a quick glance, I make out typeovers and typing errors. There are official-looking stamps all over the document. Some are in German. Some are in Russian.

I offer Brückner my lighter for his pipe.

"You realize you're now a co-conspirator in breaking your city's no-smoking regulations." Brückner flips open the lighter and draws in the flame until he's satisfied he has the pipe going properly. "I haven't seen a cigarette lighter like this in years. Do they even make them anymore?" He examines it carefully and frowns. "I see the name Carla. Would that be our Carla?" He smiles and returns the lighter.

Chapter Nine

STRENG GEHEIM—Top Secret.
EYES ONLY Reichsführer-SS
BERICHT für Reichsführer-SS
27 April 1945
THEMA: ZYKLON C
Von SS Standartenführer Karl von Goteberg
I respectfully submit my report on Operation Zyklon.
This is the sole copy and is my final report.

Upon my release from SS Hospital Wiesbaden in
March 1945, it was determined by competent medical
authorities that because of wounds I received—I lost
my left arm from a Russian mortar—I could no longer
be cleared for combat duty. Instead, I was ordered
to go directly to Berlin and report immediately to the
office of Reichsführer Himmler. On 15 March, I obtained
transport on a Focke-Wulf and arrived in Berlin at 10:20
in the morning at Tempelhof Airport. I was met there
by a command car and taken to Wilhelmstrasse, where
I spoke with Reichsführer Himmler in his private office.
    The Reichsführer dismissed his staff and gave me
my orders personally and verbally. No written record
of his orders exists. He told me I had been selected for
a special project, code named Zyklon C, because of my

outstanding combat record and my proven loyalty to
the Führer. Reichsführer Himmler acknowledged that
the Wehrmacht had experienced unexpected military
setbacks and that the outcome of the war was now in
doubt. He informed me that Projekt Zyklon would be the
decisive turning point in the war.

Reichsführer Himmler explained that a new
weapon, called Zyklon C, would allow the Reich to
defeat its enemies with a decisive blow. Zyklon was
still in development, and my assignment was to see
that the components, along with key personnel and
technicians, were brought to Berlin for final assembly
and deployment at a secure site. The Führer himself has
authorized the development and use of Zyklon. It, and
it alone, would save the Reich and the Führer himself.

Reichsführer Himmler informed me that the man who
developed Zyklon was Dr. Herr Professor Ernst Nieland,
a senior official at IG Farben. My instructions were to
create a site in Berlin where Dr. Nieland and his staff
would complete the final stages and assembly of the
superweapon under the direct supervision of Professor
Nieland himself.

The Reichsführer gave me detailed instructions
on the requirements for the construction of the site.
These included housing for thirty-three scientists and
lab technicians and a specially built area to store
Zyklon. I was required to locate and occupy a structure
in Berlin where a laboratory could be installed that
was secure from enemy bombs and artillery. I had to
provide housing and support for the SS troops I would
need for security for the site. I was to requisition
anything I needed from Dr. Albert Speer, the Minister

of Armaments and War Production, who was under personal orders from the Führer to provide everything we required.

My immediate task was to find a building that was bomb-proof. I requisitioned one of several "super fortresses" that the Führer had ordered constructed as the last defense for the city of Berlin against the enemy. These fortresses had been abandoned by the Wehrmacht by now. I took control of one of them, built of reinforced concrete, five stories high, equipped with massive gun emplacements, and, most importantly, with deep subbasements, making the structure essentially bomb-proof.

Under my command, a Wehrmacht engineer battalion began work on 22 March to prepare the laboratory and associated facilities. On 28 March, the laboratory construction work was completed. The laboratories and support facilities were placed deep underground, safe from enemy fire. Living quarters for the science staff, as well as my SS contingent, were to be housed closer to the surface. If an enemy bomb should penetrate the building, we could afford to lose personnel. They can always be replaced. The laboratory itself and its contents would be safe against enemy attack. I immediately informed Professor Nieland by secure telegram that his laboratory site was ready for occupation.

On 2 April, Professor Nieland and a crew of twenty-four men arrived at the fortress, accompanied by twelve Zvezda heavy-cargo trucks loaded with laboratory equipment. I was informed that the staff were chemical engineers and laboratory technicians. Lab work began the next day.

I was strictly forbidden to enter the laboratory area. From time to time, one of Nieland's lab assistants would appear at my office with a list of demands for more supplies and equipment. These I immediately passed on to Reich Minister Speer. As the days went on, my assignment became increasingly difficult.

On 16 April, Russian forces began their attack on the city of Berlin. We were in the final and desperate stages of the war, essentially cut off from the rest of the world by the Red Army, under the command of Marshal Rokossovsky. But despite everything, we managed to obtain the needed supplies and work on the Zyklon project proceeded.

On the evening of 26 April 1945, Professor Nieland appeared in my office.

"My work here is done," he said. "I have produced Zyklon C. With Zyklon C, the Reich will be victorious. There is one final demonstration I must complete, and I invite you to observe. Then you may inform our Führer that victory is ours."

We descended to the lowest levels of the fortress many meters below street level. Even through the thick reinforced-concrete walls, I could hear the rumble of enemy artillery. The entire building shook.

The Russians were now in the city. It would be a matter of days, at most, probably only hours, before Berlin fell. I was anxious for the Professor to finish his demonstration and allow me to leave. I did not care to become a prisoner of the Red Army.

When we reached the lowest level of the fortress, Professor Nieland took me to a large storage room constructed of reinforced concrete, with iron doors. Inside were steel cylinders stacked from floor to ceiling, each marked in stencil Zyklon C, followed by an identification number.

"This is Zyklon. It will win our war," Nieland said, then led me to the main research laboratory. We stood at the front entrance to the laboratory and looked through the sole window, made of thick glass, into the lab. Inside, more than two dozen men were packing equipment.

"They are removing all records," the professor explained. "All evidence of what we have done here has been destroyed. My discovery must never fall into the hands of our enemies. Tomorrow you are to remove all cylinders of Zyklon and deliver them into the hands of the Army High Command. Then destroy this building. Burn what remains to the ground. You must, on no account, allow Red Army troops to gain access to the building and its contents before Zyklon is deployed. The formula must be destroyed at all costs."

"There are witnesses," I said.

"There are no witnesses." Just outside the door to the lab was an iron wheel. The professor grasped the wheel and turned it slowly. For a moment, I was perplexed. I had no idea what he was doing.

When I looked again into the laboratory through its glass window, the lab assistants were writhing in agony. Some rushed to the door, flinging themselves against it, trying desperately to open it, their faces contorted in terror. They beat frantically with their fists against the iron door. They could see Nieland and me standing just outside. I could not hear their screams, but I knew they were pleading for us to open the door and save them.

Within minutes, all movement inside the lab stopped. All I could see were piles of motionless corpses on the lab floor.

"Zyklon is a success, as you can see," Nieland said. "You may inform our Führer that I have created the ultimate weapon, and he has won the war. I am certain he will award me the Iron Cross for my work here."

When I returned to my office, I summoned a signals sergeant and dictated a one-sentence message to the Führer: "Zyklon C Achieved."

I was awakened the following morning with orders to appear before the Führer to receive my final instructions. I requisitioned a staff car to take me to the Führerbunker on Wilhelmstrasse. The trip took almost an hour. We were stopped at every intersection by special SS teams searching for deserters. They examined my papers carefully, but when they realized I was on direct orders from Hitler himself, they allowed me to pass. Corpses hung from lampposts at every corner, men the SS troops suspected of desertion.

Many streets were blocked by rubble from bombed buildings, many structures were on fire. There were deep holes gouged in the streets from Russian artillery. And everywhere, there was the sound of Russian guns.

I arrived at the Führerbunker at 6:30 in the morning of 27 April 1945, and was met by Martin Bormann, the Führer's private secretary and head of the Party

Chancellery. He took me deep beneath street level to the Führerbunker itself and led me through several rooms occupied by guards, communications personnel, and secretarial staff. Finally, Bormann ushered me into the Führer's private office. Bormann closed the door, leaving me face-to-face with the man himself. I had expected Reichsführer-SS Himmler and members of the General Staff to be present, but I found myself alone with Adolf Hitler.

I had never been in the presence of the Führer before. I had seen him from a distance at Party rallies, and I thought I had a clear image of him from photographs and newsreels. The man before me was unrecognizable. His skin was sallow, his eyes sunken. His right arm trembled so that he had to hold it still with his left hand. He seemed shrunken. He sat at a small desk and held a large magnifying glass in his trembling hand as he studied a map of the city of Berlin. A large oil portrait of Frederick the Great hung on a wall behind him.

I made the Heil Hitler salute. He did not respond. There was no sign that he knew who or what I was.

"It's over," Hitler said.

"Yes, my Führer."

Hitler sat a long time, staring at the map.

"My time is over," he said at last.

"Shall I inform General Schneider?"

"There is no need."

"I assumed that the first step would be to load Zyklon into artillery shells so the Wehrmacht can mount a counterattack on the Russian forces. We can open a gap to relieve Berlin and turn the tide of the war."

Hitler looked up at me for the first time. I looked directly into his eyes. There was nobody there.

"Do you authorize me to inform the General Staff that they are to mount a counteroffensive?" I asked.

The Führer hesitated, then shook his head.

His voice was raspy. "The war is over. The Army has failed me. The Party has failed me. Himmler has betrayed me. Goering has betrayed me. The people of Germany have betrayed me. They are not worthy of me. Germany without me is nothing. Destiny has failed me."

He stopped speaking, and as he examined the map on the desk before him, he pointed at a place on the map. "This is where I was going to build the great hall 'Germania.'" His hand shook. "You are to deploy Zyklon throughout the city of Berlin. In the underground U-Bahn tunnels, in the streets, in the air raid shelters. Everywhere. Release Zyklon throughout the city."

"That will mean the death of tens of thousands of your soldiers, of German citizens, my Führer."

"That is what they deserve. They failed me. Everyone has failed me. Obey your orders. When I am gone, I want nothing left but destruction, ruins, and death."

At 7:15 that morning, I left the office and the Führerbunker. That was my last communication with my Leader.

Respectfully submitted 27 April 1945.
SS Standartenführer Karl von Goteborg

Chapter Ten

I SLIDE THE REPORT from the SS Colonel Karl von Goteborg back across the table to Walter Brückner, who carefully folds it and replaces it in his briefcase.

"What the hell happened to this so-called superweapon?" I say.

"We've been searching for the answer to that question for a long time." Brückner stares into his pipe, which seems to have gone out.

"I don't remember hearing about any superweapon used in the final days of the war."

"That's because no such weapon was ever used."

"What happened to it then?" I give Brückner my lighter again, and he fusses with his pipe.

"That's a complicated story," he says between puffs. "It's a long trail that has brought me all the way from Berlin to the Watergate apartment parking garage."

"What happened to the SS colonel?"

"Colonel Goteborg filed the report you just read at Heinrich Himmler's office. Not that Himmler or anybody important was still hanging around to read it. By that time, the Russians were just blocks away, and Himmler's senior staff knew they were all doomed. Goteborg probably handed his report to some clerk who filed it without ever reading it. Goteborg himself made a last-minute escape from Berlin to the West. He was captured a few weeks later by elements of the US Third Army and interrogated by G-2."

"What happened to Zyklon?"

Brückner hands me back my lighter.

"That's what we all want to know. Before he left Berlin, the colonel did one final act in his capacity as a ranking SS officer, something he did not mention in his official report. He returned to the 'super fortress,' called in the army engineer battalion, and ordered them to install explosive charges throughout the building structure. When the engineers left, Goteborg went to the subbasement level, where Professor Nieland was impatiently waiting to learn about Hitler's reaction to the news that Zyklon was ready to be deployed. Goteborg informed Nieland about his visit to the Führer and told him he had received his final orders. Goteborg did not tell Nieland what those orders were. He told Nieland he was making final arrangements to remove the Zyklon cylinders from the building.

"When Goteborg returned to street level, he detonated the explosive charges, and the entire fortress collapsed, burying the laboratory and Zyklon and Professor Nieland and his dead colleagues under tons of brick and mortar and reinforced concrete."

"Why did Goteborg do that?" I say. "I assumed he was a good Nazi."

"He was. But he had by then become fervently opposed to Hitler. He understood that Hitler was a mad man."

"How do we know what Goteborg did in his last hours in Berlin?"

"Because he told us. When he was captured, he was interrogated by an American G-2 intelligence officer by the name of Second Lieutenant Lionel Schwarz, attached to the American Third Army. Apparently, Schwarz, who spoke German, and Colonel Goteborg established a relationship of some mutual trust.

"Schwarz was rotated out of G-2, sent back to the US, and demobilized a few months later. But before Schwarz returned to the US, Goteborg told Schwarz what had happened during those last hours in Berlin, and Schwarz wrote it up in his report to his G-2 superiors. Goteborg had concluded that Hitler was insane and that his orders would result in the pointless destruction of Berlin and the deaths of tens of thousands of German troops and civilians. Goteborg finally realized that Hitler cared nothing for his army or the German people who were, at that very moment, dying to protect him. He cared for only one thing. Himself. And his place in history. Goteborg decided to ignore Hitler's orders and, instead, determined to destroy Zyklon so it could never be used.

"Goteborg may have known that a poison gas known as Zyklon B had been used to murder millions of Jews in the camps. Was Goteborg ashamed of how Zyklon had been used by the SS? Or was he trying to cover up the crimes the SS had committed? We'll never know. Goteborg hanged himself in his prison cell a few weeks later.

"Before he left for the States, Schwarz filed his report on Goteborg with Army G-2 headquarters, where it lay unread among mountains of reports for fifty years. Just as Goteborg's report to Heinrich Himmler, found by Russian military intelligence in the ruins of Himmler's Berlin headquarters lay untouched in the archives of Soviet military intelligence. Nobody made a connection between the two reports. Not until 1990, after the fall of the Berlin Wall and with the unification of Germany, did we in the BND see copies of the original Goteborg file, which you just read, and the Schwarz report.

"Six months ago, one of our BND researchers compared the two files and made the connection. He knew what Zyklon was, and he now knew where to find it. The researcher's name was Hugo Holst. Unfortunately, Herr Holst was a member, unknown to us at the time, of the National Democratic Party, an extremist right-wing, neo-Nazi group in Germany. Holst, we've since learned, was able to identify the site of the fortress where Zyklon was buried under tons of rubble. We assume that he informed members of his party leadership about what he discovered. The party had struck gold. For years, they'd been looking for a deadly weapon they could use to finally win the war they'd lost in 1945."

"But, Herr Brückner, Zyklon was buried under tons of concrete and steel. What use was it to them?"

"Remember what was happening in Berlin after the fall of the Wall. There were construction projects everywhere. The city was being rebuilt. The right-wing organization found a man who was head of a large construction company and sympathetic to right-wing causes and persuaded him to excavate the site and remove Zyklon."

"That must have been an enormous undertaking and cost a fortune."

"It was. We believe a man, extremely wealthy and powerful, financed the excavation of the site of the fortress and the recovery of the Zyklon cylinders. Zyklon had survived the destruction of the building, and the cylinders were found intact."

"Where are the Zyklon cylinders now?"

"The man you tried to interrogate told you 'Zyklon has come.' That means that Zyklon has been secretly transferred to somewhere here in the United States. We believe Zyklon is now in the hands of an organization called Black Sun."

"What is Black Sun?"

"It's a global neo-Nazi organization. Its purpose is to install Nazi regimes around the world."

"What does Black Sun plan to do with Zyklon?"

"It looks like Black Sun plans to create a catastrophic attack on the US government."

"What would be the purpose?"

"We think Black Sun plans to reduce the US—the government and society—to ruins, at which point the man financing all this will buy what's left."

"Why would anyone want to do that?"

"If you're so rich you already own everything—the yachts, the homes, the businesses and industries—what is there left to buy? Perhaps your own country."

"That's monstrous. You can't just buy a country!"

"If you're rich enough, you can buy anything. But it helps to be crazy."

"Our county is not for sale."

"I'm afraid it's on the market to the highest bidder. In today's social and political conditions, it's all too possible. Black Sun can seize control of the levers of power, using militia forces where necessary. The man behind this plan—the man with enough money to finance it, will become Black Sun. And ultimately the new Hitler."

"Can this be stopped?"

"Our immediate objective is to get hold of Zyklon. Without Zyklon, Black Sun and its leader can do nothing."

Brückner gives up on his pipe and replaces it and the tobacco pouch in his jacket pocket. "Zyklon is a neurotoxin gas developed in Germany in 1938. It's a precursor to what is known these days as sarin. In the 1940s, the SS, on Hitler's orders, contracted with Nieland to produce large quantities of the gas for use as a military weapon. What Nieland developed is what we call Zyklon C. That is what we're searching for. That's what the man you tried to arrest was telling you."

"I thought sarin was outlawed."

"It is. That doesn't mean it doesn't exist. Sarin was used by an extremist group in Japan in 1995 in a terrorist attack in the Tokyo subway system. In 1997, the Assad regime in Syria used sarin to suppress domestic opposition. More than a thousand people were killed in that single attack."

"Do you believe sarin gas, or Zyklon, is now in the hands of this Black Sun?"

"I believe that a substantial amount of Zyklon C has been secretly shipped into the United States and is under the control of Black Sun. We think it is now hidden, probably somewhere not far from Washington." Brückner removes a piece of newsprint from his briefcase. It's a tear-out from the *Washington Post* Style section, print edition. It includes the crossword puzzle.

"Look at sixteen across," Brückner says. "Read the clue."

I already know what it says. "'Winds rotating counterclockwise in the South China Sea.' Cyclone? But 'cyclone' doesn't fit. Cyclone has seven letters. The puzzle has space for only six."

"Try the word using the German spelling. Zyklon. It fits perfectly."

"What does all this mean?"

"The word 'Zyklon' is a signal."

"A signal for what?"

"For end times. For Armageddon to launch."

"I'm not a believer in conspiracy theories."

"You should be. Sometimes they're actually true." Brückner reaches into his briefcase and removes a photograph. "Two nights ago, one of my agents was able to enter a warehouse where Black Sun had hidden Zyklon. Somewhere in Virginia. He managed to take a single photograph of the stockpile of cylinders with his cell phone and transmit it to our headquarters in Berlin. That's why I'm here today."

Brückner pushes the photo across the table. The picture is dark and grainy. I make out a stack of what seem to be cylinders. Standing in the shadows is a single man. He stands with his back to the camera.

"There's something written on the cylinders," I say.

"We've had our graphic technicians in Berlin work on the photo. They deciphered the stenciled text. The top line reads Zyklon C."

"Who is the man in the picture?"

"That is Black Sun. The man who financed this entire operation. My agents have been able to photograph the man on other occasions. His face has always been obstructed, so we can't identify him. We shared this photograph yesterday with your Department of Homeland Security. Their agents located the site somewhere in Virginia this morning. But the Zyklon cylinders were gone. Zyklon has once again vanished."

"Your agent penetrated the Black Sun organization. Can't he tell you where Zyklon is now?"

"We have not heard from him since he transmitted the picture. We must assume he was exposed and killed."

"Why am I involved? Until today, I'd never heard of Zyklon. Why was I attacked in the parking garage of the Watergate apartments?"

"Because a man whispered the words 'Zyklon has come.' And warned you about Black Sun."

"That doesn't mean I know anything about this plot."

"You know more than you think you know. You heard the word 'Zyklon.' You know that Black Sun is connected to Zyklon. What Black Sun doesn't know is whether the man you tried to arrest told you the name of Black Sun himself. He cannot take that chance. Not before Inauguration Day. I'm afraid, as a result, you are deeply involved with Zyklon and with Black Sun, whether you like it or not."

Chapter Eleven

I HAVE A SECOND MARTINI while Brückner tells me about Black Sun but nothing about the wealthy man who is paying for all of this. At one point while Brückner tries to fire up his pipe, I call Latasha. I get her voicemail and leave her a brief message. "In investigating the crossword puzzle lead, try spelling 'cyclone' in the German manner. 'Zyklon' with a 'Z.' Good luck."

What I learn from Brückner leaves me cold sober, but I'm probably over the blood-alcohol limit. That's all I'd need to end a perfect day—a cop pulling me over and tagging me for DUI. It's dark when I leave the Peking Palace and say goodbye to Brückner and the waiter, Zhang. I drive home—slowly and with caution—through snow-clogged streets. Only when I get home do I find my perfect day isn't over yet.

A black sedan blocks the entrance to my driveway. After what Brückner told me about werewolves, I'm cautious, and I consider driving past my home and coming back later. But then I see the sedan's license plate. I silently curse as I climb out of my MG, walk around the black sedan, and rap on the window of the rear passenger door. I don't bother speaking to the two armed men sitting in the front seat. They're just window dressing.

"Get in, Marko." Carla Lowry opens the passenger door for me. "Quick. Don't let the cold air in."

"It's late. I've had an eventful day. Can't this wait until tomorrow, Carla?"

"No, it can't—as you know perfectly well."

There's no point in arguing. Carla's wearing a stylish outfit, professional and conservative, with a bit of discreet silver jewelry. She never loses her allure. She's obviously come from some classy social event given by and for the elite. The kind of event I'm not welcome at.

"What kind of mischief have you gotten into now?" she says as I take the seat next to her and give her my disarming smile. She doesn't wait for a response. "This afternoon, there was a gunfight in the parking garage in the Watergate building. My forensics people are examining the scene. They found a machine pistol under one of the parked cars. Not the weapon of choice for carjackers. There were traces of blood on the garage floor. Looks like there was a major firefight."

"Why are you telling me all this?"

"Every time there's an unexplained act of violence in Washington, I immediately think of you. Why is that, I wonder? I know you were at the Watergate this afternoon, visiting Vice President-elect Grant. Were you involved in this shootout as well?"

How does she know I met with Grant? Is Carla having me tailed these days? That shows a disappointing lack of trust. "Carla, how can you even ask?"

Carla squints, as she always does when she knows I'm lying.

"Were there any victims?" I ask.

"None we could find. That doesn't mean there were none. My people tell me that it looks like the scene was cleaned up. Professionally."

"What's the problem, then?"

"You're the problem, Marko."

"You're being terribly judgmental."

Carla barely suppresses her irritation. "What trouble have you gotten yourself into this time?"

"You worry too much."

"Don't bullshit me, Marko. I'm not asking out of idle curiosity. Right now, I'm dealing with a major national security fuckup. Tell me what's going on. If not, I may have Anthony or Jesse"—she gestures toward the two men sitting in the front seat of the car—"beat the crap out of you."

"You'd never do something like that."

"Don't tempt me. Why were you seeing General Grant?"

"Secretary Fletcher told me to call on him."

"What did Grant want?"

"He wants me to provide protection for him."

"Ridiculous."

"That's what I thought."

"Okay. What else have you been up to?"

"I met with Cosmo Hunter this afternoon."

"You what?"

I can see I've taken Carla's breath away. It's not often I get to surprise her about anything.

"We had tea. He wants me to help find the man responsible for the Friendship House bombing."

"I don't get it."

"Neither do I. He implied the police, the FBI, and Homeland Security will screw up the investigation."

"He may be right. I hope you accepted his offer."

"I didn't. Cosmo Hunter was lying to me."

"What makes you say that?"

"He told me he lives by a code of honor he learned from his parents on a farm somewhere. That's crap. You don't become the richest man in the world by observing some code of honor. You don't become a billionaire by playing by the rules and being a nice guy. You become the richest man in the world by fucking people over."

"You're being very cynical."

"I don't know why he's wasting time with a dumb cop."

"Maybe because he knows you're an exceptional crime investigator. Maybe because, despite everything, you can be trusted to do your job and to tell the truth. Sometimes."

It's time to level with Carla about what else happened. "I also met with an old friend of yours. Walter Brückner."

"What's Walter doing in Washington?"

"Ask him."

"I will."

I decide to leave out the incident in the parking garage. I'll let Brückner explain that away.

"Walter and I are old colleagues," Carla says. "We're mostly on the same side. Not always, but mostly. As a courtesy, we usually keep each other informed when we're on the other's turf. What's Walter up to?"

"You don't trust him?"

"As much as he trusts me. What does he want?"

"He's looking for something he called Zyklon C."

"Oh, Christ." She puts her face in her hands. "That's not good. Walter told you about Zyklon C? That was indiscreet."

"You know about Zyklon C?"

"I know enough to be very frightened."

"He told me Zyklon has been brought into this country and hidden somewhere."

"Did he say where?"

"He said agents of the Department of Homeland Security

raided a place in Virginia this morning. Zyklon had been hidden there but was removed before the agents arrived."

"Homeland Security made a raid this morning?" Carla is almost breathless with shock. "Liz Fletcher didn't tell me about the raid. Or about Zyklon being in this country. I just spoke with her. The bitch never said a word."

"Maybe she doesn't like you. You have that effect on some people."

"Fuck you, Marko."

"I'd say whoever brought Zyklon into the country must have been tipped off about the raid. Probably by somebody inside Homeland Security."

"Of course they were. Who brought Zyklon into this country?"

"Brückner thinks it's a neo-Nazi terrorist organization called Black Sun."

She shuts her eyes, as if in pain. "You're not supposed to know about Black Sun either. Did he say who Black Sun is?"

"He said he didn't know the name. Brückner believes Black Sun plans to use Zyklon to assassinate the new US president and trigger a revolution."

"Go on."

"Brückner had an agent inside the Black Sun organization."

"Had?" she says.

"Brückner's pretty sure the agent was exposed and killed. What do you know about Black Sun?"

"Stay out of this, Marko. This is way above your pay grade."

"I'm already involved. Yesterday when I tried to arrest a man, he told me 'Black Sun' had arrived and is watching me."

"That's it?"

"There's something I want you to see."

I take out the copy of the letter I found on my desk.

LASCIATE OGNI SPERANZA, VOI CH'ENTRATE.
YOU WILL FIND ME HERE,
BUT YOU WILL NEVER ESCAPE.

Carla reads it. Twice. "What's this about?"

"Beats the hell out of me."

"Why are you showing it to me, then?"

"I need the Bureau's help in analyzing this letter. There's something strange about it."

"I can tell you it's in old Italian."

"I know that. It's the font I'm curious about. I want your wizards at the Bureau to examine this letter and tell me when and where it was typed."

"Do you think this note is related to Black Sun?"

"Of course it is. Do this for me as a favor. For old times' sake."

"I'll see what I can find out."

"I also need to know who Black Sun is."

"I'd advise you to stay away from Black Sun. But of course, you'll ignore me. As usual. If you really want to know about Black Sun, there's one man who could give you some answers. If he feels like talking to you. Which he probably won't."

"Who is the guy who could tell me about Black Sun but maybe won't?"

"He's a professor who used to teach modern history at Princeton. He's retired now, living here in Washington. He knows all there is to know about right-wing, neo-Nazi organizations."

"Have you talked to him?"

"I've tried to. He won't talk to me. He thinks I'm a fascist witch. He doesn't talk to anybody in the FBI. Or from Homeland Security. Or the police, for that matter. He's convinced we're all members of a modern-day Gestapo. If you can persuade him that you're not a part of some right-wing conspiracy planning to put him and all other right-minded people like him into concentration camps, he might talk to you."

"He sounds like somebody I'd like."

"This is serious shit we're facing, Marko. You could get hurt. Leave Black Sun to me." She sighs. She knows that won't happen.

"Give me his damn name."

"His name is Severin Fairfield. Persuade him you're one of the good guys. Tell him you'll share your Pete Seeger record collection with him. Maybe he'll talk to you then."

Chapter Twelve

AN OFFICIOUS VOICE on my cell phone announces, "The Secretary must speak with you. Now!"

I haven't had my morning coffee, so I'm not at my most personable, and the peremptory tone ticks me off. My desk is covered with investigation reports and messages that have come in overnight. After some annoyed reflection, I figure the voice on the phone probably belongs to the bespectacled man I saw in the office of the Secretary of Homeland Security. Which makes the "secretary," the Secretary of Homeland Security, Liz Fletcher herself.

Twice in two days. I should be honored.

I'm not.

I consider ignoring the summons. I need my coffee. Need time to think about what I've learned in the last twenty-four hours. I know that won't work. One must always answer a summons from Mount Olympus. Even before morning coffee. Otherwise, be prepared to be zapped by a thunderbolt.

"The Secretary is expecting you now," the voice informs me. I'm given an address—not that of the headquarters of Homeland Security. The reports on my desk and the phone messages will have to wait.

From the outside, the place looks like an ordinary town house and is located not far from the White House. In this area of the city, the streets have been plowed and are mostly clear.

I've been to this place before. This is a safe house used by US intelligence agencies. Nothing good ever comes of such visits.

I'm escorted by armed security guards into an ordinary-looking office. At a desk sits the bespectacled young man with his hair parted in the middle. I seem to remember his name is Arthur, the same man who was holding an umbrella for the secretary when I first spotted her at the bomb site "You took long enough," he says.

"What's this all about?" I say.

"Follow me. And learn." Arthur leads me through a warren of narrow corridors and small offices, all empty at this early hour, until we reach a closed door. Two uniformed, armed guards sit at small desks on either side. One of the guards, who wears a plastic ID that says Smitty, instructs me to empty my pockets. I dump my wallet, watch, and car keys into a plastic container. Reluctantly, I add my cigarette lighter.

Smitty instructs me to walk through a metal detector arch, then checks me out with a handheld detector wand. The whole scene is mostly déjà vu. It's the same routine I went through when I visited General Grant—except there was no detector arch and Grant's Secret Service agent was cuter than Smitty.

"She's in a bad mood," Arthur says under his breath. "Be careful."

He opens the door, and I step into an empty room. Except it's not a room at all. And it's not really empty. It's a shell that contains another complete room within it. This inner room is brilliantly lit by racks of fluorescent lights that emit a faint humming sound. The walls of the inner room are constructed of transparent plastic, as are the ceiling and floor. The entire edifice is raised two feet above the existing concrete floor, resting on transparent plastic blocks. This is a room designed and constructed to prevent any possibility of electronic eavesdropping or any other unwanted device being brought in unseen.

I've been in safe rooms like this before. They're routinely used by security agencies when carrying out super-secret consultations. I'm not reassured. I walk up the two plastic steps and enter the brightly lit inner sanctum. Mr. Peepers closes the door behind me, leaving me alone with Liz Fletcher. The room is furnished with a transparent plastic conference table and four transparent molded plastic chairs. Liz, dressed in a severe, well-tailored dark suit—not transparent—sits at the plastic table. She wears horn-rimmed glasses.

On the table in front of her lies a thick manila folder that she closes quickly when I step into the plastic room.

"Good morning, Madam Secretary. I didn't expect to have the pleasure of seeing you again so soon."

She removes her glasses and points with them at one of the molded plastic chairs. "Believe me when I say that pleasure has nothing to do with our meeting this morning. Sit down."

"Why are we meeting here rather than in your lovely office?" I ask as I sit across from her. "I rather liked your fake fireplace."

"There have been serious developments since we last talked. I've deemed it prudent to increase security precautions."

"Would those 'serious developments' have anything to do

with the fact that you managed to lose a deadly poison gas called Zyklon?"

"Zyklon!" She almost chokes. "Zyklon is classified. Way above your clearance level, Detective. Where did you hear that word?"

This would explain her bad mood Mr. Peepers told me about. Losing a cache of weapons of mass destruction somewhere in Virginia can ruin your day.

"Did General Grant tell you about Zyklon?" she asks.

"I'm not at liberty to say."

Her right arm twitches, knocking her reading glasses to the floor. "I must remind you," she says, snatching up the glasses, "I'm responsible for our nation's security. As long as I am, you will do as I say."

"That's not the way it works, ma'am. I'm an officer of the District of Columbia Metropolitan Police Department. I report to the chief of police."

Fletcher takes a deep breath. "You forget that I put you on temporary assignment as an acting Secret Service agent. You work for me now. Not Kelly Flynn. Have you joined General Grant's security detail?"

"No, ma'am. He told me not to."

She leans forward in her chair as though she didn't quite hear me properly. "He told you what?"

"He has a different assignment for me."

"Did Bobby Grant instruct you to investigate the man responsible for the Friendship House terror attack?"

Holy batshit! "Have you been bugging my private communications?" I say.

"Consider it your tax dollars at work."

"That's illegal!"

"I say what's illegal in this town. I repeat: Did General

Grant order you to find the man responsible for the bombing of Friendship House?"

"That's between the general and me."

Her face flushes. "That's outrageous," she says. "Have you forgotten who I am?" She shakes her head in disgust. "I've reviewed your military file, Detective Zorn. As I noted when we first met, the file I saw was highly redacted. I now know General Grant had you court-martialed, did he not?"

"He tried. He failed."

"What charges did he bring against you?"

"Refusal to carry out a direct order."

"What was the order?"

"I'd prefer not to talk about it. It's ancient history and irrelevant to the present crisis."

"Around here, I say what's irrelevant. Under the circumstances, it seems odd that he wants you, of all people, to join his security detail."

"Seems odd to me, too."

"You have ample cause to resent General Grant. Even hate him. He destroyed your Army career. In my book, that makes you a threat to him."

"I had no career prospects in the military by that time. By then, I was finished with the Army. And the Army was finished with me. There were no hard feelings."

She takes a gulp of air. "What do you know about Zyklon?"

"I know that it's a poison gas. Cylinders of it have been brought secretly into this country and hidden somewhere. Your agency was informed about Zyklon's location. You found it, until your people lost it. That's sort of embarrassing, isn't it?"

"You're speaking about highly sensitive intelligence—highly classified information."

"I must point out that the word 'Zyklon' was recently featured in the *Washington Post* crossword puzzle, a copy of which I saw on the desk in your office. Does that count?"

She glares at me. "Who told you about Zyklon?"

"If I tell you, will you tell me about Black Sun?"

"Listen to me, Zorn. Listen carefully. Never, and I mean never, mention 'Black Sun' again. To anyone. Have nothing further to do with Grant, regardless of what that damn fool wants. I'm pulling rank. I'm instructing the Secret Service to deny you access to Robert Grant. Do not, under any circumstances, take orders from him. Do not undertake any actions on his behalf. I'm firing you as an acting Secret Service agent. I know what you are. You're a grifter. I have no use for grifters in my organization. But before I throw you out, I have one question for you. Who is Black Sun?"

"I haven't a clue."

She studies me intently, then sits back in her plastic chair. "I didn't think you knew."

"So, why am I here then?"

"I had to be sure."

"You believe me?"

"Actually, I do. As much as that goes against my better judgment."

"Why?"

"Because if you really knew who Black Sun was, you'd be dead now."

Chapter Thirteen

THE SKY IS LEADEN, heavy with snow. It's dark; the few cars still moving on the streets have their headlights on. Latasha and Celia, the assistant chief medical examiner, are waiting for me in the lobby of the medical examiner's building. Usually bustling with people who have business with the dead, the space is mostly empty today. Almost tomb-like, you might say.

Latasha and I follow Celia through to the police morgue. We stop at a locked door labeled Office of the Chief Medical Examiner, Examination Room, Authorized Personnel Only. Celia punches in a code on a cyber lock and the door opens. 9-12-17-4-20. As I usually do, I observe the code Celia uses and memorize it. You never know.

When we step into the morgue, Celia throws a switch, and lights flicker on. We're standing in a room furnished with a half dozen steel examination tables. A body lies on one table, covered by a heavy blanket. Celia picks up the clipboard attached to the end of the table.

"Deceased. Name unknown."

"Quiet day?" Latasha asks, looking around the empty room.

"The snow is keeping everyone at home. Even the dead. Of course, we had a massive input from the Friendship House bombing. We finished identifying the last of the victims late last night."

"What did you want to ask us about?" I say.

"There was an incident at the Potomac Avenue Metro station a short time ago." Celia examines the clipboard. "A man fell off the platform and was crushed by an incoming Metro train. The body arrived here an hour ago. I saw your report about your encounter at the bomb scene. The Metro train victim looked like someone who might be your guy." She moves one corner of the cloth cover revealing the face of a young man, horribly disfigured.

Latasha gasps and steps back. She's still not used to seeing the victims of violent death and is pained by the sight. I hope she never gets over that. She should never become so hardened that she doesn't feel sick when she sees the damage that can be done to a human body. I hope she never becomes like me.

"Show me his feet," I say.

Celia pulls the cloth away. He's wearing mustard-colored Air Jordan high-tops.

"Did he have a cell phone on him?"

"No phone."

"Does anybody under the age of fifty leave home without a cell phone these days?"

"The Transit Police think he may have been robbed just before the accident."

"He fell off the Metro platform?" Latasha's voice is laced with skepticism.

"That's what the Metro Transit Police told me."

"Were there any witnesses?" I ask.

Celia looks at the clipboard. "They told me the station was almost empty at the time, as schools, government offices, and many businesses are closed because of the snow and the Friendship House bombing. There was one woman on the platform near where this man fell. She told the Transit Police officers she had her back turned when it happened."

"Any ID?"

"The victim's pockets were empty."

"Did the Transit Police get the name and description of this woman who didn't see anything?" I ask.

Celia examines the clipboard.

"A Mrs. Edna Emanon. She has a Baltimore address."

"Latasha, please have the Baltimore police check out the witness. Not that they'll find anything. Edna doesn't exist."

"Why not?"

"Because 'Emanon' is 'No name' spelled backward. The address will turn out to be an empty lot. Somebody's playing games with us."

"There's something else you need to see." Celia removes the blanket, revealing the dead man's upper torso. He's still wearing the hoodie, now stiff with his blood. Beneath the hoodie, there's a green denim shirt that's been torn open, showing what's left of the man's chest. Celia points to a tattoo on the man's left shoulder. It's small and hard to read, but I make out two concentric circles connected by twelve broken lines. In the middle is a black circle.

"I've seen this tattoo before," Celia says. "All on dead white men. The tattoo is always on the left shoulder. Does it mean anything to you?"

Am I looking at a werewolf? It seems somehow appropriate that this perpetrator will be resting, at least for a few days, among the victims from the bombing of Friendship House. Serves him right.

Using my cell phone, I take a picture of the tattoo while

Celia collects the metrics from the unknown man lying on the slab, including height, weight, and skin and eye color. Latasha takes his fingerprints on an electronic gizmo and sends the data electronically to the central police crime reporting center with a request that identification be given highest priority.

My cell phone rings. "What progress are you making on our enterprise, old man?" General Bobby Grant doesn't bother to introduce himself. Probably just as well. Who knows who's listening?

"A couple of guys were waiting for me in the parking garage in your building and tried to kill me. If you call that progress."

"Great! You've attracted their attention." Grant doesn't ask whether I was injured. "You're drawing them out into the open. That's a good thing."

I pause before going on. "You should know, Liz Fletcher called me to one of her offices this morning."

"What did the bitch want to know this time?"

"What you and I are up to."

"Don't tell the lady shit. The attack on you puts everything in a new light. You and I need to talk. Meet me at the Army and Navy Club. Join me in the bar at six. We can talk tactics."

"I thought the Army and Navy Club was exclusively for commissioned officers. Should I sneak in through the service entrance?"

"The club's management will lower their standards this once and let you in the front door. At my personal request. After all, it's still the Christmas season. One mustn't lose the Christmas spirit."

General Grant hangs up before I can say, "humbug."

Chapter Fourteen

After checking my coat at the front door of the Army and Navy Club, I join General Robert Grant in the Daiquiri Lounge. I nod to the pretty Secret Service agent sitting at a table near the bar's entrance, whose name, I seem to remember, is Susan. It doesn't look like Susan's received orders from Liz Fletcher not to let me near Robert Grant. If she has, Grant has countermanded the order.

Tonight, Susan's watching those of us who enter the bar, prepared to intervene, by force if necessary, if anybody should disturb the general's peace. She regards me with cool distrust, doubtless recalling Bob Grant's warning about the kind of person I am around beautiful women. Another agent—male—stands near the bar, surveying the room. Almost certainly there are other agents posted at strategic locations throughout the club.

I'm not a frequent visitor to the Army and Navy Club. Sometimes, as is the case tonight, I'm here as a guest of some club member. Even then I feel like an intruder. Membership in the club is limited to commissioned officers. I'm afraid I'm an enlisted man at heart. I can't seem to get over that.

Usually, when I'm invited, it's for lunch or dinner in the oak-paneled dining room. At one end of that room is a large mural depicting a bunch of naked women cavorting in what I suppose is an ocean. Maybe they're sea nymphs or some such mythic marine creatures. It's always struck me that the picture is not very martial in character. I hope this doesn't mean our military leaders are going soft.

The Daiquiri Lounge is almost empty this evening, maybe because of the weather. A man in a poorly cut tweed suit is talking to the bartender. He's maybe forty and has a narrow face and an aquiline nose. He reminds me of a Roman bust I saw years ago in a museum. A man in a tuxedo and an attractive blonde woman in a low-cut dress sit at the bar speaking softly to one another. The staff, all men of color, are keeping a close eye on Bobby Grant. They'll see that no tourist or inebriated club member disturbs the general. If someone should break through Susan's defensive lines, Grant is well protected.

"What are you drinking, my boy?" Grant asks as I sit at the table.

"I'll pass."

Bobby Grant shrugs. "Who attacked you in the Watergate parking garage?"

"We weren't introduced. I believe they call themselves werewolves."

Grant nods as if the name is familiar to him.

"They work for an outfit known as Black Sun," I add. "Black Sun has possession of a dangerous weapon—a poison gas developed by the Nazis at the end of World War II. It's called Zyklon. Some of this gas has recently been smuggled into the States and been hidden somewhere in Virginia."

Grant signals to a waiter, who rushes to our table. "Another Manhattan, Antoine. Why doesn't the government just seize the damn poison gas and get rid of it?" Grant says. "How hard can that be? From what I understand, these neo-Nazi types are made up of redneck yahoos incapable of doing anything more complicated than flushing a toilet."

"Liz Fletcher's people were close to locating the Zyklon gas," I explain, "but Black Sun was tipped off and moved it before her agents were able to take possession."

"Liz Fletcher lost this damn poison gas? Jesus! No wonder this country has gone to the fucking dogs. What is Liz doing about it?"

"She didn't take me into her confidence. I don't think she likes me much."

"With good reason, I'm sure. Why did she want to talk to you?"

"She wanted to know whether I knew the name of the man responsible for the terror bombing of Friendship House. A man she referred to as Black Sun."

"Do you know?"

"Not yet."

"Don't screw around. I need the name of Black Sun. But don't tell Liz shit. Understand?"

"I'll keep it between us. She also fired me. I'm no longer a Secret Service agent."

"Outfuckingstanding. Don't let Liz fuck things up again."

"She also doesn't want me to take orders from you."

"Then you better get moving fast, Zorn. Don't dick around. We don't have much time. Black Sun must be identified and destroyed before Inauguration Day."

Bob Grant does not look like he's upset with the news about Zyklon or the fact I don't know who Black Sun is. I have the impression it's all old news to him. He looks more like a man who's thinking it would be nice to have a drink with Susan.

I get up from the table, nod to Grant, then to Susan, who gives me back an icy stare, and leave. I collect my coat from the hatcheck girl at the club's front entrance and step outside, where it's cold and windy. A small cluster of men and women huddle on the front steps, waiting for their cars or Uber rides. Some of the men are in dress uniform. Several of the women wear mink stoles around bare shoulders. They look cold. There's no sign of the man in the tweed suit. The streets are dark and empty. In the distance, a lone dump truck pushes a snowplow, working its way slowly along K Street.

The door behind me opens, and the couple I saw at the bar—the blonde woman and the man in a tuxedo—step out and join the crowd. The woman's evening dress shows off her ample bosom. I worry she's going to catch cold. A third man steps out the front door and bumps slightly into the couple. The woman stumbles forward a bit and presses against me.

"I'm so sorry," she whispers, and smiles. I feel the warmth of her body and inhale her perfume. There's a quick exchange of apologies as a black limo arrives, and the man in the tux and the blonde climb in quickly and are gone.

There are half a dozen other people waiting for their rides, and I realize I may be here for a long time before I get a cab. It's too cold for me to stand around waiting, so I decide to walk a bit and look for a cab.

Farragut Square is a small urban park—not much to look at, especially not in midwinter. Tonight, it's just a barren space with benches half buried in the snow. A few distant streetlamps on Connecticut Avenue cast a dim light over the deserted park.

I'm halfway across the park when I become aware it is not

as deserted as I thought. Two men appear in front of me at the end of my path and stand motionless, watching me. Why would two men just stand in a park on a dark winter night? Nobody does that.

I stop and decide to return to the club. When I turn, my way is blocked by two more men walking quickly toward me, both holding what look very much like guns.

I reach for my cell phone to call for backup.

My phone is gone.

I always carry my phone in my left inside jacket pocket. There's no point searching further. I know I've been robbed. The woman with the blonde hair and ample bosom must have done the dip while I was distracted by the feeling of her body pressed against me. She would have passed the phone to her accomplice, the man in the tuxedo. They're both long gone now. Along with the dude who "accidentally" jostled her. A classic hustle, and I was the mark. The couple was waiting for me at the bar when I arrived. Somebody knew I was coming.

I have more immediate things to worry about right now.

I know I'm dealing with the werewolves Brückner told me about, and I know I'm in deep shit. Unless I do something fast, this will not end well. I can't call for help because there's no one around, I can't get back to the club for safety, and I can't fight.

I have one option—run like hell.

I step off the walkway and sprint across the empty park, stumbling and sliding through knee-deep snow.

There's a shot from behind me. Then another. I have nowhere to hide or find shelter from the gunmen. All I have to protect me is darkness. And speed. And as much dodging and twisting as I can manage in the snow. Twice I stumble, then scramble to my feet. I don't look back. I know the gunmen must be close behind me, but they're having the same trouble I'm having, getting through the snowdrifts in the dark. I run into a bench, half buried in the snow, hitting my shin. There are two more shots from behind. One from my left. One from the right. The werewolves are closing in fast.

I reach the far sidewalk. There's no one nearby. No taxi. No private vehicle. No group of late-night revelers I can join. Certainly no police. There's never a cop when you need one. Nothing is moving except the snowplow now a block away.

I race toward the truck with the plow, dodging among parked cars and bicycle racks. I'm limping; my shin aches. Blood pounds in my ears. My pursuers are gaining on me. Soon they'll be within easy shooting distance. Except it's hard to aim well if you're running through drifts of snow.

I reach the snowplow and lunge for the truck's passenger door, high above the street, praying it isn't locked. I yank the door open and climb up, grasping a heavy metal handhold on the side of the cab, and pull myself into the passenger seat and slam the door closed.

"Who the fuck are you?" the driver demands. He's an elderly Black man wearing heavy work clothes—probably a sanitation worker in his day job—now drafted into a snow-clearing crew. He has a neatly trimmed white beard and mustache. He stares at me, open-mouthed.

"I'm a police officer. Don't stop! Keep moving. Fast! There are gunmen after me."

At that point, one of the gunmen catches up to the truck, trying to locate me through the passenger side window, now almost opaque from condensation. We're high off the ground, and he can't see me clearly, so he can't aim well. He tries a shot, and the round hits one of the truck's side panels. A second man appears in the headlights in front of us. He fires twice, holding his gun in both hands. He's in a better shooting position than the first man. The windshield shatters. I feel splinters of window glass and freezing air on my face.

That aggravates the driver, who slams his foot on the accelerator, and we lurch forward toward the shooter. The truck, with the snow blade lowered, crowds in on the man, now caught between the plow blade and the snow piled on the side of the street. The driver scoops the shooter up and dumps him into a large snowbank.

"That man tried to break my damn truck," the driver yells, followed by furious curses. He moves the truck forward and pulls into the street. I catch a quick glimpse of one of the gunmen leaping to one side, slammed into a snowbank where he flails.

We drive at what feels like a high speed but is probably no more than twenty-five miles per hour. Cold wind and snow pour through the shattered windshield.

"They shouldn't 'a done that," the driver yells. "This rig's the property of the District of Columbia Department of Public Works. Damaging public property is a crime. Who's gonna pay for that?"

"Send the bill to the mayor. Tell her Detective Marko Zorn sent you. They know me downtown."

The driver turns on Twelfth Street. "We got company," he says.

In the side-view mirror, I see a black sedan immediately behind us with its headlights off. The sedan driver tries to pull up alongside us but can't get by because of the snowdrifts.

The street is down to two lanes, and the opposite lane is blocked.

We're barreling along Seventh Street now, nearing H Street and approaching the arch marking Washington's China-town. I tell the driver to stop.

"In the middle of the street?"

"In the middle of the street. Don't move your rig until I get away. I don't want the car following us to be able to move around you until I'm gone."

The driver stops the truck.

"You take care," I say as I pop open the door and leap for the street. I land in a snowbank and have to struggle to get out. I then run, limping, under the ornamental Chinese arch, down the empty street. The sidewalk has been mostly cleared by the business owners, but I must dodge patches of invisible ice. The restaurants and stores are locked up for the night. The street is empty.

There are footsteps behind me. With my bum leg, I know I can't outrun my attackers. I see the sign for the Peking Palace and dive down the steps and push open the front door. Most of the interior lights are out. There's just a faint light from the lurid dragon over the bar. I hear voices. Someone is coming down the steps. I lock the door behind me.

"Are you in need of help, Detective Zorn?" a voice from the dark asks. It's Zhang, the waiter who served Walter Brückner and me. He's standing in the shadows, his voice calm.

Someone pounds on the door, demanding to be let in.

"There are men outside," I say. "They're armed, and they want to kill me."

"Herr Brückner said you would be back." Zhang is hold-ing a white dishtowel in his left hand and a cooking pot in his right. He calls out in what I assume is Chinese. The doors to the kitchen swing open, and three men emerge, all wearing stained aprons, each holding ten-inch butcher knives.

"Nothing to worry about, Detective. Everything is under control. Go into the kitchen, and don't come out until I tell you it's safe."

I dive into the kitchen. Behind me, Zhang unlocks the front door. "We're closed," he calls out.

"Out of the way!"

Then there's a scream of pain. I look back and see one of the intruders covering his face with his hands, trying to wipe something off. I expect it's boiling oil from the pot Zhang holds. A second man, holding a gun in his hand, pushes through the door and steps over his buddy, who is crouching on the floor now, whimpering. Zhang grabs the new man's gun hand, twists it violently so the attacker is turned around, and smashes his head into the wall. The man's knees buckle, and he's on the floor, dazed. Two more attackers burst through the door. The three cooks, armed with the butcher knives, swarm the werewolves.

I don't wait to see what becomes of them.

Chapter Fifteen

"YOU LOOK GRUMPY." Latasha places a large cup of coffee on my desk. "I mean, you always look grumpy this early in the morning, but you look especially grumpy today."

"I had a bad night.

"What happened?"

"Some thugs attacked me."

I know she's about to say that proves I should be armed, but she checks herself. She knows that will only annoy me. Instead, she says, "You should have called for backup."

"I would have except somebody stole my damn phone."

"Was this part of our investigation into the Friendship House bombing? Is the investigation getting into dangerous territory?"

"I think it probably is."

She must see the discouragement in my face.

"We're going to beat this," she says. "We're going to find out who's responsible for the bombing, and when we find out, we'll crush 'em."

"I certainly hope you're right. At the moment we seem to be at a dead end."

"I think I may have a possible lead. I believe the terrorists placed the clue in the crossword puzzle in the paper. I know you think it's unrelated, but if we could discover who placed it, it could help us trace back to the terrorists themselves.

The tip about the correct spelling of Zyklon you left on my voicemail last night helped. I've learned who created the crossword puzzle and made an appointment at eleven for us. We can go together."

"Fine. Let's go for it. I don't have any better ideas."

"You don't have to do this investigation alone, Marko. I'm your partner. You know I have your back. We're a team."

"I know that."

"So what's bugging you?"

"There was a photo on my phone directly linked to the bombing. Now I've lost the phone and the photo."

"You can always replace your phone."

"Admin's already given me a new phone."

"So what's the problem?"

"The photo on that phone. That photograph may have been why I was attacked and the phone stolen."

"We can always get it back. It's in the cloud, you know. You can reinstall it on your phone right now."

"I have no idea how to do that."

"Oh my God! You're hopeless, Marko." Latasha takes the phone from my desk and punches keys.

She passes me back the phone. "There! All fixed."

I check my photo file. There it is.

The cell phone I'm holding in my hand rings. "Mr. Zorn?" The voice at the other end of the line is soft, almost gentle. "We must talk."

"Now?"

"I'm in Nebraska at the moment," Cosmo Hunter says. "Or to be exact, around thirty thousand feet above Nebraska. Or possibly it's Iowa. I arrive at Dulles International Airport at 10:15 this morning, your time. Meet me at 10:35."

"Can't we speak on the phone?"

"Considering what happened to you last night, the phone is not advisable. My enemies are listening. Yours, too."

I'm about to say I don't have any enemies, but that would be silly.

"My driver will pick you up at police headquarters at 9:30."

The Rolls is waiting for me. Once again, I sit in the front passenger seat with Drago Escher.

"Mr. Hunter's been under great stress in the last twenty-four hours," Escher informs me. "Please be careful when you see him."

"I've been under some stress myself," I say.

"I understand you were attacked last night."

How the hell does he know that?

"I'm informed you never carry a weapon. Why is that?"

"Why do you care, Drago? May I call you Drago?"

"I prefer that you address me as Doctor."

"Okay. Doctor it is. Why do you care about whether I carry a weapon?"

"I'm told you never kill your opponents," Dr. Escher says. "That seems strange for someone in your profession."

"Are you psychoanalyzing me?"

"I'm just looking out for Mr. Hunter's interests. Is your objection to killing political or moral?"

"Neither. It's personal."

"I've never observed that condition before."

"Consider this your lucky day."

We drive in silence the rest of the way to Dulles Airport. Dr. Escher takes us to a private terminal where a Gulfstream G700 is waiting. Ken and Barbie, in spiffy pastel uniforms, wait for me at the bottom of the landing ramp. The words Hunter Industries are embroidered on each of their blouses. They escort me onto the plane and into its luxurious interior.

"Mr. Hunter will meet you in the board room," Barbie tells me with a warm smile. I follow her to the rear of the aircraft and into a room with a conference table with a Brazilian rosewood top.

"Please make yourself comfortable. Mr. Hunter will be right with you," Barbie whispers reassuringly.

Barbie, whose real name, according to her name tag, is Laura, serves me coffee with warm brioches in a basket covered by a white linen cloth. Despite being almost murdered last night, I haven't lost my appetite. The coffee is outstanding, as is the brioche. I eat one and am tempted to eat a second but decide that would be gauche.

As I sink into the soft, buttery leather of the seat, I detect something in the air—the merest whisper of the scent of a perfume. *Strange*, I think. *This doesn't belong here.* A woman must have just left the cabin. The scent is not sweet and flowery. It's not a Barbie scent. This is something for an older woman. It's dense, luxe, kind of insolent, even brazen. Very expensive. And dangerous.

An inner door opens, and Cosmo Hunter enters, dressed in jeans and a collarless shirt. He wears loafers but no socks.

"Thank you, Laura," he says. "Inform the flight crew we depart in fifteen minutes."

Hunter sits in a chair across the table from me and places a manila envelope on the table between us. "Have you had your coffee? I'm told it's first-class. I never drink coffee myself. I'm unable to tolerate stimulants."

He seems tense. Is this the result of the stress Drago Escher mentioned? Or was it something I did when we first met, when I looked directly into Cosmo's eyes?

"What did you want to speak to me about?" I say. It has taken me forty-five minutes to get to the airport, and what with morning traffic and the bad weather, it will probably take another hour to get back into town and to police headquarters. I'm scheduled to meet with Latasha to investigate a crossword puzzle and, later, to get a lecture in history. I've got a full day ahead of me. Meanwhile, Cosmo has allowed just fifteen minutes for us to meet. I'm seriously annoyed.

"Sorry for rushing off like this." Cosmo must sense my irritation. "I'm having dinner this evening in Venice with George and Carolla. But I had to see you before I left. Something quite urgent has come up." Cosmo opens the manila envelope and takes out a glossy photograph which he pushes across the table toward me.

"This man was my chief of security. His body was found in a culvert shot in the back of the head early this morning."

It's a photograph of a man. The man with the aquiline nose I saw in the bar when I spoke with General Grant. The man who was watching me and reminded me of a Roman bust. Perhaps one of the late Roman emperors.

"Why are you showing me this?"

"It means Myland has come."

"Who is Myland?"

"You will meet Myland soon enough, I'm sure. He can't be missed. He has a very distinctive facial feature. Quite memorable, in fact."

"What am I supposed to do when I meet this Myland?"

"Cyclone has come, so you must kill him, of course. Do not hesitate." Cosmo sighs. "Except you don't kill people, do you?" He shrugs. "That's your funeral."

It comes back to me where I've heard the words. The man in the mustard-colored high-tops told me "Cyclone has come." Is Cosmo telling me that Myland has something to do with Cyclone? Does he mean that Myland is Black Sun?

"His presence here in the city is a warning," Cosmo says.

"A warning to me? Or to you?"

"Both of us."

"Are you afraid of this Myland?"

"I'm not afraid of anybody. But you should be."

"You know him?"

"Many years ago, when we were both young and innocent, I knew him. Intimately. We have had nothing to do with one another in years. Myland is wealthy. His only motive in life is to prove he's better than me—richer, more powerful. Stronger. Owns more things. He'll do anything to destroy me."

"Where does Myland live?"

"Everywhere. Nowhere."

"How am I supposed to find this Myland?"

"He will find you. More coffee?"

"I should be getting back to the city. I have a busy day."

"I'm informed that the chief of police has assigned you the lead investigator into the Friendship House bombing. That was a sound decision. It will make our task easier."

"I'm not so sure."

"I also understand you were attacked last night by armed bandits."

"It was a close thing."

"The game is afoot. It means you're getting close."

"Much too close, I'd say."

"Did you tell Liz Fletcher that you do not know who Black Sun is?"

"That's right."

"Did she believe you?"

"Who knows? She a complicated woman."

"You don't know the half of it. Liz is an 'old bitch gone in the teeth for a botched civilization.'"

"Is that what you really think?" I say. "You believe we live in a botched civilization?"

"Don't you? Liz has spent her entire adult life defending this corrupt civilization. Such a waste."

"Is Black Sun the enemy of this botched civilization?"

"He may be, or he may be its savior."

"Do you know who Black Sun is?"

"I know that Black Sun is a dreamer," he says. "A dreamer who dreams fearful dreams. He has become lost in them."

"Is Myland the leader of Black Sun?"

"Certainly not!"

"Are you an admirer of the poet Ezra Pound?"

"Why do you want to know?"

"You just quoted a line of Pound's poetry when you referred to Liz Fletcher as an 'old bitch.'"

"I can't say I care for Pound's poetry."

"What about his politics? He was a Fascist, you know. An admirer of Benito Mussolini."

"Ezra Pound was a man of profound understanding." Cosmo glances at his watch. "I must leave now. I'll be back in the States in a day or so. Find Black Sun and cut off his head. Or I'll have Dr. Escher take care of that detail. He has special skills."

Cosmo is on his feet, and Ken and Barbie are at the door, ready to escort me off the plane.

I snatch up the remaining brioche.

Dr. Escher is waiting for me at the bottom of the plane's ramp and escorts me to the Rolls. On the trip back to the city, I once again ride in the front seat.

When we arrive at police headquarters and are out of the Rolls, I say, "Mr. Hunter wants me to find somebody called

Myland. And someone he refers to as Black Sun. A man he says dreams great dreams. Are they the same person?"

Escher shrugs. "You must do as he says. Find Black Sun."

"He wants me to kill Black Sun," I say. "Why doesn't he just have you do that? That's what you do. Right?"

"I do what Mr. Hunter asks."

"Should I be afraid of you? You don't appear to be carrying a gun," I say.

"Nor do you." Suddenly Escher is holding a switchblade knife. *Where the hell did that come from?* "If I had to, I could easily use this. Of course, as you are an employee of Mr. Hunter, I would try to avoid a vital organ."

"All my organs are vital."

Escher puts away his knife. "I just wanted you to understand that I'm prepared. Are you?"

"I'm not a hired gun," I say. "I don't use guns. I assume you don't have any scruples about using that knife."

Drago shrugs. "I find it gets easier with practice."

Chapter Sixteen

T HE WOMAN at the door wears a terrycloth bathrobe and dirty pink slippers. She looks to be in her early forties, once pretty, now looking a bit faded. Her hair is black, curly, and wildly dense. We'd come in a police cruiser. My MG was making strange new noises this morning, and I didn't trust it. It sometimes has days like that.

"Sorry to disturb you, ma'am." Latasha uses her usual, cheerful tone and flashes a warm, nonthreatening smile. I've asked her to take the lead at the start of this interview. Latasha was the one who tracked down the crossword puzzle maker. "We're with the Metropolitan Police. My name is Latasha Powell. This is my partner, Marko Zorn. We have a few questions for you."

"Zorn, did you say? I've been wanting to use 'zorn' for so long. I'm crazy for the letter 'Z.' Am I in trouble?"

"Are you Zenobia Jones?" Latasha asks. "Are you the one who creates crossword puzzles?"

"I'm a cruciverbalist, yes, which means I construct crosswords. What's this about?"

"We have a question about one of your puzzles."

"I knew this day would come. I confess I cheated on one of my clues. It was 'perihelion,' wasn't it? Come on in."

Parked on the street behind us is the police cruiser we arrived in with two heavily armed, uniformed police officers watching us closely. After last night's events at the Peking Palace, I figured we could use backup. I wave at the sergeant in the front seat, and we step through the door.

I'm still limping from my run-in with the park bench.

After wiping our feet on a thick doormat—which reads Word Wise—Latasha and I follow Ms. Jones through a messy living room and into an even messier kitchen. The sink is full of dishes. One end of the kitchen counter is heaped with a large pile of books, the huge *Webster's Second Unabridged Dictionary* among them. The kitchen is clearly Ms. Jones's workplace and study. A colorful print hangs on the wall. The legend reads Words Fail Me.

"Sorry about the mess," Ms. Jones says. "I wasn't expecting guests." She doesn't sound sorry, just embarrassed. "Can I offer you some tea?" Without waiting for an answer, she goes to the range and puts on a kettle.

"I'm a great admirer of yours, Ms. Jones." Latasha sits at the kitchen counter.

"You do crosswords?"

"Whenever I get a free moment."

"I've always thought detective skills must be an advantage in solving crosswords." Ms. Jones places three Lipton tea bags in three mugs. "Of course, there are no crimes in crossword puzzles."

"I wouldn't be so sure," I say.

Ms. Jones glances at me.

Latasha's cell phone rings. "Excuse me, I have to take this."

While Latasha speaks on her phone, I ask Ms. Jones, "What did you mean when you said you always wanted to use 'zorn?'"

"It has a 'Z.' I love the letter 'Z.' And zorn could be made into such a nice clue."

"Only if you speak German," I say. "Your name is Zenobia with a 'Z.' Maybe that accounts for your partiality to the letter 'Z.' Are you Zenobia, the Queen of the Desert?"

"I'm afraid you're standing in the only kingdom I have. Here I'm queen, but I have no desert. No palace. No legions. Just a pile of dirty dishes."

"Zenobia's a rather unusual name, isn't it?"

"I have my mother to thank for that." She glances toward the ceiling above us. "Mother taught history in high school. Zenobia was queen of the Kingdom of Palmyra in the third century." Ms. Jones pours boiling water into the three mugs. "She thought the name Zenobia was something I could aspire to. Zenobia was a warrior queen, you know. Her palace was in the middle of the desert, where she thought she was safe from her enemies. At one point, her empire incorporated what is now Syria and Egypt. She challenged Rome in the West and Persia in the East. Some lady! Do you think I'm safe from my enemies here?"

"That depends on your enemies," I say.

Latasha returns to the kitchen, putting away her cell phone. She speaks to me quietly. "We've got a fix on the man in the morgue. A name and an address."

"Ms. Jones was just telling me about her namesake, Zenobia, queen of Palmyra," I say.

"I'm not sure how great an example Zenobia was for me," Ms. Jones says. "She was a success until her antics became too much for Rome to tolerate. She thought the desert was her fortress until the emperor Aurelian sent his legions across the desert to Palmyra and defeated her army. Aurelian captured Zenobia and brought her back with him to Rome in chains of gold. Or so the story goes. The lesson is, don't mess with powerful people, no matter what protection you think you have."

"Do you mess with powerful people?" I ask.

"Not if I can help it."

There's a voice from somewhere in the house, from an upper floor. A thin, elderly voice, querulous and impatient.

Ms. Jones gets up from the counter. "Excuse me." She steps out of the kitchen and calls upstairs. "It's all right, Mother. I have guests . . . No, there's nothing wrong. I'll be right up with your tea. No, it's not the same lady."

Ms. Jones returns to the kitchen counter. "Sugar?" she asks. "I'm afraid I'm out of milk. It's on my grocery list."

She brings the mugs to the counter and places them in front of us, shoving away a yellow foolscap legal pad covered with minuscule writing. She pushes a sugar bowl across the counter to us. "What can I help you with? I don't suppose you're here to get a tutorial on constructing crossword puzzles."

"Maybe a little," I say. "We're interested in one specific puzzle. A puzzle that appeared in the *Washington Post*. The title was 'Dutch Treat.'"

She sighs. "I suppose you want to know about sixteen across."

"It seems like you cheated a bit," Latasha says. "Using a German word in an English-language puzzle."

"The name of the puzzle was Dutch Treat. Dutch as in Deutsch. German. Get it? That was to alert those working the puzzle there'd be German language words used. There are other German words in the puzzle as well."

"Why did you use the word 'Zyklon' in the puzzle?" I say.

"I did Dutch Treat more than a month ago." She runs

her fingers through her thick black hair. "I'm not sure I can remember."

Latasha leans close to her and speaks in a low, soothing voice. "I don't mean to be rude, Ms. Jones, but I think you do remember. We're investigating the terrible bombing attack. I'm sure you've read about Friendship House."

Zenobia nods.

"We think the word 'Zyklon' may be an important clue about the people who planted the bomb. What gave you the idea to include 'Zyklon' in your puzzle?"

"Am I in trouble?"

Latasha squeezes Zenobia's hand. "Just tell us what happened."

Ms. Jones sighs deeply. "I was sitting here at the counter one morning about a month ago. The front doorbell rang. It was very annoying. It disturbs my concentration."

"Just like we did," Latasha says.

"It was a woman. A stranger. 'I must talk to you,' she said. No 'good morning.' No introduction. Nothing like that. She just waltzes into my home as if it were hers. I know it's not much, but it's all I have. This woman just walks into the kitchen here, and I follow as if I were a guest or her employee. I try to protest, but she just cuts me off like she's in charge of my life.

"'You're to do something,' the woman said to me. 'You are to include a word in a crossword puzzle you're doing for the *Washington Post*.' I tried to argue, but she paid no attention. She took one of my notepads and wrote out the word 'zyklon.'"

"'Zyklon.' A word with a 'Z,'" I say.

"Exactly. Include zyklon in the crossword puzzle that will

appear in the *Post* on January second. I don't care what clue you use. Spell zyklon just as I have written it. There must be no alteration. And it must appear on January second," she said.

"I told her I can't do that. I don't control the date the puzzle appears. That's up to the puzzle editor.

"'Just include the word zyklon,' she said. 'Don't worry about the editor. Do as I say.'"

"I tried to argue with her. Mother was here in the kitchen with us. This woman frightened Mother."

Zenobia stops speaking and runs her fingers through her hair. We let her sit in silence a moment to collect herself.

"Did this woman threaten you?"

"She threatened Mother. Not in so many words, but she looked directly at Mother. 'You live here with your mother?' the woman said. 'What a nice place. I'd hate to see your living arrangements disrupted.' It was absolutely clear she meant that to be a threat. Mother was upset, frightened for days. The woman was very scary."

"So, you went ahead and used the word 'zyklon'?"

"I had no choice. I rewrote the entire puzzle to accommodate that damn word."

"Can you describe this woman?" I ask.

Zenobia bites her lower lip. "It was a long time ago."

"Try. Any detail will help," Latasha says.

"She wore bright crimson lipstick. It made her look quite old-fashioned. Know what I mean? And it made her mouth look like a scar—cruel and scary. Her fingernails were black. Otherwise, she was well put together. She wore designer clothes and had large, dangly gold earrings. But what I remember most is that she had white hair."

"Was she an older woman?" I ask.

Ms. Jones frowns. "I don't think so. I couldn't really see her face all that well. She wore bangs cut just above her eyebrows and oversized, round sunglasses that covered her eyes. But I don't think she was old. From what I could see, she had one of those timeless faces some women have. She could have been twenty or seventy."

"Sunglasses? Inside the house?" Latasha says.

"She wore them the whole time. The lenses were dark green, and the frames were large and round."

"Was she wearing perfume?" I ask.

"It's funny you should ask. Now that you mention it, she did wear some kind of perfume. It was heavy and dark. Know what I mean? Kind of funky. I hated it."

"Did she give you her name?" Latasha asks.

"She refused to tell me."

The voice from somewhere upstairs calls out. Ms. Jones is obviously anxious to go. "I must speak with Mother. She gets easily upset."

"Thank you for your time." Latasha rises. "You've been most helpful." She places her business card on the counter. "If you think of anything more, please call me. Especially if you get any threats."

"Would you mind if I use the word 'zorn' in some future puzzle?" Zenobia asks me as we stand with her at her front door. "'Zorn' means 'wrath' or 'anger' in German. Is that right? You don't look like an angry person."

"You should see him when he's having trouble with his computer," Latasha says.

"By all means, use my name. It might get me a free drink at a bar."

Latasha checks a text on her cell phone. "We've identified the man who was killed in the Metro incident. His name was Billy Collins, and he lived in a one-bedroom apartment in the Adams Morgan area. I'm going to check it out now and talk to his neighbors. I'll find out who his visitors and friends were."

"I'd go with you, but I have an appointment to get a history lesson. You go ahead with the cruiser. I'll catch a cab. Be sure to take a uniformed officer with you when you investigate. Be careful. We're dealing with dangerous people."

Latasha rolls her eyes at me as if to say, *I know what I'm doing. Don't bug me.*

Chapter Seventeen

"At heart, we're all Fascists." Professor Severin Fairfield looks at me with amusement. *Is he serious? Or is he just being provocative to get a rise out of me? Sorry to disappoint you, Professor, I didn't come here for a graduate seminar.*

"Not me," I say. "I reject all totalitarian forms of government. Left or Right."

"Even you, Detective Zorn. You just won't admit it to yourself. Everyone wants to be a slave and be told what to do and what to think."

"I don't take orders from anybody."

Fairfield shrugs. He wears a worn tweed jacket with leather patches at the elbows. He has gray hair in serious need of a haircut. His horn-rimmed glasses are perched at the end of his nose. According to my Google search, he's written a dozen books on political movements. He's a highly respected expert on Hitler and Mussolini, on Japan in the 1930s, on Russia and Hungary today. He's working on a new book on contemporary American politics.

"It's been said that it's better to live in chains than to be free," Fairfield says.

"Who said that?"

"I think it was Franz Kafka."

"Well, Franz Kafka was dead wrong."

"Don't you ever tire of having to make hard decisions yourself, Detective? It's exhausting, always doubting, always second-guessing. Don't you ever wish someone would make those decisions for you? Now that we are in late stage capitalism, chains can be quite fashionable. You can order them online."

We're sitting in his cozy home in Georgetown, surrounded by books in multiple languages, some on shelves, some lying on a nearby table, some stacked on the floor near his chair, all with bits of torn paper sticking out as bookmarks. He's poured me a glass of sherry—a small glass. There's a fire in the fireplace with just a few logs left smoldering. Fresh logs are stacked nearby. Through a window, I can see snow-covered trees in his small garden.

"I've come to you to learn about neo-Nazi political movements," I say.

"Why should I talk to you?" Fairfield asks cheerfully. "About anything? Read my books. Everything I know is there. And it's all indexed and has footnotes. My books are all available on Amazon."

"I don't want footnotes." I'm impatient, but I try not to be rude—always an effort. "I'm a police officer investigating a horrific act of terror—the bombing of Friendship House."

"That was terrible, but I know nothing about what happened or who was responsible. I do not associate with killers and terrorists. My life is books."

"You can tell me what kind of organization would do such a thing."

"I'm sorry. You're a policeman. You're part of the establishment. In fact, you *are* the establishment. You're the enforcer. That makes you my opponent. Nothing personal."

I can see that I'm dealing with an unreconstructed radical from the 1960s. He was probably once a member of the Weather Underground and maybe a buddy of Abbie Hoffman. I'm tempted to take Carla's advice and offer to share my Pete Seeger record collection to prove I'm a good guy. Instead, I say, "I'm trying to prevent a neo-Nazi group from committing another act of terror."

"What makes you think neo-Nazis are involved?"

I show Professor Fairfield the photo on my iPhone of the tattoo—two concentric circles linked by lightning bolts, a black sphere in the center. "Does this image mean anything to you?"

Fairfield adjusts his glasses, studies the photograph. "Oh, my God," he whispers. "Where did you get this?"

"It's a tattoo on a dead man. What does it mean?"

Fairfield takes a deep breath. "It's an ancient Nordic rune adapted by the Nazis in the 1930s. It's known today as the Wewelsburg Mosaic. The Nazis used it as a key to their mythology."

"Does anybody buy this hokum?"

"Tragically, many do. And you'd better take it seriously as well, young man, if you hope to survive."

"This is all nonsense. Right?"

"Of course it's nonsense, but that doesn't mean it's not dangerous." Fairfield gives me back my cell phone. "I'd be careful who I showed that to. We're not living in a Nazi regime, not just yet, but we're moving in that direction. These days, it's more like 'fascism lite.'"

"With respect, Professor, you exaggerate."

"Our social fabric is fraying. Law and order is breaking down. One-half of the country hates the other half. Social norms are failing, and we're awash in racism and misogyny. America is arming itself for the coming civil war, driven by anger, resentment, and grievance. We're close to plunging into a nightmare abyss. All it will take is some cataclysmic event to push us over the edge. America is inexorably moving toward the wilder shores of madness."

"I don't see any of that."

"Truth has become irrelevant in public discourse. We live in a cult of irrationality. Public figures lie with impunity—and the bigger the lie, the better. As Adolf Hitler explained in *Mein Kampf*, the masses will believe a big lie more easily than a small one. Cartoonish politicians become, at best, entertainers, amusing and distracting the people with outlandish claims and conspiracy theories. While the people are being entertained, the apparatus of oppression and control is being constructed."

"I think I would have noticed that."

"You should have if you were paying attention. You should be afraid."

"Are you afraid?"

"I'm too old to worry about what will happen to me when they take over. But that doesn't mean I'm not their enemy."

"Why are you the enemy?"

"Because I read books."

"I don't believe the country is at risk."

"It's right there before your eyes. It begins with overt hate of the 'other'—Jews, people of color, immigrants, minorities, gay and transgender people—whatever marginalized group can be blamed for whatever is perceived as wrong with the world. For a while, after the Second World War, people stopped being overtly anti-Jewish in public. Adolf Hitler gave anti-Semitism a bad name. Today, you see race baiting in public discourse once again. People now freely say aloud their private, poisonous thoughts. It's the beginning of the end, my friend."

"We live in a democracy. The American people will never accept a dictatorship."

"Trust me, it can happen here. There are extremist movements in this country today that call for an American civil war. America is digging its own grave."

"Should I take all this revolution talk seriously?"

"You damn well better. Extremists have declared war on America—on all our traditional institutions—church, science, education—even the State itself. Reason itself. Truth is unmoored from reality. The neo-Nazis foment civil instability and large-scale civil breakdown by creating a stew of victimhood and grievance. To adapt Shakespeare's words, they will soon unleash the dogs of insurrection and violence. There's a seething subterranean force tearing our country apart. When the time is right, the true believers will take up arms. They're just waiting for the signal to mobilize. A sign that will spark large-scale civil disobedience and civil unrest."

"A sign, something like the bombing of Friendship House?" I ask.

Fairfield takes off his glasses and polishes them nervously. "That was just a signal to prepare, to arm themselves. The vigilantes—the militias—are gathering even now, waiting for the sign. The signal will be a major political disruption."

"Who are these people who plan to overthrow our government?"

"Those who feel they are the victims of an unfair system. Many are young men. Until recently they thought they were masters of the universe. Now they are the losers. They think their jobs—their futures—are being stolen. By immigrants. Black and Hispanic people. Gay people. And by women."

"That's crazy."

"You think these surface disturbances are only temporary, but beneath the surface, deep tectonic social shifts are taking place in our society. These shifts will result in the cata-strophic collapse of liberal democracy and the installation of dictatorship."

"No reasonable person wants to live in a dictatorship."

"For thousands of years, people had God to tell them what to think. In 1882, Friedrich Nietzsche wrote God's obituary. Science and rationalism were supposed to replace God. De-mocracy has always been a messy business, but politics have gotten worse in recent years. Today, politics is a blood sport. Public discourse has coarsened. People don't dispute issues. Instead, they mock and demonize their opponents. Com-promise is treason. Many believe society is being taken over by their enemies—external and internal. People demand a 'strong man' to fix things and save the country. A strong man who doesn't believe in rules. Rules are for losers. A man who has the will to power. The Savior. The Anointed One. And he is coming."

"I don't get the appeal."

"Never underestimate the allure of evil and cruelty. Fascism provides the pageantry of power—the jackboot. It's all basically sexual. For many, the Nazi image is erotic— the black uniforms, the leather—it's the pornography of violence, the fetishism of power, the rapture of death. Re-member the words of the poet Sylvia Plath—'every woman adores a Fascist, the boot in the face.'"

"Not any of the women I know. What does any of this have to do with the tattoo I showed you?"

Fairfield stares into his empty sherry glass. "In 1933, Heinrich Himmler, then head of the Nazi SS and the architect of the Final Solution, acquired Wewelsburg, a castle in Germany, intending to make it the center for the new Aryan world order. Himmler had a mosaic installed on the floor of the castle's great hall, where he planned to meet with the assembled leaders of the future Nazi world empire. The mosaic consists of two concentric circles, each linked by lightning bolts. It represents the spiritual essence of the Nazi movement. There's also some Hindu mythology thrown in to add an exotic flavor. The tattoo you showed me is the Wewelsburg Mosaic. In the center of the circle is a black disk. That is Black Sun. The Wewelsburg Mosaic is the esoteric key to Black Sun and the belief that Adolf Hitler will return."

"What is Black Sun?"

Fairfield closes his eyes and takes a deep breath. "Black Sun is a secret international organization created at the end of the Second World War by a group of SS and Nazi elites. Its purpose was to establish a new Reich after Germany's defeat in the war and to prepare for the return of the Führer, a new Hitler. The key to the neo-Nazi Zeitgeist."

"I'd say their Zeitgeist sucks. Do you know who Black Sun is—the new Führer?"

"I don't know the name. I just know it will be the end times."

"What's supposed to happen when he appears?"

"He will emerge from the flames of ruin and destruction. A new Führer even now is waiting to appear."

"Why would anyone want another Hitler? Wasn't one enough?"

"The followers long for the Chosen One. They demand someone to bring order to the world in chaos."

"So any smart person could seize power if he were ruthless enough?"

"You've got it all wrong, Detective. The Chosen One is typically an ignorant fool. The leader need not be smart. In fact, thinking is a handicap for a dictator. Thinking leads to reflection. That can lead to doubt and hesitation. And hesitation is fatal. People want a man who acts on instinct. The leader is a man of action. Hitler called what he did 'sleepwalking.' All a dictator needs is a willingness to lie and deceive and bully his opponents. And to never hesitate."

"How can we stop this from happening?"

"It may already be too late to wake the country. In the sleep of reason, we create our monsters, and the monsters are already among us. There is only one way now. Stop Black Sun."

My cell phone rings—it's Police Chief Kelly Flynn.

"Marko, get back to headquarters. Immediately."

My heart sinks. I know something bad has happened.

"It's Latasha. She's been murdered."

PART TWO

Chapter Eighteen

CHIEF KELLY FLYNN waits for me at the entrance to police headquarters, her face pale and drawn.

I'm trembling as I get out of the taxi. I can't seem to breathe right.

"I'm so sorry I had to break the news to you like that." Kelly grabs my arm. "But you had to know. Your life depends on it."

"There's no good way to tell someone their friend and partner has been murdered."

"We're going to take care of this." Kelly rushes me through headquarters' front doors. "Latasha and Sergeant Findley were shot down. We'll get who did this."

I'm gutted by remorse. Or guilt?

I say to Kelly, "She was an inexperienced officer. I insisted she remain my partner. It's my fault she's dead."

"She was a trained police officer. She knew what she was doing. She knew the risks."

"She's dead. How can we ever fix that?"

"We can't fix it, Marko. But we can get justice. And we need you for that."

There is a sense of shock everywhere. Officers glance at us but stay away, saying nothing, not wanting to intrude. Two police officers shot down in cold blood. That's never supposed to happen.

An elevator is waiting for us, the door held open by a uniformed cop.

"I was just with her. Two hours ago." I can barely breathe. "How could this happen?"

"Latasha was investigating the man you tried to arrest. She and Sergeant Findley were on their way to the man's apartment. It looks like they were heading up a flight of stairs when a figure appeared above them and shot them both. In cold blood. Without warning. Neither even had time to draw their weapons."

"Jesus!"

"Latasha was shot in the head. Findley was shot in the chest. An EMS team took them to George Washington University Hospital. Latasha was dead on arrival. Sergeant Findley died an hour later."

"This was not a random shooting," I say. "Just two shots fired. Both fatal. This was done by a professional."

Memories from many years ago rush through my mind. The moment I first saw my sister dead. Bitter anger raging through my body. Fury at my helplessness—that I couldn't do anything to protect her. I feel that same rage now. It brings back that moment when I finally faced my sister's killer. The moment I found myself.

"I should have been with her at the end," I say to Kelly.

"She never regained consciousness."

"I'm going to requisition my service weapon."

"No, Marko, you're not going to do that."

"I'll investigate her death and find her killer."

"No, Marko, you're not investigating Latasha's death. That's an order."

I remember moving through a grove of maple trees and emerging into a small meadow. I'm looking for footprints, broken branches. A sign the man passed this way. I know this territory well. I'd been hunting these woods since I was a boy. I need to stop and drink some water. Not yet. I'm close. On the far side of the meadow is a small stream. This late in the season, it's not much more than a trickle. On the other side of the meadow is a thick stand of elm trees. A perfect place for a man on the run to hide.

"I can't just stay here and do nothing," I say to Kelly. "I should be at the crime scene now. We've lost two officers."

"I don't want you anywhere near the crime scene. In your present state, you're in no condition to be out in the streets. Certainly not armed."

Deep down in the recesses of what's left of my mind, I know she's right. I should not be near a gun. I take a deep breath.

"Were there witnesses?" I ask.

"A couple of neighborhood kids, but they can't give us a good description. The shooter was white. Uncertain age. We'll talk to the witnesses again and show them a photo array. But I don't expect to learn much. They're just kids. And scared to death."

"Let me talk with them."

"That's not going to happen, Marko. You're off the case. Frank Townsend is at the crime scene now and is in charge of the investigation. You'd only get in the way."

The elevator doors slide open.

The man hiding in the shadows is expecting me. I think it's almost a relief to us both as we stand face-to-face. He points a revolver at me. He hesitates.

"Come with me," Kelly says. "There are people who need to talk to you."

Waiting for us in Kelly's office are Carla Lowry and Walter Brückner. He's leaning back in his chair, legs crossed. His brown briefcase is resting on the floor at his feet.

This is the only time I've been in the same room with Kelly

Flynn and Carla Lowry at the same time. They don't look at each other. They look at me. I can't help wondering whether each knows about my relations with the other. They probably do. Women have an instinct about these things. Both women are supremely professional and would never allow personal issues to interfere with work—especially not today. Not with the deaths of Latasha and Findley haunting us all.

"I'm truly sorry about your partner, Marko." Carla Lowry is the first to speak. "I never met Latasha Powell, but I know what it's like to lose someone killed in the line of duty—someone you've worked with. I've been through that myself. It's tough." Carla sounds genuinely shaken and grieved. This is out of character for her. She's not the sentimental type. I'm grateful for her words.

Kelly Flynn says, "Latasha was investigating the man you tried to question at the bomb site. His name was Billy Collins, known as Charming Billy. He was a low-level thug with an undistinguished rap sheet, mostly assault and extortion. We've learned he was a member of a neo-Nazi group who call themselves werewolves. He was a subscriber to several Nazi publications, including *The Storm,* and was an active follower on extreme right-wing websites. Incidentally, we're convinced his death was no accident. He was certainly pushed in front of a Metro train arriving in the station."

"By a woman who was standing on the platform just by chance, I'll bet."

"That's the way it looks."

"Let me start by outlining the situation," Carla says. "The Secret Service is convinced there will be an assassination attempt on the president on Inauguration Day. But we have no idea how this will be done. The Secret Service and CIA are attempting to uncover the plan and identify the leader.

Of course, the Metropolitan Police are doing all we can as well. The Capitol Police are on full alert, as are the Metro Transit Police—as are all law enforcement agencies in the Washington metropolitan area and nationally. Right-wing crazy communications on the web are being monitored twenty-four seven. Anyone who has posted any threat to the president-elect or any public figure is being rounded up for questioning. Are you with me so far?" Carla asks.

"On Inauguration Day," Carla goes on, "all traffic will be blocked at least a mile from the Capitol reviewing stand, the parade route, and the White House."

"I'm calling in all police resources for street patrol and as backup for the Secret Service," Kelly says. "As are the FBI and CIA. In addition to the blockade of all unauthorized road vehicles, Washington's no-fly zone will be fully activated by the air force. Fighter jets will be scrambled in advance of the swearing-in ceremonies, flying out of Joint Base Andrews with the 316th Wing fully deployed and armed, in case there is an attack by air, with orders to use whatever force is needed to neutralize the threat. The Navy and Coast Guard will patrol the Potomac and Anacostia rivers. All nonofficial watercraft will be barred from using both waterways during the inauguration ceremonies. The Army is bringing in National Guard troops to create a secure perimeter around the president and his party."

"It sounds like you've got the situation all buttoned up," I observe, unconvinced.

"I'm afraid not," Carla says. "We're missing something vital. We don't know what, but we're overlooking something. The opposition knows what resources we have and how we'll deploy them. I fear the opposition is one step ahead of us."

"Cancel the inauguration then," I say.

"The president-elect has been briefed on the security situation and was advised to cancel all outdoor inauguration events. He adamantly refuses. He says he will not be bullied by what he calls a bunch of right-wing bozos. The inauguration will take place as scheduled."

"I assume you have a plan," I say.

"That's where you come in," Kelly says.

Showtime! I have a bad feeling about what's coming.

Walter Brückner clears his throat. "There is only one way to prevent disaster. Someone must infiltrate the Black Sun organization and locate and neutralize the weapon they plan to use—a poison gas called Zyklon. I believe you know all about Zyklon and what it can do. First we must determine who Black Sun is."

"I don't suppose you have a description of Black Sun," I say.

Brückner shakes his head. "We have some photographs, but they're useless. His face is always obscured or turned away. I had a man on the inside, but I've lost him. We've got to get somebody else in to replace him."

"Can you really do that?" I ask.

"Hard, but not impossible," Carla says. "Herr Brückner managed it. Once."

Brückner stuffs tobacco into the bowl of his pipe with his thumb. "That's true, but the circumstances were different. It took us months to infiltrate the organization. We have no time left. We've identified some of the leaders, but not the top man. We were able to target some of their meetings—but only from a distance. About a year ago, we figured out a way to track the location of Black Sun himself. He moves constantly, conferring with his senior lieutenants. We have even been able to photograph him. A little more than a month ago, one of our operatives finally made contact with a woman high up in the Black Sun organization."

"Don't tell me," Carla says. "He seduced her, and she revealed all their secrets in bed."

"Actually, she seduced him. And she revealed no secrets. We now think she suspected he was our agent and had him executed. Or, more likely, executed him herself."

"Why are you telling me all this?" I ask.

Carla takes a deep breath. "The president has authorized the Executive-Action protocol."

Kelly sits up straight in her chair. She knows what the Executive-Action protocol means, and she doesn't like it. She's a police officer. Her job is to prevent crime and punish criminals. Not to take part in a conspiracy to commit murder.

"I can't believe this," I say, shaking my head. "That can't be right. The Executive-Action protocol can only be activated in time of war."

"We *are* at war," Carla says.

"How can it be activated when we don't know who Black Sun is?" Kelly asks.

"We'll just have to find out who he is," Brückner says. "For that, we need to get someone inside the Black Sun organization."

"Show us your photographs," Carla says.

Brückner reaches into his briefcase and takes out a packet of glossy photographs, which he passes to each of us. The photos, obviously taken with telephoto lenses, mostly show a man with his back to the camera or his face obscured by a hat or in the shadows.

He appears to be a big man and overweight. The photos have been marked on the backs with a date, time, and location. They go back several years, and the locations are all over the world. One was taken on the island of Corfu. Another in front of a bookstore on Madison Avenue in New York City. Two with what looks like a Japanese temple in the background—marked Kyoto. Two are in front of the Capitol Building in Washington, both dated March 12 at 11:45. And then there's one in Mexico City on the same date and time.

"There's something wrong," I say.

"I know." Brückner sighs. "The dates."

"What's wrong with the dates?" Kelly asks.

I shuffle through the photos. "The picture taken on Corfu is dated June 26 of this year. Time is 10:42 in the morning. The photo in Kyoto is also dated June 26. That's the same date as the one on Corfu. He seems to have been in Greece and Japan on the same date. All within an hour of one another. The photos taken in Washington are dated March 12 at 11:45. The one in Mexico City is dated the same day at 3:15 in the afternoon."

"Well, Walter," Carla says. "Did your photographer screw up the locations and dates?"

Brückner shakes his head. "Not possible. The date and location stamps are correct. The photos were transmitted to Berlin the moment they were taken. There can be no mistake about date, time, or location."

"So according to your records," Carla says, "Black Sun has been in several places at the same time, halfway round the world. That's not possible, unless he's some kind of demon or has magic wings."

"Could he have traveled by private jet?" I ask.

"That doesn't work." Brückner looks discouraged. "We've checked. Even the fastest commercial jet couldn't get him those distances in those times. I can't explain how he did it. Maybe it's a decoy."

"So, our opposition has access to a magic carpet," Carla says. "You should know, it looks as though he may also be capable of time travel as well." Carla takes papers from her folder. "Marko received this from an anonymous sender." She passes copies to Kelly and to Brückner.

LASCIATE OGNI SPERANZA, VOI CH'ENTRATE.
YOU WILL FIND ME HERE,
BUT YOU WILL NEVER ESCAPE.

"That sounds like a threat," Kelly murmurs.

"If it's a threat, it's a seven-hundred-year-old threat," Brückner says. "'*Lasciate Ogni Speranza, Voi Ch'entrate*' is from Dante's *Inferno*, written around the year 1300. The words are inscribed above the gates of hell. They mean 'Abandon all hope, ye who enter here.'"

"I've had my forensics people analyze this letter," Carla says. "It was not printed from a computer or on a modern printer. This was done on a typewriter. Specifically, a 1952 Remington Super-Riter Standard. It looks like this note to Marko was written seventy years ago.

"I don't believe in demons or witchcraft. Or time travel," she says. "But we don't have time to figure out how he did it now. The threat against the president-elect is real and is immediate. And the only way to stop this threat is to neutralize Black Sun—now! We can worry about his travel arrangements later."

"And the only way to neutralize Black Sun is to have someone infiltrate his organization," Brückner says.

"That would be insane," I say.

"Totally insane. Only an insane person would try." Carla looks directly at me. "That's why we immediately thought of you, Marko. We want you to become a werewolf. Go under-cover and make friends with Black Sun."

"You said this involves an Executive-Action protocol. That leaves me out. I'm a dumb cop, not a professional assassin. I don't do Executive Actions."

Carla and Brückner look at each other. I can't read their thoughts. Does Brückner understand why I do not kill? Carla does. Because, in a moment of weakness, I once told her. Late at night in her apartment. About what happened that day in the woods. She understands.

"We know you will not kill," Brückner says. "We just need you to identify Black Sun and locate Zyklon. Liz Fletcher can find someone else to do the dirty work. Or we can outsource the Executive Action ourselves."

Carla clears her throat nervously. "Will you do it, Marko? Will you go underground?"

"Black Sun will never believe I've defected to their side. I'm a cop."

"No, Marko. You're not a cop. You're a gunslinger. Just one without a gun."

That reminds me of what Cosmo Hunter said: *I'm an outlaw.*

"We're certain Black Sun is responsible for Latasha's death. This is the only way to get justice for Latasha," Kelly says. "Do this for her."

"It's the only way to prevent the assassination of the president-elect," Carla adds.

"Even if I should agree, why would they let me get close to Black Sun?"

"Because," Brückner says, "the organization desperately needs men with combat experience. Black Sun plans to go to war in a few days. We know Black Sun is actively recruit-ing men with military experience. The men in their ranks now are, at best, weekend warriors. They're mostly clueless civilians whose only military experience is running around in the woods, shooting paintballs at one another. Black Sun needs a man with real combat and leadership skills. You fit the bill perfectly."

"You were trained as a special ops Ranger," Carla says. "On top of that, you were almost court-martialed. You're the perfect candidate for them."

"They'd never believe I've defected to their side."

Kelly nods. "That's true. Unless ..."

"There is a way to convince Black Sun to trust you. You'll have to become a criminal pariah," Carla says.

"You will commit a crime, in the name of Black Sun, that's so despicable, so heinous, that you will become a social and political enemy of the country," Brückner adds.

"You'll have to commit a crime so awful that the DC police, the FBI, the Secret Service, and every law enforcement agency in the country will be after you," Kelly adds.

"I suppose you have a plan for that," I say.

"Of course we do," Kelly says. "We'll arrange for you to kill someone. A murder so brutal there will be no room for sympathy for you in the public and in the law enforcement community. We'll make it clear that you committed this crime to protect Black Sun, because you're a secret Nazi sympathizer and wish to join the ranks of Black Sun—to be part of their new Reich."

"That simple?"

"I'm afraid it's more complicated than that," Carla says. "You'll have to complete this mission in less than two weeks—that is, before Inauguration Day. And you'll have to do it while every law enforcement agency in the country is hunting for you."

"I'm afraid it gets worse," Kelly goes on. "You must be identified as a vicious killer who is armed and dangerous."

"You mean so every cop and law enforcement agent will be authorized to shoot me on sight?"

"I'm afraid that's the way it's got to be. Anything less will make Black Sun suspicious."

"What crime will I have to commit?"

"You're not going to like this," Kelly says.

"I already don't like it."

Kelly looks away from me for the first time, almost as if she's embarrassed. "I'm going to charge you with the murder of Latasha Powell. And of Sergeant Findley, as well."

"No. Absolutely not! There's no way …"

"You will be charged with shooting them both in cold blood."

"You realize what that means. Every police officer in the country will be out for my blood."

"That's the point," Carla says.

"What will my motive be?"

"Your motive is that you realized Latasha was about to expose Black Sun as responsible for the Friendship House terror bombing. You had to stop her."

"Nobody who knows me would believe I'm capable of killing a fellow police officer. Least of all my partner. And I'd never hurt a woman."

Kelly nods. "Those of us in this room know that. Other people know nothing about you, except that you're a rogue cop—unpredictable and dangerous. But we'll provide something more to convince Black Sun you are ready to join them. We'll add a charge of espionage in addition to murder to sweeten the deal. Those are the kind of charges that Black Sun won't question."

"I suppose you have a plan for that, too."

"Of course," Carla says. "You're going to love this. You're going to give Black Sun a top-secret FBI file containing all the information the US government has on the organization. The US government's most secret and sensitive file. This will be pure gold for them. It will, of course, be a violation of the Espionage Act. And I will have to charge you with espionage."

"How am I supposed to get hold of this FBI file?"

"Easy. I'll give it to you," Carla says.

"Will the file be genuine?"

"It will be genuine. I will take the folder on Black Sun from my personal files, and it will have all the proper routing stamps and notations on each document. The classified documents will have notes and comments in my handwriting, and my fingerprints will be all over the file."

"Aren't you worried that Black Sun will learn sensitive information they can use?" I ask.

"That's a risk we must take. It will be the complete file. Enough to convince Black Sun the file is legitimate and that you are a traitor to your country. However, the file won't contain the one piece of information they most need—the identity of Black Sun himself. We don't know who he is, so it's not in the file."

"How am I supposed to get this file into the hands of Black Sun?"

"The FBI has identified a confidential contact," Carla says. "It's a law firm here in Washington that does covert business with Black Sun. If you get the file to that firm, they'll pass it on to Black Sun. I'll get you the FBI file before midnight tonight. You must put it into the hands of the lawyers no later than noon tomorrow."

"What's the urgency?"

"Because" Kelly says, "at five o'clock tomorrow evening, I will publicly announce the charges against you for the murder of Latasha Powell and Sergeant Findley."

"At the same time," Carla adds, "I will announce that you are wanted for the theft of a top-secret FBI file. We will leak the story to the press that you are a secret Nazi. With that, you're done for. You will be a fugitive from justice. Every law enforcement agency in the country will be after you. We'll see to that."

"There's one more thing," Kelly says. "You'll have to contact a Black Sun operative tomorrow before your arrest warrants are made public at five. You'll find your contact at the Hellfire Club."

"What's the Hellfire Club?" I ask.

"It's a network of sports clubs. They claim to be athletic clubs, but their real function is to be a feeder to Black Sun. There's a Hellfire Club in Falls Church, Virginia. Go there tomorrow. Introduce yourself. They'll take it from there."

"Are you in, Marko?" Kelly asks.

I take a deep breath before I answer. All three are watching me closely.

"I'm in," I say at last. "For Latasha. It's the only way I can see to take down the fuckers who killed my partner. When a man's partner is killed, he's supposed to do something about it."

I'm pretty sure that sounded better when Humphrey Bogart said those words in the movie *The Maltese Falcon*.

Chapter Nineteen

THE OFFICES of McKenzie Sullivan & McKenzie are located in a building in downtown Washington—not in a sleek high-rise building on K Street, like its powerhouse competitor law firms. Its two-story building is discreet, almost modest, and non-declamatory. This is a strictly old-school firm that assures its clients they'll never have to see the inside of a real courtroom or stand before an actual judge.

The offices are decorated with bookshelves, and the books are bound in genuine leather. A great deal of money has been spent on creating a setting from the nineteenth century. I half expect to see doddering elderly men with muttonchops clutching briefs. On the walls are tasteful Currier and Ives prints.

No noise penetrates the corridors of these offices. No sounds of telephones or office equipment or eager young interns intrude. Here it's sepulcher quiet.

A man wearing an expensive double-breasted suit and a deep blue tie adorned with tiny white polka dots sits at the end of a mahogany conference table. He's in his sixties, flush-faced and jowly. Next to him, yellow pad in hand, sits a sallow young man. The older man smiles guardedly at me.

"I'm Justin Wilberforce." The man glances quickly at a piece of paper lying on the table in front of him. "You are Markus Zorn, I understand."

"It's Marko Zorn. I'm with the DC Metropolitan Police Department, Homicide Branch."

"When you called for an urgent appointment this morning, it wasn't clear why you wished to consult us. We don't handle criminal cases here at McKenzie Sullivan & McKenzie." His eyes crinkle with distaste.

"I'm not here to consult about a criminal case. I'm here to make an offer to one of your valued clients."

"The names of our clients are strictly confidential."

"I have a gift for Black Sun."

Wilberforce's head snaps back, and he glares at me. The associate with the yellow pad seems to shrink back into his chair.

Wilberforce catches his breath. He was not expecting to hear those words, and he's not happy. He scratches the side of his nose and glances at his young associate. "Mr. Andrews, would you be so kind as to excuse us for a moment? I must speak privately with this gentleman."

Mr. Andrews looks anxious and a bit annoyed, but he knows his place, and he knows when he's being kicked out. He glances carefully at Wilberforce to be sure he's got the message right, shrugs, and collects his yellow pad. "I'll be in my office," Mr. Andrews says, not very graciously, and leaves.

"We have no client by the name of Black Sun," Wilberforce says as soon as Andrews has left.

"That's unfortunate. I have something for him. Something Black Sun needs." I open an expensive leather briefcase I bought this morning at a luggage supply store on my way to the appointment. I withdraw a thick manila envelope and place it on the table in front of Wilberforce. "Tell Black Sun I have here a copy of a top-secret FBI file on the Black Sun organization that will be of interest to him. He's mentioned often in this file."

I carefully open the envelope and withdraw its contents. It's a thick, pale gray file folder marked Top Secret on the top and the bottom. The words EYES ONLY. Distribution Restricted to the Director, Deputy Director, and Executive Assistant Director, National Security Branch are printed in large, bright red letters on the cover. The file label reads BLACK SUN Most Restricted.

"This must be seen by Black Sun himself—urgently," I say.

"May I ask how you obtained this file?" Wilberforce asks.

"Of course you may ask. But I won't tell you. All you need to know is that this file is authentic and must get into the hands of Black Sun urgently."

Justin Wilberforce never takes his eyes off the file. I swear his eyes are watering.

"If you're really unable to help," I say, "I suppose I will have to take this file back with me."

"No. No." Wilberforce leans over the table, his beautifully manicured hands clutching at the air. "That won't be necessary."

I grasp the file, snatching it away from him, and start to slip it back into the manila envelope.

"I may recall that name now," Wilberforce says, stuttering. "I will get this file to him."

"Give me his name, and I can deliver this in person."

"I'm afraid I don't know his real name. He prefers to remain incognito."

"His address then."

"Again, I'm unable to help you. Black Sun has no fixed address. He moves constantly."

"But you can get this to him today?"

"Absolutely. It will be in his hands by six o'clock this evening. Guaranteed."

"Pass on a message to Black Sun. Tell him that, in return for this file, I want to join Black Sun."

"You?"

"I have the skills and experience and the information that is vital to the cause. Tell him that."

Wilberforce nods. "I'll inform Black Sun." He snatches the file back and holds it to his chest. "Have no fear, sir. He will have the file by six."

Chapter Twenty

THE HELLFIRE CLUB is a typical gym with the usual equipment: treadmills, rowing machines, elliptical bikes. In the center, there's a boxing ring where two men are sparring listlessly while a few bored gym rats watch. They're all young, all male, and all white. To one side of the ring is a man working a punching bag.

On the wall near the front door is a sign that reads White Lives Matter. A Confederate battle flag hangs over the water cooler.

The place smells like a gym—chlorine, talcum, and the musky scent of men working out. It brings back dark memories—the barracks of the Third Ranger Battalion, men returning from a combat mission, dirty and sweaty, still pumped from the action. Men who've just come off combat smell different from others. Maybe it's fear. Maybe the readiness to kill.

"Hello, my friend." A middle-aged man wearing a white T-shirt with the words Hellfire Club stenciled on the front approaches, smiling broadly. He's about five foot nine, muscular and toned, probably a former college athlete. His blond hair is trimmed in a crew cut. "This your first time at Hellfire Club?" His tone is warm and friendly. "I don't remember seeing you here before."

"I thought I'd check you out."

"You're welcome to look around."

"I've heard good things about Hellfire Club. Some friends tell me good men come here."

"You got that right, pal."

"I'm talking about right-thinking men. If I'm going to join a group, I want to be sure what kind of people I'm mixing with."

"Absolutely. You can't be too careful. If you're interested, we have meetings every Wednesday at nine. You know, to talk about what's happening in the news. What's wrong with our country. Why things are going to the dogs. You know. You can meet the guys."

The man in the white T-shirt eyes me reflectively. "These are all great guys." He holds out his hand. "I'm Gary. Welcome to Hellfire." We shake hands.

"My name's Marko. What happens when a guy comes here, you know, a Black dude? What if he wants a membership or something. Or maybe just to look around."

"We're very polite. That's what the law says. We don't throw him out or anything. But we make it clear he's in the wrong place. We suggest he try another club where he'd feel more at home, with people like him."

"How about if a woman wants to join?"

"They take one look around, and they're out of here. They have an instinct. Not a problem."

"And gay men? I understand they like to work out. Stay in shape. Look sharp."

"Do you see any queers here? They're not welcome. I can see you demand a select clientele. Hellfire is the place for you, my friend. Of course, we'd have to ask you a few questions first. Hellfire is very particular. Who are the friends who recommended us?"

I ignore the question.

"I'd need to be sure you'd fit in."

I point to the boxing ring. "Maybe I could try a little sparring. You have somebody I can work with?"

"Mell is available." He gestures at one of the two men who shuffle around the ring.

"Is that the best you got?"

The man scratches the back of his head. "There's the Turk. He was once a pro wrestler."

"You hire immigrants here?"

"Never. Only white Anglo-Saxons. The Turk is just his professional name. Actually, he's from Arizona. But he doesn't have a drop of spic blood."

"I'll try the Turk, then."

Gary nods and disappears into a back room. When he returns a few minutes later, he's accompanied by a big man, probably six four, well over two hundred and fifty pounds—but too much of it is fat. He's let himself go. He has massive arms and shoulders, and his head is clean-shaven. A swastika is tattooed just above his right eye. A Hawaiian sports shirt falls over his torso, and its brilliant greens and golds are so bright they make my eyes hurt. Because of the shirt, I can't see whether he has the tattoo that so troubled Professor Fairfield.

"The Turk will do," I say.

"Just sparring," Gary says. "No heavy hitting. I don't want to see no one get hurt."

"I'll try not to do any serious damage," I say.

The Turk stares at me. Angry. He doesn't promise not to do any serious damage to me. I walk up to the Turk and look him up and down. He has three inches on me, and he smiles malevolently through broken teeth.

"I don't do fancy-pants boxing," I say. "Bare-knuckle."

"My favorite." The Turk grins, flexing his fingers.

Gary looks anxious. "I don't carry liability insurance."

"I'll try to be gentle," I say. I think the Turk is about to haul off and slug me right then before we even get into the ring. The first rule: get your opponent mad. They get careless that way.

The Turk climbs into the ring and waits for me, arms crossed over his chest. I take off my jacket, being careful to remove my gold cuff links from my shirt and put them in my trouser pocket. I add my Rolex, then climb into the ring. Nobody offers either of us headgear or mouthguards. A small crowd of regulars gathers around the ring to watch, hoping for some entertainment.

I stand in front of the Turk while we take the measure of each other. I know he's going to try to take me out with one or two powerful punches. That would be the smart thing to do. We both know if he manages to reach me, I'm done for. This is going to be a short bout.

As we move, he gauges my style, determining whether I'll lead with my left or right. Will I move away from him or come in close for a clinch? What signs will I give?

We dance around each other for a couple of minutes, and the Turk takes a few easy jabs at me, testing my responses. Nothing serious—just to see my reaction. I jab at him twice, which he easily brushes away. He's not sweating this bout. He's sure he'll win. He thinks I'm an amateur, a desk-bound lightweight, and inexperienced. Maybe it's the expensive suit and the silk shirt I'm wearing. Maybe it's my haircut. He thinks he's already won, so he's just playing with me. I know I have to end this right away. The longer I stay in the ring with him, the more chances he'll get in a lucky punch and put me away. He's strong enough to do that. But he's overconfident. And he's angry, which makes him sloppy.

I'm acutely conscious of the time. How long have I got before every cop in the country is looking for me? I'm not safe here in the club. Some of the men in the Hellfire Club are probably off-duty cops.

I step back as if in fear and feint with my left. The Turk blocks, and that opens him up. I hit him hard with my right—dead center on the swastika above his right eye. He wasn't expecting that. His head snaps back, and he loses his footing—just for a second. That's all I need. I hit him with my left, aiming for the nose.

The one-two works. The Turk's face is covered with blood. His nice Hawaiian shirt turns crimson. He covers his face, or what's left of it, with his hands and stumbles backward against the ropes, his nose gone.

Bout over. Ring the damn bell.

The crowd is silent. Not the fun they hoped for.

I climb out of the ring. My right hand hurts, and I hope I didn't break anything. That's the trouble with bare-knuckle fighting. You can get hurt. Gary passes me a sort-of-clean towel, and I wipe my face, now covered with sweat and some of the Turk's blood. Behind me, the Turk is staggering out of the ring, leaving gobs of his blood on the mat. I flex my right hand. No broken bones. My hand seems to be working okay.

"How much do I owe you?" I ask Gary. "I think I may have ruined the Turk's nice sports shirt."

"I think you may have ruined his face. It's on the house, friend."

I replace my cuff links and put on my jacket.

"I've never seen anyone take the Turk out like that. You've had experience."

"A long time ago." I give the manager a piece of paper with the number of my cell phone. "My name is Marko Zorn. I may be looking for some action. You can reach me at this number."

"There's somebody you got to talk to. I'll ask him to give you a shout. He may have some ideas."

It's 3:45 in the afternoon.

Chapter Twenty-One

I RETURN HOME and go immediately to my basement office. I open the floor safe where I place my house keys, wallet and IDs, credit cards and Rolex, as well as the wad of three hundred dollars in cash I normally carry with me—in case I must consult one of my informants or leave a cash tip. There will be no need for cash where I'm going. I peel off thirty dollars in fives and ones from the wad as a reserve for tonight.

I add my reading glasses to the safe—I figure Nazis don't read much. Finally, I deposit my cigarette lighter. I know the FBI will search my house, and Carla will probably join the search team. She, too, must play her role in this charade—that of an FBI leader determined to ferret out a traitor and murderer. And her curiosity will be too much for her. She's always wanted to explore the secret recesses of my home. Will they be able to break into my safe? That will be tough, but I never put anything past Carla and her FBI associates. Will she find the cigarette lighter there? Will she know what it means to me?

Upstairs, I locate an old pair of trousers in the back of my bedroom closet. It has an ancient stain which looks suspiciously like hoisin sauce I've never been able to remove, so I can't wear them in public. They'll do for tonight. For footwear, the best I can do is an old pair of Ferragamo moccasins. I put on the oldest and most worn topcoat I have. For the next few hours, I need to pass as a bum. This is as close as I can get to looking homeless. Of course, in a sense, that's what I am.

I'm ready to go dark.

The clock in my kitchen reads exactly 4:10. I have less than an hour.

The police and the FBI will come to my house first and stake it out for as long as it takes. Obviously, I can't go anywhere near my office at police headquarters or any of my usual haunts. I can't seek shelter with any of my friends— I don't want to put them in danger. Every hotel in town will be covered. There will be men and women patrolling the streets searching for me in any place that's warm and out of the snow. I can't even hide among the homeless shelters and flop houses. They'll be searched, and the residents would spot me as suspicious and inform the police immediately. The train station and airports are out. Both are saturated with surveillance cameras, not to mention their special cops. I'll have to figure something else out.

In the meantime, my first requirement is food. God knows when I'll eat again. The FBI and the police will know all my usual haunts—they'll have a list of the bars and clubs I frequent, and their guys will be there, comfortable and warm, chatting up my favorite bartenders while I'm out in the snow and wind, freezing my ass off. I must find a place where I'm not known, where nobody will think to look for me.

My immediate problem is transportation. I can't drive the MG, and I can't rent a car. Uber and Lyft are out. Either would leave a clear record of where I'm going. Taxis keep records of their pickups and discharges too. The Metro trains are no good—too many cameras. My image will soon be distributed everywhere, and I'd be identified by the hordes of agents who will be monitoring surveillance camera feeds. That leaves Metro buses. At least in the short term they'll be safe, until copies of my picture are distributed throughout the city to all bus drivers. That will take, at most, two hours. Maybe less. Carla Lowry and Kelly Flynn are super efficient. And they must make the search look good.

I lock up the house and head out. I catch a series of buses, each trip short enough that the driver is unlikely to remember me. I end up in the far southeast part of the city. This is an area I know well—a high-crime district with a lot of heavy drug activity—and I'm often called here, but I've never worked this particular street, so I'm unlikely to be known. On the other hand, in this part of town, a cop can be spotted a block away. I don't have much time.

I locate a small diner, the kind that serves breakfast twenty-four hours a day. The place is almost empty. I take a seat at the counter, facing a TV set, which currently features a basketball game. I hunch over and try to look like a derelict homeless person. I suspect my disguise isn't really working. The Ferragamo moccasins are a giveaway. Or maybe it's my hundred-dollar haircut. But the few customers pay no attention to me. I'm just some white guy. The middle-aged African American lady who takes my order shows no interest in me. Instead, she chats with the short-order cook about the basketball game.

I order two eggs, bacon and sausage, extra toast, a double order of wedge potatoes, and coffee. While I wait for my food, I take an inventory of the diner and its occupants. In addition to the counter, there are four booths, one of which is occupied by a middle-aged African American couple. To my left, there's a door to the restroom. To my right, there's a swinging door leading to the kitchen. I can't see into the kitchen, but I know there will be a door opening onto a back alley used for deliveries and to dump kitchen waste. Good to know, just in case.

The waitress places my order in front of me, smiles, and turns to watch the game.

I'm about halfway through my meal when the basketball game on TV suddenly disappears. There's a groan around the diner from the waitress and the middle-aged couple. A red crawl chyron appears at the top of the TV screen: BREAKING: MAJOR SECURITY ALERT. A ticker text appears that reads POLICE ANNOUNCE SEARCH FOR ARMED GUNMAN. There follows, in smaller letters, an announcement that the Metropolitan Police and federal agencies are searching for a man who killed two police officers. He's described as a white male and is reported to be armed and dangerous. The public is asked to be on the lookout for the killer.

It's 5:05. *God, Carla and Kelly are efficient.*

The TV screen goes back to the game, to the relief of those in the diner. Five minutes later, the game is once again interrupted. Police Chief Kelly Flynn appears on screen. She's in full-dress police chief uniform, brass buttons and all. She's seated at her desk, backed by an American flag and the flag of the District of Columbia. She looks very stern and mad as hell. Kelly announces, in a sober tone, that a former police officer by the name of Marko Zorn has been charged with the murders of Latasha Powell and Charles Findley, both police officers. My picture appears on-screen. It's from my official police ID. Not flattering, but good enough for me to be easily identified. Kelly gives a brief physical description—height, weight, coloring—and announces that Marko Zorn is armed and considered very dangerous. The "armed" part is an unnecessary embellishment. So is the "dangerous." Kelly warns her listeners not to approach Zorn but to inform the police immediately if he is seen. She makes me seem like some kind of psychopathic monster on the loose. I think she's overdoing it a bit, but maybe that's called for. She looks good. She always looks sexy in her uniform, particularly when she's mad.

Back to hoops.

I sense no response among those in the diner. No urgent whispering. No fingers pointed at me. I was right to come to this part of town. If I were in a white suburb, there'd be agitated talk about what's gone wrong with the police department and the city administration that allowed such a thing to happen. In this part of town, they don't expect much from the city government or the police.

Then the basketball game is interrupted again. More groans. Some male announcer's head appears and tells us what we've just heard from Chief Flynn, but more breathlessly. He makes Marko Zorn sound like a crazed killer at large.

Lock your doors. Hide your daughters in your cellar. Grab and load your AR15s.

Then the TV shows pictures of Charles Findley and Latasha Powell, and the mood in the diner changes. The victims of this deranged killer are not just some abstract police officers. One of them is an average-looking Black man in a police uniform. He could be anyone's neighbor. The other, an attractive young Black woman with a beautiful smile. She could be anyone's sister or daughter. It breaks my heart to see her.

Without looking around, I sense the atmosphere in the diner has changed. Everyone is now standing behind me, looking at the pictures of the two victims. The mood is somber. Angry.

The basketball game returns, but the cheerful mood does not.

Should I make a break for the door now? I decide not to. No one seems to be paying any attention to me. They're seeing the back of my head, not my face. They're not making a connection with what they just saw on the screen and this lone white guy. No one is reaching for their cell phone. The customers return to their places in the booth and ignore me. I decide not to draw their attention by leaving, so I play it cool. I even ask for a second cup of coffee. So far, so good.

The door to the diner opens, and a freezing draft chills the room. There are two male voices. Heavy footsteps stomp on the linoleum floor to loosen snow that has stuck to their boots.

I know absolutely they're police—two officers on patrol stopping in the diner to get warm, for a coffee break, or maybe to get a bite to eat. Their police radios crackle. They speak familiarly to the waitress and say hi to the couple in the booth. This is a place where they all know one another. I'm tempted to turn and look at them. Are they officers I know? Will they recognize me? Have they been given flyers with my photograph, warning that I'm a vicious killer? I don't turn. I try to act nonchalant, even though my heart is pounding.

I ask for the check, and behind me, I hear the waitress speak with the cops. She's asking whether they know any-thing about the criminal policeman who's on the loose. I can't hear their answers.

I'm feeling desperate for the waitress to bring me my check so I can get the hell out of here without looking like I'm trying to escape. Instead, the waitress stands at the booth, talking with the cops. I'm beginning to wonder whether I could take them. That would be tough. Even if I got out the door without getting shot, the cops would call in reinforcements, and the neighborhood would be flooded with police in minutes. I'm already thinking like a wanted criminal.

Fuck! I am a wanted criminal.

"Would you like something more?" The waitress is standing in front of me, a pad in her hand.

"That will be all. Thank you."

She tears a slip of paper from her pad and places it in front of me. "Crappy weather," she says. "Try to stay warm." She thinks I'm homeless. She thinks I'm going to sleep under a bridge somewhere, and she sounds genuinely concerned for me. Moving slowly, deliberately, I reach for the bill, peel out some cash, just enough to add a tip, a small one. Not enough to make her remember me, a homeless man, carrying cash.

I rise from the counter, keeping my back to the two cops in the booth studying their menus. I sneak a quick glance. One is white. One Black. I don't recognize either. They must be from the nearby precinct—not operating out of headquarters. Neither looks up at me. I shrug into my topcoat and walk slowly to the door.

Outside, I'm hit in the face by a cold blast of wind. My breath turns to white vapor as I walk away from the diner. Not fast. Expecting any minute to hear shouted commands from behind. *Hands up! Where we can see them!* I hear nothing. Just cold wind.

There are a few people on the street hunched over, watching the ground in front of them, careful where they step. No one looks at my face. But I know I'm not safe for long. A lone white man in this part of town after dark draws attention.

At the next intersection, a two-door Civic stops for a

traffic light. I step into the street and pull open the passenger door. I slip into the front seat, pulling the door closed behind me.

"What the fuck?" a young white guy in the driver's seat yells at me.

"Take me to Union Station."

"Get the fuck out of my car!"

"Sorry. Can't do that. The light has changed. Go!"

"Is this a carjacking?"

"It can be if you want. Now go!"

The car moves. The driver is trembling.

"Can you make it a little faster, buddy?" I say. "I've got a train to catch."

The car moves steadily. The driver makes quick, fearful glances at me. He must be wondering whether I'm going to kill him.

"Turn left on Massachusetts Avenue. Stop in front of the main entrance."

The young driver pulls up and stops in front of Union Station. There are no police in sight. Who knows what's waiting inside.

"Thanks for the ride, buddy," I say, and slip out of the car. "Drive safely."

The panicked driver speeds away. I move as if to enter the station but stop at the main entrance until I'm sure the car is out of sight. I turn and walk quickly away. I'm pretty sure my terrified driver will be on his phone by now, reporting me to 911. I figure I have maybe five minutes before a fleet of squad cars descends on the station. My driver will be shown my photo, will identify me, and police will flood the zone.

He'll report that I said I had a train to catch, so the police will start with the Amtrak waiting room and departure areas and probably search the trains standing in the station. Union Station is a large building with countless places to hide—restaurants, snack bars, restrooms, luggage rooms. And the trains waiting to depart for Richmond or Baltimore and points north and south. It will take an hour or more to sweep the station. Then the nearby Metro and bus stations. This is a big place to search. I estimate I have maybe an hour max before they give up and widen the search into the surrounding neighborhood. I can't hang around.

The rest of my trip will be on foot. In the snow and shadows.

When I reach the building of the Office of the Chief Medical Examiner, an ambulance is parked at the back of the building. Two emergency medical service men stand just inside the doors, smoking. I nod in a friendly manner and slip through the double doors. I don't recognize either of the EMS guys, and they don't know me. They wouldn't have been on the distribution system for the flyers with my picture. And they won't see the TV announcements about me until they get off shift. The only people who normally use this entrance are dead, and they don't care.

I am, at first, lost, until I find a sign that points to the morgue. I go down several corridors and have no idea where I am until I find myself standing in front of a door with a large sign that reads: Office of the Chief Medical Examiner, Examination Room, Authorized Personnel Only.

Using the electronic code I saw Celia Moore use when I last visited the morgue, I punch in the numbers—9-12-17-4-20—and the door opens.

The examination room is dark. A single lamp sheds a gloomy light.

I'm alone—except for the corpses resting in their chill cubicles along one wall.

Half a dozen steel autopsy tables are ranked in rows, all empty now. Waiting for the arrival of fresh victims sometime tomorrow.

According to a large clock on the wall, it's now 10:10, and there's still no phone call. So there's nothing for me to do now but wait. I decide I might as well make myself comfortable.

There's no point pacing around the morgue, feeling spooked by those I'm sharing the place with.

I select one of the steel slabs, climb on top, and roll myself in the heavy blanket. I wonder who the last user of the blanket might have been. For some reason, I can't sleep.

The call comes at 4:18 in the morning.

A voice I don't recognize announces, "You're in serious shit, Zorn. There's an all-points search for you going on right now. If you stay in Washington, you'll be arrested before morning. Or shot on sight."

"Who are you?" I ask. I don't really expect an answer.

"I can arrange for you to get safely out of town. But this a limited time offer. First we need to talk in person."

"How do we meet?"

"Be on the Taft Memorial Bridge at five this morning. Wait in the center of the bridge, on the east side of the roadway. If I see anybody there but you, the arrangement is off, and you can deal with the police on your own. Is that clear? Be there on time. I won't wait."

Chapter Twenty-Two

I'M STANDING in the middle of the William Howard Taft Bridge in a snowstorm. Nothing is moving—not a car or bus, no flicker of distant headlights. No late-night revelers trying to find their way home. As a fugitive from justice, I'm feeling exposed right now. The man I'm supposed to meet chose the middle of the bridge so he can observe me and confirm I'm alone. He's probably watching me right now from somewhere at one end of the bridge or the other. He'll wait until he's sure I'm not being followed.

I toss my phone over the side of the bridge and watch as it disappears into the snowy darkness below. Maybe in the spring, some hiker will find its remains. No one will care then. In the meantime, I don't want my new friends to search my phone and learn who I've been talking to.

The Taft Bridge links downtown Washington to the upper Northwest across Rock Creek Park. At either end of the bridge, concrete lions protect it—I don't know from what. Decorative cast-iron lampposts shed a dim light through the snow. Above and below the bridge is impenetrable whiteness.

After almost half an hour, two headlights appear through the swirling snow. A black Volvo station wagon slows and stops a few feet from where I'm standing. The back doors swing open, as does the one on the driver side. A single man moves out from behind the wheel, wrapped in a heavy leather coat. Two more men climb out from the back seat.

"Don't bother to get in, Mr. Zorn," the driver says. "We can take care of business right here on the bridge."

The two men from the back seat immediately surround me. They've done this maneuver before. They're trained, and this is not an exercise. Before I can move, they've gripped my arms on either side.

"Take him," the driver says and the next thing I know, I'm being hauled to the bridge railing—half carried, half dragged. I struggle, but there's no way to break their iron grips. This is not going to end well.

I'm pushed against the railing, then lifted off my feet and pushed over the edge, suspended over the abyss, held by my wrists, the ground 130 feet below me.

A voice speaks to me. "Can you hear me, Mr. Zorn?"

"I hear you," I shout back.

"Now pay close attention to what I say. I won't repeat myself. In three minutes, these gentlemen will release you and let you drop. They're looking forward to that. They have a deep antipathy to policemen and will happily let you go, unless I order them to pull you back up. I will ask you four questions. If you answer me truthfully, you may live. If you equivocate or lie, I will know, and it's over for you, Mr. Zorn. Are you listening?"

"You have my undivided attention," I yell back.

"First question, has the Executive-Action protocol been activated?"

"Yes," I yell.

"Are you the protocol?"

"No."

There's silence. "Who has the protocol been activated against?"

"Against Black Sun."

"Who is Black Sun?"

"I don't know."

I dangle over the edge, trying not to struggle. I don't want the two men to lose their grip on my wrists.

The driver speaks again, and I'm pulled roughly back over the railing so I'm standing on the pavement on my own two feet. The goons release me, and I grab the bridge railing to steady myself and try to breathe normally, my heart pounding. My mouth is dry, and I can't seem to swallow. I am deathly afraid of heights.

The driver spins me around and looks intently into my eyes. "Who is Black Sun?"

The man facing me looks somehow familiar.

"Who is Black Sun?" he repeats.

"I don't know. Nobody knows."

"Does that mean the Executive-Action protocol is moot?"

"It's moot until Black Sun is identified, at which time, the protocol will be activated."

The driver says something, and the next thing I know, the goons are gone, lost in the snowstorm.

The driver gestures for me to get into the car. He takes the driver's seat, and the car moves into the blinding snow. I rub my chafed and bruised wrists where the two primates held me as I dangled over the abyss.

"What's your name?" I ask.

"You can call me sir."

"I don't call anybody sir."

"That's going to be a problem."

The driver says nothing more until we're well off the bridge. He turns onto a side street, pulls into an empty parking spot clear of snow, and stops. "Sorry for the business back there on the bridge, but I had to know."

"Know what?"

"Whether you know who Black Sun is."

"You could have just asked."

"It would have taken too long. I needed to get your attention in a hurry."

"Do you believe what I said about Black Sun?"

"I believe you don't know who he is."

"I could have been lying. Hanging over the edge of the bridge like that, I would have told you anything."

"You weren't lying. I know when a man is lying. I'm like you. We both have instincts about things like that. We both understand the soul of the outlaw."

Outlaw? Who else talked to me recently about being an outlaw?

"Are you an outlaw?" I ask.

"I am an outlaw from the corrupt society in which we live." The driver turns in his seat to study me. "You look frightful. I'd been told you were a smart dresser with sophisticated taste in clothes and lifestyle. A metrosexual. Right now, you look like a homeless bum."

"If I'd known I was being invited to my own execution, I'd have worn a tie." I study his face. I'm sure I've seen him before. And recently. But where? "Why didn't you have me killed at the bridge?"

"Killing you was never my purpose," the driver says. "I need you."

"Does that mean you trust me not to be the Executive-Action assassin assigned to kill Black Sun?"

"Carla Lowry and Walter Brückner are determined to

destroy Black Sun, but they would never entrust that act to you. I know you do not kill in cold blood. Carla and Walter want Black Sun dead. So you cannot be their instrument."

The driver's a big man. He's tall, heavily built, and a bit fat. He looks to be about fifty or sixty.

Where the fuck have I seen him before?

"You said you need me. Why?"

"All in good time, Mr. Zorn. First, some questions. Is it true you served in the US military?"

"The Rangers."

"What unit?"

"Third Ranger Battalion. Seventy-fifth Ranger Regiment."

"You were awarded a Bronze Star."

"So?"

"And the Purple Heart. You were highly regarded as a unit leader in combat."

"That was long ago."

"No comments. Just answers. It will save us both time. You were also almost court-martialed. Why was that?"

"Ask General Grant."

"I'm asking you."

"I was charged with failure to obey a direct order."

The driver turns to look directly at me again. There's a vivid white scar on the left side of his face running from just under the eye to the corner of his mouth. It's an old and angry wound.

"Why did you steal the FBI file?" the man asks.

"I want to be on the winning side."

"You think Black Sun is on the winning side?"

"I think it should be. Is this an interview?"

"But you're a police officer."

"That does not define me."

"So I've heard. You wish to join an organization that is opposed to all you stand for?"

"I believe in law and order. In America today, there is no law and no order anymore. I want to see order restored to our country. For that, the nation needs a strong leader. I've lost faith in the politicians who run our country. They're weak and feckless and have no vision. I have faith in Black Sun."

"Even though you don't know who he is."

"I have faith in what Black Sun stands for. Someone told me recently Black Sun has dreams—great dreams—heroic dreams. I trust men who have great dreams."

"You do not believe in authority. You obey only your own rules. There is no room for such a man in the new Reich."

"I can do as ordered for the right cause. For the right man."

"That's not what you said at your court-martial hearing."

"Wrong cause. Wrong man."

The driver almost smiles, but his mouth is distorted by the scar, and it comes out a grimace. "Time to go. We mustn't be late."

We drive silently through the blinding snow, the wipers struggling to keep the windshield clear. After almost half an hour, he pulls the car to the curb. In front of us is a passenger bus painted orange with a blue logo and the name Sun Valley Farms on the side.

"The bus leaves in exactly seven minutes. Be on it. Don't talk to the driver or to the other passengers."

"Where will the bus take me?"

"To where the bus is going. Beginning tomorrow morning, you will begin training along with other recruits. Leave everything behind, including any scruples—although I doubt you have any left."

PART THREE

Chapter Twenty-Three

THE PASSENGERS on the bus are all men, mostly in their twenties, all white, half of them with mohawk haircuts. A few are older, in their thirties and forties. They all look anxious. Some are openly frightened. From the look of them, for many, this may be their first time away from home. They've been told … what? They're going to have an adventure. With guns. Maybe with death. They're just now realizing they don't know what they've gotten themselves into.

Some glance at me furtively as I pass by, searching my face. I'm older than the other passengers. They wonder whether I know something they don't. Most stare dully at the seat in front of them. A few clutch brown paper bags, probably containing lunch for the bus trip, prepared by anxious mothers. I take a seat at the back of the bus. The windows are opaque with condensation.

One last traveler arrives. He's younger than most. Short and a little chubby, he wears a ball cap turned backward and looks lost as he settles into the seat next to mine. The driver, wearing dark-brown fatigues, moves along the aisle carrying a clipboard, checking names. When he arrives at our row, my seat companion pulls the cap from his head in a gesture of respect.

"Name?" the man in fatigues demands.

"Apple," my seatmate murmurs. "Charlie Apple."

"Zorn," I say. "Marko Zorn."

The driver returns to the front of the bus, takes his seat, and the bus moves off into the snow-clogged Washington streets, along Constitution Avenue, over the river, and into Virginia. We travel along Route 50 for a while. The highway has been plowed and salted overnight, so it's smooth going. After about ten miles, however, the bus turns off the highway and onto some Virginia state road. I try to memorize the route we're taking, but I can't see much of anything through the opaque windows. There's more snow here, heaped into large snowbanks on each side of the road, so only two lanes are passable.

I examine my seat companion. He appears to be around seventeen, maybe even younger. He wears a North Face parka, somewhat stained. The bus's heater is on full blast and it's getting warm, and my companion struggles out of his parka, which he folds carefully on his lap.

I turn and hold out my hand. "Hi. I'm Marko." I smile in a friendly way.

The boy shakes my hand indifferently. His grip is weak. "We're not supposed to talk," he whispers.

I ignore his admonishment. "It looks like we have good weather for our trip. I was afraid we might get stuck in a blizzard."

"Whatever," he mumbles without looking at me.

He's around five foot six or seven and a bit overweight. He has a round baby face, and his hair is cut short. He has brown eyes, and his eyelashes are long, which gives his features an almost feminine cast. He's wearing a Hawaiian shirt even though it's freezing outside. His bare arms are covered with tattoos, including a crudely drawn Iron Cross. Next to it are the words in bright red ink, Fuck Me Babe. The tattoo is clearly aspirational, I think.

"Do you know what to expect when we get to camp?" I ask.

"I know all that shit."

He's not entirely shutting me out.

"You know all about Hitler?"

"I know all about the Führer—the old Führer and the future Führer."

"Where did you learn all that?

"Mr. Holland explained it to us."

"Who's Mr. Holland?"

"He's our gym teacher."

"Is he a member of Black Sun?"

The boy looks at me sharply. "We're not supposed to say those words. Ever," he whispers. "It's top secret."

"So how do you know about it?"

"Me and my friends meet once a week, and Mr. Holland teaches us all that stuff."

"Are you a werewolf?"

"You have to be over twenty-one for that."

"Will Mr. Holland be at the training camp? I'd like to meet him."

"I'm not sure. It's all secret stuff, you know. Mr. Holland is way up in the hierarchy."

"Did Mr. Holland ask you to join Black Sun?"

"Sure. Me and my friends. Stan was supposed to come with us today, but his mother wouldn't let him." Suddenly the boy looks anxious. He's said too much. He turns away and sinks back into his seat in sullen silence.

The bus is now traveling through open country. Occasionally, we pass a small town or a farm. There are sometimes horses standing stiffly in snowy pastures. I think we're rising in altitude and are now probably in the Virginia foothills somewhere. Judging by the location of the sun, we're traveling south by southwest.

After almost two hours, we pull into a compound in a shallow valley. The bus stops. The driver opens the front doors, letting in a blast of cold air, and yells, "Everyone out!"

Stiffly, we shuffle down the center aisle and step outside. It's cold, and there's a brisk wind. We all shiver as we stand next to the bus.

We've arrived.

Chapter Twenty-Four

FACING US ARE SEVEN MEN.

We are all silent, each group watching the other. Charlie Apple stands, or rather slumps, in line a few yards away from me. The bus moves off, disappearing into the snow-covered hills in a cloud of blue exhaust.

One man steps forward to address us—the same man I met last night on the Taft Bridge. He wears black fatigues with a gun and holster at his waist. He seems to be a little over six feet but is fat—middle-aged fat. He stands ramrod straight, but despite his posture, he looks unimpressive. The sides and back of his head are shaved in a high skin fade while the hair on the top of his head is cut in a short buzz cut. His small blue eyes dart from one of us new arrivals to another. They seem to settle on me. Or am I imagining that? The scar disfiguring the left side of his face is not a traditional dueling scar you sometimes see on the faces of men of a certain age in Germany. This scar was carved into the man's face in a frenzy of rage.

Crouching at the man's feet are two large rottweilers. The dogs eye us with deep suspicion. I observe, with unease, that neither dog is on a leash.

Surrounding us are half a dozen wooden buildings. Facing us is an exercise field with a single flagpole at one side. There is no flag. I'm pretty sure this was once a US military air base left over from World War II or the Korean War, long ago abandoned. A few hundred yards from where we stand there is a large concrete one-story building with a flat roof that looks like it might once have been an airplane hangar. There are several antenna arrays on the roof. Surrounding the building is a barbed-wire fence. I make a note of all this—the building will require my personal attention.

Behind the hangar is an open field on which two trailer homes are parked.

The fat man raises his right arm and makes the Nazi salute. "Heil, comrades! Welcome to Camp Rockwell."

We, the busload of recruits, don't know how to respond to this, and we stand uncertain and silent.

"As of this minute, you are under my personal command. I am Commandant of this camp. Remember that. I am your Commandant, and you should be afraid. I am the air you breathe. The blood beating in your veins.

"For the next ten days, this will be your home. Here you will forget everything you've ever been taught. Here you will learn everything you will ever need to know. It will be an ordeal. I warn you now. You will undergo physical, intellectual, emotional, and moral training. The worthy among you will become warriors in the most important struggle in human history. You will be princes in the new kingdom. You will join the historic ranks of destiny's leaders—or destiny's martyrs. Those of you who survive this training will become rulers of a new world order. Cruel. Heartless. You will learn to be merciless."

The dogs shift restlessly.

"You will now be assigned your camp leaders, and you will follow their orders without question. Any violation will be severely punished. If any of you cannot handle the discipline and think of trying to desert ... understand you will be punished. This is not a summer camp."

He leans down and pats the head of each of the two dogs. "Meet Bruno and Ingrid. They like to roam through the camp at night. If they should find any of you out on your own, Bruno here will rip your face off. Ingrid will drink your blood. Welcome to Camp Rockwell."

Six men step forward and stand before us at "parade rest." I recognize the type.

I understand these are noncoms whose function will be to destroy any remnants of humanity we, the recruits, may have. That includes attachment to friends and family and lovers, to community, to church, to our former selves. These noncoms' mission will be to turn us into mindless killing zombies.

"The men standing before you are your instructors. They will be your family," the Commandant yells. "For the next ten days, these men will be your leaders. You are to do whatever they say. Fear them. They will tell you when to get up in the morning. When to go to bed at night. When to eat. When to shit. They're here to make men of you. When they address you, stand at attention and yell 'Heil.' When they tell you to sit, you sit. When they tell you to stop, freeze. For the next ten days, you live and breathe for them. You are all worthless maggots. Maggots beg to be stepped on. They beg to be ground into the mud. Understood, maggots?"

There are a few uncertain responses.

"I asked you maggots a question. Did you not understand me? Are you all as stupid as you look?"

A few more answers. A few weak "heils."

"I can't hear you! Louder!"

Again, more heils. Louder this time.

"Louder, maggots. Louder!"

The troops are getting the message now. The ranks yell "heil" over and over again. Louder and louder. Standing in the snow, we become a mindless unit. I join them. That's my mission. I yell "heil" louder than anybody.

The rottweilers look bored.

We, the new arrivals, are divided into small groups. The leader of the group I've been assigned to is a tall man whose name, according to a tag on his chest, is Porter. The stripes on his sleeve indicate he is a sergeant. He marches us to one of the barracks buildings.

Inside, the place is lined with double-decker metal bunk beds. Stacked on each bunk are brown fatigue uniforms, underwear, thick woolen socks, hats, and coats. Pairs of heavy black combat boots are set out on the floor at the foot of each bunk.

Porter orders us to undress, leaving our civilian clothes in a pile on the floor. All connection to our past is stuffed into heavy plastic garbage bags and hauled away, presumably to be dumped in the trash and burned. I'm going to miss my Ferragamo loafers.

We're herded, naked, into a large shower room, where we take a collective cold shower. I suppose that's intended to make us men. It just makes me cold. When I return to my assigned bunk, I dress quickly in my new brown uniform. The fabric is coarse and stiff. A label sewn to the left breast tells me my name is now Nelson.

We're ordered to stand for inspection—uniforms, heads, and bunks—and for the proper stowing of pillows and blankets. Porter seems particularly concerned with bed-wetting which, it seems, is not a Nazi thing.

"Nelson's not my name," I say to Sergeant Porter when he reaches me.

"It's your name now," he says. "Today, you are a new man, with a new man's name—Nelson. How do you address your superior?"

"Heil."

"Again. Louder. Like you mean it."

"Heil!" I yell, like I mean it. I figure I'd better show him I'm gung ho.

"I'm keeping an eye on you, Nelson," Porter yells at me, his face inches from mine, red from rage. "You're already making trouble. Do not complain about your name. Do not complain about anything. Or I will personally make it my business to give you something to complain about. Is that clear, insect? Give me twenty!"

I drop to the floor, lie prone, my nose inches from Sergeant Porter's boots. I do twenty vigorous push-ups.

"You're a pathetic insect," Porter says. "Twenty more."

After another ten push-ups, I begin to feel the strain in my arms and shoulders. I didn't realize how out of shape I am. Too many nights at local bars. Too many dry martinis and salted peanuts. Thankfully, Sergeant Porter loses interest in me and moves on to torment some other poor son of a bitch.

After inspection, Porter quick marches us to a nearby building where we are to get our meals. He instructs us not to complain about the food because that will upset the cook. Anyone who complains will be denied that meal and assigned latrine duty.

It's dark by the time we leave. On our way back to our

barracks, I see two figures loping through the snow. They stop and stare at us, their eyes unnaturally bright. It's Bruno and Ingrid on their nightly hunting rounds. They keep a close eye on us.

Back inside the barracks, Porter strides from one recruit to another, looking for anything out of order, such as a messy bunk, unbuttoned tunic, or misplaced socks. He gigs anyone who falls short in any way, which means they'll be assigned additional duties, mostly distasteful ones. I pass with no problem. I know how to do this kind of inspection and square away my bunk and gear. I went through inspections like this many years ago. I know how the system works. Sergeant Porter is annoyed when he can't find anything wrong with me. He'll try harder next time.

After half an hour, he orders lights out. We're to be up and dressed by 6:30 in the morning. I've heard it all before. I've given those instructions myself in wooden barracks not unlike the one we're in now.

I nod to my bunkmate, a tall man with a gaunt, haunted look, and try to engage him in conversation. I need to find out who he is, where he comes from, what he thinks he's doing here. He answers with monosyllabic grunts. The label sewn on his uniform tells me his name is Howard. He looks to be in his late twenties. He's missing two upper front teeth. Not that it matters. He doesn't smile much.

Howard takes the lower bunk. I take the upper one. The mattress is thin. So is the pillow. There's a threadbare woolen blanket folded at the foot of the bed.

I sit for a moment on my bunk and survey my new world. It's not a happy one.

At the pillow end of the bunk is a wall made of rough, scarred wood, covered in old peeling paint. Generations of men have left their marks on this wall. A few names remain: Sandy, Cramer, Ben. I wonder how old these are, whether the men who carved them are still alive. Did they survive whatever war they were in? Somebody diligently carved "Kilroy is here" but with devil's horns added.

Just beneath Kilroy, there's an empty space about ten inches by twelve square. Using the brass buckle on my newly issued uniform belt, I scratch a square into the empty space and divide it into thirty-one cells. I etch an "X" into one of the empty cells—marking today—my first day at camp. I have exactly twelve days before the twentieth day of the month—Inauguration Day. That means I have twelve days to locate Zyklon. Twelve days to find Black Sun and stop him. Twelve days to save the country.

I roll myself in my blanket and fall asleep in minutes.

Chapter Twenty-Five

THE LIGHTS in the barracks are switched on at six, waking the groggy recruits from their wet dreams. Sergeant Porter is yelling, and we're herded into another cold shower. We dress, and after breakfast, Porter leads us to a building where our hair is cut. The only style the barber offers is to take most of our hair off, using large electric clippers. So much for my hundred-dollar haircut. A man with a red face, using a large push broom, sweeps up the hair trimmings, which include a lot of dead mohawks.

We're marched to another building where a man in a once-white tunic gives us a medical exam to confirm that we have an adequate number of arms and legs. He checks our scalps for lice, then gives each of us an injection of some kind. It's obvious he hates me and the other trainees. Several recruits faint while being given the shots. So much for the master race.

When Dr. Mengele is done with us, Porter marches us to the drill field. Snowflakes prickle my now-almost-hairless scalp. We go through some physical training. After an hour of this, my knees start to complain, but at least I'm still standing. Most of the recruits fade fast. These are guys who probably spent their lives playing video games and hanging out in bars trying to pick up girls, watching sports on television, and drinking beer. Three men collapse and are hauled off the field where they're made to sit up with their heads between their knees. Charlie Apple, a few yards away, hasn't collapsed yet, but he looks close.

Porter then marches us to one of the larger buildings in the camp. Inside, the walls are adorned with Nazi icons and regalia. There are flags and images featuring the swastika and various military emblems. Inspirational music plays on the loudspeakers. It's kind of jaunty, until I recognize it as the *Horst Wessel-Lied*, the anthem of the Nazi Party. It loses its charm for me then.

The walls are covered with photographs of Nazi leaders. I recognize Göring and Himmler and Hess. A large color photograph of Adolf Hitler, looking fierce, adorns one wall. The other men pictured do not look at all impressive. I must admit, though, that the senior SS officers do look kind of cool. They should; their uniforms were designed by Hugo Boss, a leading designer of high fashion menswear in Berlin in the 1930s.

Once we've taken our seats, the Commandant appears, now wearing a black SS uniform. He strides onto the stage, stands before us, and gives us the Nazi salute. "Sieg Heil!" He wears a swastika armband and polished boots and peaked cap with the Death's Head insignia — the full Nazi bling. He holds in his right hand a riding crop, which he taps against his boot. His left thumb is hooked into his belt.

The Commandant informs us that we're about to take a solemn oath of allegiance to our true Leader. Once we've taken the oath, we must salute the Commandant and senior members of the force with the Nazi salute. He shows us how to extend our right arm stiffly from the shoulder, upward at a forty-five-degree angle, palm facing down and parallel to the arm. We practice this salute several times. With each salute, we're supposed to yell "heil" loudly and with enthusiasm while clicking our heels together. No limp arms. No mumbled "heils." We're to salute as if we mean it. I try to make my heils sound enthusiastic. I can't manage the heel-click thing.

We are now "comrades."

Someone from the ranks asks, "Can we say, 'Heil Hitler'?"

"Not until you've proven yourselves worthy of the Führer," the Commandant answers.

Next comes the oath. The Commandant reads from a card, and we're supposed to repeat his words. I don't pay much attention. I'm not much of an oath person myself. There are mentions of destiny and duty and blood. It doesn't say whose blood.

At that moment, there's a sound overhead, drowning out the proceedings. It's the whump-whump of a helicopter flying low over the camp. For a moment, I wonder whether Carla has located me and organized an extraction operation, but I quickly discard the idea. This is a small helicopter—not the kind that would support a team of Rangers. From the Commandant's reaction to the interruption, I can tell this is no hostile intrusion. Rather, it's expected and routine. The sound fades, then cuts out. I assume, the aircraft has landed somewhere nearby.

Once it's quiet again, the ceremony resumes. Another officer describes the program for the coming days. He tells us we will receive intense physical training "to make men out of you," to become worthy of the Führer. There will be lectures on the National Socialist Party and its history and politics. Nothing is said about our mission. I'm disappointed to note the word "Zyklon" is not once mentioned. Nor is the name Black Sun.

We're dismissed and return to the exercise field where we're ordered to run around the field five times. Several of my fellow recruits don't make it beyond the third circuit. There are further orientation classes in the afternoon, which I pay no attention to, then dinner.

After dinner, Sergeant Porter marches us back to our barracks and yells, "Lights out!" We climb onto our bunks. I carve an "X" into the next empty cell on my wall calendar. Another day gone. And nothing to show for it.

My bunkmate, Howard, begins to speak—a disembodied voice in the dark. "Those men giving the lecture made a lot of sense."

"You think?"

"Damn right! We've got to stop the hordes invading our country. We can't let them replace us. We won't let them take our country. Our women. We've got to resist." There is silence from the bunk below. Then he asks, "Aren't you too old for our struggle?"

He's got a point. I'm old enough to be the father of some of these kids.

God! I hope not.

"How did you get connected to this outfit?" I ask.

"I was a member of the *Atomwaffen Division* for two years in Florida. I decided it was all talk. So I joined Black Sun. This is where the real action is."

"What kind of action do you expect?"

"We're going to create an 'ethno state.'"

I don't want to know what an 'ethno state' is.

"They're taking over my country."

They?

"Building fucking windmills everywhere. Windmills cause

autism. You know that. It's a proven scientific fact. They're trying to kill us with windmills. We have to stop them before it's too late."

"How will you do that?" I ask.

"Create a unified operations force. With the jackboot." Pause. "You're a college boy, aren't you?"

"A long time ago," I mumble.

"I'll bet you've never worked a day in your life."

I don't know how to answer that.

"You don't learn shit in college." I hear the loathing in Howard's voice. "The stuff they teach you rots your brain and turns men into queers."

Should I try to explain to Howard how important it is in life to be able to solve quadratic equations and to know the names of the English metaphysical poets? At the moment, I can't seem to remember why it is.

Chapter Twenty-Six

U P BEFORE DAWN. A cold shower. Calisthenics. We've been designated Bravo Company, and Sergeant Porter divides us into squads of twelve men. Charlie Apple is one of the twelve in my squad, along with my bunkmate, Howard.

It's the third day, and our ranks are beginning to thin as the failures and weaklings are weeded out. There's at least one candidate in my barracks, a young kid named Lewis. He's a nice-looking boy, but he's frequently late, his uniform is often untidy and stained with food particles, and his boots are not properly shined. He often argues with Sergeant Porter, his heil salutes lack conviction, and he complains about the food and the cold showers. He's one of those people who can never get with the program—a classic fuckup. There's always one in every military unit I've ever been in. He'll never make a proper Nazi trooper. I wouldn't want to serve with him in combat. He'd get us both killed. Apart from that, though, he's my kind of soldier.

After lunch, we march, raggedly, around the parade ground, then are sent to the lecture room where we're told about the history of National Socialism. There's a lot of talk about autobahns and heavy industry and national pride and the villainous Treaty of Versailles. And the Jews, who caused the two World Wars. And how evil Winston Churchill was and how the Jews controlled Roosevelt. The lecturer neglects to mention the concentration camps and the fact that the Nazis lost the war. And how the allies beat the shit out of Hitler's Wehrmacht.

After the lecture, we're told we have fifteen minutes of personal time. I take the opportunity to get as close as I can to the large building—the one I think is the camp operations center. I make mental notes about entrances, doors, and the fence that surrounds the building, which turns out to be made of razor wire and is nine feet high. Two sets of armed guards patrol the front entrance. There's also a roving guard circling the building. I try to determine the timing of their patrol schedule. That's hard to do without a watch.

Is this where Zyklon is stored?

Somehow, I doubt it. It doesn't feel right. But I'd better find out.

Not far from the operations center, a robin's-egg blue Sikorsky helicopter is parked.

I'm trying to organize all this in my head when I'm suddenly aware that I have company. The camp's two Nazi rottweilers are crouched just a few yards away from me, eyeing me with loathing. I don't know anything about dogs, but these look to me as if they are about to attack and tear me to pieces. Their jaws are open, teeth bared. I guess they're really fangs. They certainly look like fangs to me. The beasts tremble with fury and snarl loudly. I don't think they like me.

"Popcorn!" a woman's voice calls out from somewhere. I can't see anyone and am puzzled. I haven't seen a woman in the camp. I assume the word "popcorn" is an order for the beasts to back off their prey. An order they've been trained to obey. Something like "stand down." The beasts slink sullenly away. I decide to leave the area in case they change their minds. Who was it that ordered them not to attack me?

I pass a group of recruits standing in a circle yelling at someone in the middle. These things happen fast in any organization such as prisons, schools, and armies. The formation of groups of oppressors and oppressed is instinctive and happens automatically. Victors and victims are formed overnight. And it usually ends badly for somebody.

In this case, the somebody turns out to be Charlie Apple, the kid I met on the bus. The Charlies of this world are born victims. Charlie stands now, hunched, almost crouching, as his oppressors close in on him, yelling and cursing. I can see Charlie's trying not to cry. If he does, he's done for.

"You boys have a problem here?" I shout as I push my way through the ring of cursing men. "Is this man giving you trouble?" I point to Charlie as if he were the culprit.

"Just having a little fun," one of the attackers shouts at me.

"Have fun another day." I grab Charlie roughly by the arm and pull him away from the angry crowd. They reluctantly fall back.

Who the fuck does this guy—meaning me—*think he is?* they're asking themselves.

I have no rank or official position. My only authority is that I'm older and act as if I have authority. And I yell loud. Sometimes that's all it takes. I sense their resentment about a stranger spoiling their fun, but they're a disorganized rabble. Nobody dares say anything or challenge me. A mob like this can form in seconds and vanish just as fast.

I haul Charlie to the edge of the parade ground. "What was that about?"

"They were making fun of me 'cause I'm short and fat."

"You've got to stand up to people when they bully you."

"They might hurt me."

"Let 'em. It doesn't matter if they hurt you. If you're afraid of being hurt, you'll always lose. If you don't stand up to them now, they'll do it another time. Only it'll be worse next time. Sometimes you've got to be hurt. If you fight back, they'll go find someone else. Of course, it's better if you hurt them."

We stand on the edge of the parade ground. "Hit me," I say. "Hit me as hard as you can. Try to hurt me."

"Why should I hurt you?"

"Because I'm telling you to."

Charlie looks bewildered.

"That's the Nazi way, Charlie. Didn't Mr. Holland explain that to you? It's time you learned, if somebody in authority tells you to hurt someone, you go ahead and hurt them. You don't need a good reason. Or any reason at all. You don't ask why. If you want to be a real Nazi, just do what you're told. Hit me. Hard."

Charlie takes a deep breath and swings at me. A soft punch. I swat it away. "Hit me like you mean it."

He swings at me, aiming for my upper chest. I dodge, and his fist just glances off me.

"Aim for my face. Not the chest. Unless you're a professional, you'll never do any damage hitting your opponent in the chest. Hit me in my face. Try to take my eye out."

Charlie looks scared but swings at my face, and I block him with my left arm. His swing is fairly strong. If he'd hit me, it could have caused a real bruise. He's not as soft as he looks.

"That's a good start, Charlie. We'll try again another time. Remember the lesson for today."

Charlie looks blank.

"Don't ever be afraid to be hurt or to hurt somebody. If you run into one of those guys again, hit him! Hard. Never pull your punches. And never hesitate. That's the secret to life."

Back at the barracks, Porter calls Bravo Company to attention just outside the front door, and we wait until a truck arrives. Two recruits open wooden crates, loaded with M-1 rifles. The weapons are passed down from the truck and we're each assigned one weapon. But no ammunition. Besides being out of date, the weapons are badly beat up from years of use and neglect. This is army surplus at its worst. The M-1 will be okay for marching, but not for much else.

Chapter Twenty-Seven

I T'S THE END OF another day, and I'm carving a new "X" into my wall calendar when a young officer appears. He gives me a snappy Nazi salute. Judging from the insignia on his collar, he's an *Obersturmführer*, which makes him something like a lieutenant. His black SS uniform and white kid gloves are spotless, his brass is polished, his leather glowing. This young man will go far in the new Nazi Reich.

"You are to come with me," the young officer says loudly. "You are to report to the Commandant. Immediately." He clicks his heels. "Sieg Heil."

Howard, on the bed below me, must be grinning. He's sure I've done something unspeakable and am about to be shot. Or worse.

I follow the lieutenant out of the barracks and into a waiting Mercedes command car where I'm seated alone in the back seat and driven across the campgrounds in a matter of less than five minutes. We drive through the front gates of the operations center building. The gates are held open for us by a phalanx of men armed with AK-47 assault rifles. The lieutenant parks the Mercedes in an empty storage bay and escorts me into a room.

A large color photograph of Adolf Hitler dominates one wall. Desks have been pushed out of the way to make room for a table set for dinner for three, with porcelain dishes, silver serving ware and stemmed wineglasses. Each piece of tableware is decorated with a swastika—I suppose to give the setting a festive air. At one end of the table, a board with chess pieces has been set up.

This does not look like a room organized for a court-martial. At least not any I've ever been hauled to before.

The Commandant is waiting for me, dressed in full Nazi SS rig. His service cap and sidearm lie on a nearby desk. "I invited you here this evening because I thought we should get to know one another better. Over dinner and a bottle of wine. Don't you agree?"

"It looks like you're expecting a third guest."

"My guest has been delayed. I suggest we play a friendly game of chess while we wait."

"It's been a long time since I've played chess."

"Just a friendly game."

"Is this an order?"

"Of course not. I'll make it easy for you. If I can't check you in ten moves, you win."

"I'll agree to play your game if you'll answer me one question."

The Commandant looks baffled. "You have a question?"

"Just one. Were you in Washington on June 12 of this year?"

He reflects a moment. "I was in Mexico City on that date. What's this got to do with our chess game?"

"Nothing."

"Then let's play. Let's say we make the game more interesting, shall we? Maybe a small bet on the side?"

"You know I have nothing to wager."

"You do have something of value. If I win, you help train my troops."

"And if you lose?"

He sort of laughs. "What do you suggest?"

"Issue me a standard issue US Army bayonet."

The Commandant looks startled. Then doubtful. "Why would you want a bayonet?"

"I know you would never issue me a gun of any kind. But if you want me to help train your troops, I need some badge of authority. A bayonet would serve."

The Commandant reflects for a moment. "Very well," he says. "If I don't mate you in ten moves, I'll have a bayonet issued to you. Understand, I never lose."

He sits at the table. I take the seat opposite and wonder about the missing guest.

I can now observe the Commandant at close range and in a bright light. He's about sixty—somewhere in that waste-land of advancing middle age. His smartly cut SS uniform does nothing to camouflage his aging body. His small eyes dart around the room, checking to make sure everything is in order. His eyes are an intense blue. He has full, pink, pouty lips, which he licks nervously. In the light of the fluorescent bulbs, his raw facial scar stands out.

Once again, as I did on Taft Bridge, I have the feeling I've seen him somewhere before—that I should know him.

"Have we met, Commandant?" I say. "You look familiar."

"The night on that bridge in Washington was the first time we ever saw one another."

"Perhaps I've seen your face on TV or the papers."

He shakes his head. "My image is never seen on TV or in the press. I make a point of it. I don't much care for my appearance." He touches his scarred face. "You play white. I prefer to play black. You understand. You open."

I move a pawn to Bishop Three. He moves a pawn to

Knight Six. A conventional gambit. It's clear he's following a strategy—one he's learned from a book on how to play chess.

In the distance, there's the sound of a helicopter.

I move my knight to Queen Three. My opponent is baffled. That move wasn't in his chess book, and it doesn't make sense to him. He does something with his rook. I move my bishop to Queen Four. He takes a long time trying to figure out what I'm up to, then moves his pawn to the center of the board. I return my bishop to Bishop Two. I sense his mind racing: *What the hell is going on here?*

I move a rook and then on my next turn, I launch my castle to no apparent purpose. By now, the Commandant is hopelessly confused. As we continue, he can't figure out what I'm doing. The truth is, I'm not doing anything. I'm just creating chaos and confusion—something I'm particularly good at. The Commandant thinks I'm doing something clever, maybe even brilliant. But he can't figure out what it is. He panics, and his game falls apart.

In any conflict try to panic your opponent, or at least confuse them.

"Game over," I say. "You've just made ten moves. You haven't checked me. You lose."

"That's ridiculous. That's not how the game is played."

"Your game, Commandant. Your rules. You owe me one bayonet."

At that moment, the door opens, and a woman enters the room, accompanied by a gust of freezing wind and snow. She's wearing a black alpaca topcoat, leather gloves, and a sable fur hat. She snatches the hat off and drops it on a desk near the door along with her gloves and begins to unbutton her coat. "It's fucking cold out there. You should have sent a sleigh."

"Lieutenant!" the Commandant orders.

The young officer jumps forward to help the woman with her coat. He's clearly intimidated by her and almost cringes when she looks directly at him. As soon as he's collected her coat, he backs away quickly.

The woman is wearing oversize green sunglasses, which she now removes and tosses onto the nearby desk with her hat. She has white hair cut in a bob, with bangs cut just above the eyebrows, and she wears dangly gold earrings, lurid red lipstick, and black nail polish.

Her beauty takes my breath away.

She points an accusing finger at me. "What's he doing here?"

"Mr. Zorn is our guest for dinner this evening, my dear. There is nothing to fear. He is one of us."

"Bullshit."

"Detective Zorn will help us in our coming struggle."

"Double bullshit."

"Mr. Zorn, allow me to introduce my guest, Mrs. Davenport."

"It's a pleasure to meet you, Mrs. Davenport," I say.

"Detective Zorn and I have already met," she says.

The Commandant looks baffled. I probably look baffled as well. I can't imagine how I could have met this extraordinary creature and forgotten her. We stand staring at one another for a long moment. She does look vaguely familiar. But from where?

"Detective Zorn and I were just finishing a game of chess." He turns to me. "Let's call our game a draw."

"Let's not call it a draw. You lost. You owe me one bayonet."

Mrs. Davenport looks down at the chess board. "Did the Commandant cheat?" she asks me. "He usually does, you know."

"Do you play chess, Mrs. Davenport?" I ask.

"Certainly not. I never play games. But I love the Queen. She's the strongest piece on the board. She can destroy anybody, and I adore her."

"You know," I say, "sometimes, in order to win a game, the Queen must be sacrificed."

Her eyes widen in feigned horror. "Certainly not! Don't even think such a thing."

The young lieutenant enters and whispers into the Commandant's ear.

"Dinner is ready," the Commandant says, almost with relief. He takes one final, puzzled look at the chess board, making a last attempt to figure out my secret strategy.

"Please, sit down." The Commandant holds a chair for the woman he calls Mrs. Davenport.

"Is there a Mr. Davenport?" I ask.

"Not so you'd notice."

"You say we've met," I say, sitting at the table opposite her. "You have the advantage. I confess I do not remember the occasion."

She smiles. "It was shortly after the bombing of Friendship House. Perhaps you were distracted at the time, trying to arrest someone."

It comes back to me. The woman who helped me to my feet after I was nearly knocked unconscious. "Are you the one who hit me on the head with a rock?"

"It was a brick, actually." She studies me carefully. "I hear you've been a naughty boy, Detective."

"Why do you say that?"

"You murdered two police officers and committed an act of treason. All in one day. Where do you find the time?"

"No talking business during dinner," the Commandant

cuts in. "I have a treat for us tonight." He removes a wine bottle from a wicker basket and shows us the label. A vintage Burgundy. He pours wine into our glasses. The Commandant then rises to his feet and faces the portrait of Adolf Hitler. He raises his glass. *"Mein Führer."*

Mrs. Davenport looks bemused and glances at me as if we've shared a joke.

When the Commandant takes his seat, the woman sips her wine and makes a face. "An inferior year. I expect you bought it from that Armenian in Geneva."

The Commandant looks stricken. He turns to me. "Women don't have the refined palette that men do. They cannot appreciate fine wine. Don't you agree?"

"The wine is fine," I say.

Mrs. Davenport gives me the finger.

At this point, the anxious lieutenant serves our dinner. Throughout the meal, Mrs. Davenport studies me closely, obviously trying to figure me out. We talk about wine and snow.

"I don't see my purpose here," I say when coffee is served. "You have armed troops ready to deploy. Why do you need me?"

"Don't play games," Mrs. Davenport says to the Commandant. "It's time you told this man the truth. If you insist on having him to dinner, at least be honest. Zorn is useless to us unless he knows what's going on."

The Commandant sighs and drains his wine glass. "I have formed my militias, the signal has been sent, and they have been put on the alert, standing ready to take action."

Signal? Was the destruction of Friendship House the signal to his militias?

"But the situation has changed in the last few weeks. I originally thought that moderately trained militias would be adequate. All they had to do was look menacing and secure unprotected facilities like certain government buildings, communications centers, university campuses. That kind of thing."

"What's changed?" I ask.

"We have recently learned that we may face organized armed resistance. I'm afraid we may have to deal with trained and well-armed opposition."

"If so," I say, "your militias will fold the first time they face hostile fire."

"I'm aware of that. That's why we need you."

"To do what?"

"To provide training—and expert combat leadership. You have that experience."

"Yes, he does have that experience," Mrs. Davenport says, "but remember that he was almost court-martialed for refusing to obey an order."

"He's explained that to me," the Commandant says.

"You're a fool, Myland. You may trust this man. I certainly don't." She turns and looks me directly in the eye. "Why should I believe you?"

"I'm convinced Black Sun will win in your coming struggle. I prefer to be on the side of Black Sun rather than his enemy."

"But you claim to not even know who Black Sun is," she says.

"I don't need to know his identity to be loyal to him."

"What makes you think Black Sun will win?"

"Because Black Sun is a dreamer. I'm told he has

magnificent dreams. Dreams that will change history. In my experience, men with great dreams will always defeat a man with no dream to fight for."

Mrs. Davenport studies me suspiciously.

"What kind of resistance do you expect to encounter?" I ask the Commandant.

"A single brief, but intense firefight—during a critical moment in the final stage of our plans."

"Commandant, why are you in this war?" I ask.

"We live in the cesspool that is America today. The decadent, the corrupt, the immoral run our government, our universities, our society. Our country was built by yeomen farmers. The founding fathers were right. Don't give the mob the vote. Decisions should be left to high-status males." Mrs. Davenport glares at the Commandant. "Slaves and servants, the rabble, the mob—none of them have the character to rule. Today, America has become a garbage heap where the ignorant have opinions and demand to be heard. Even Jews and Negroes and people from other countries who don't even speak English."

Mrs. Davenport rises to her feet, tosses her napkin on the table, and collects her coat, hat and gloves. "I've heard enough. You want high class males to run society. See where that's gotten us! There are no women leaders in your future. I've heard your nonsense rant before, and it bores me." She stops at the door and looks directly at me. "Watch your step, Detective Zorn. I'm keeping an eye on you."

She's out the door and gone.

Evening's entertainment over.

"What do you think of Mrs. Davenport?" the Commandant asks me.

"Unusual."

"You don't know the half of it. She's known as the Bride of the Apocalypse. That's on her good days."

"And on her bad days?"

"She's called The Angel of Death. I try to avoid her on her bad days. Goodnight, Detective."

The last I see of the Commandant, he's standing at the table studying the chess board and our unfinished game, trying to figure out where he went wrong. I have to walk back to the barracks through the snow, on my own. No escort. No fancy car.

Until an hour ago, I thought I knew who Black Sun was. Now I'm not so sure.

Chapter Twenty-Eight

WHEN I RETURN to my barracks after breakfast the next morning, I find a cardboard box on my bunk. Inside is a US Army standard issue M-7 bayonet with a metal sheath. A handwritten note is attached. "I do not concede. We will meet again to finish the game when we have achieved victory." It is unsigned.

The bayonet is dull, and I know I'll have to fix that. We are in the end game, and I'm pretty sure I'm going to need an edged weapon soon. I attach the bayonet in its sheath to my web belt. I'm now properly dressed as a pretend soldier.

A man standing nearby is studying the wall next to my bunk.

"Is there something I can help you with?" I ask.

"I was just admiring what you've carved into the wall," the recruit, Lewis, says without shifting his gaze from the wall.

"You like my graffiti?"

"Actually, it's a graffito. There's only one of them. It appears to be a fragment of a calendar. Am I right?"

"That's possible."

"My guess is that it must be the month of January. This year?"

"Could be."

"But it stops on what appears to be Monday, January 20.

What happens to the rest of the month? Not to mention the rest of the year?"

"You'll have to be patient and wait and see."

Lewis smiles. "Sergeant Porter would not be pleased if he knew you were carving his wall."

"Are you going to be the one to inform him?"

Lewis laughs. "Me? Perish the thought. Sergeant Porter and I do not communicate well."

"So I've noticed."

"That obvious?"

I'm suddenly intrigued. This man is an outlier and doesn't belong here at Camp Rockwell—like me. He's obviously well-educated and does not look like a zealot. What's he doing in a Nazi training camp? I'd better find out.

"My name is Zorn. That's my real name."

"Tim Lewis."

We shake. He studies me with suspicion.

"You don't look like someone whose life dream is to be a Nazi storm trooper," I say.

He shrugs.

"Where do all these kids come from?" I ask. "How did they ever get caught up in this nightmare?"

Lewis glances around the barracks. We're alone. "Social media mostly. These are kids, mostly in dead-end jobs—in dead-end lives. Everything they know they've learned on the internet."

"Why would that drive them to wage war against society? That makes no sense."

"They come from broken families. Drugs. Alcohol. A lot of abuse."

"How do you know that?"

"I've been talking to them. And to some noncoms." Lewis gestures around the barracks room. "This is their escape. Their refuge. They're low-hanging fruit for people like our Commandant to harvest."

"You don't look like low-hanging fruit."

"You never can tell." He shrugs. "I can't wait to see how January turns out."

"Neither can I."

"Good luck with whatever you're doing." Lewis smiles and walks away.

A moment later, Porter enters. He studies Lewis suspiciously, then calls Bravo Company to attention. He establishes a rotating roster for guard duty. He doesn't tell us what it is we're supposed to guard and against what. I'm assigned guard duty for tomorrow night. A lucky break for me.

Next we gather on the exercise field and go through an hour of drills using our M-1 rifles. I'm careful to wear my newly issued bayonet. We don't get much beyond "Present arms," "Order arms," and "Port arms." The exercise is sloppy. After we stumble around in the snow for an hour, a truck picks us up, and we're driven to a firing range a mile from the main camp for live-fire training. We're issued two clips with .30-06 cartridges. A sergeant counts the rounds in each clip. A new guy gives instructions on firing the M-1. It all seems hurried and superficial. The troops soon lose interest and look bored. Most of these kids have grown up with firearms— a lot more powerful and dangerous than the M-1.

I've never fired an M-1 Garand myself. In my day, I mostly used the MK12 SPR, but I grew up hunting with a Remington 700. How hard can an M-1 be? I figure, with some care, I can hit the targets.

As we proceed through the firing exercises, many of the weapons jam, and the shooters are taken off-line. The equipment we've been issued hasn't been maintained and the unit gets low scores. But so do all those using the range today. If these weapons are being issued to the Commandant's militias, they would be better off using them as clubs rather than trying to shoot them.

After completing the live-fire exercise, the sergeant collects the ammunition clips and counts all unused rounds. Obviously, Command doesn't trust any of us with a loaded weapon.

We're ordered to stand down and wait for the truck to take us back to barracks. After a few minutes, I sense I'm being surrounded by a dozen men. Not in a happy "let's get together and be friends, kumbaya" kind of way. But in an angry, "we want to beat the shit out of you" kind of way. Some among them are the men I saw who were trying to torment Charlie Apple.

Lewis stands some distance away, arms crossed, watching us with amusement.

"You need to be taught a lesson." A tall man's lips curl in a snarl. "My friends here don't like your attitude, bitch."

"I can't say as I like yours."

I sense two men are silently circling around behind me. I expect their plan is to grab me by the arms and hold me while the tall man beats the crap out of me. I have a better plan.

"Why don't we all just settle down and relax?" I say. "No need to get all huffy. Let's talk this through. Okay? Sorry about any misunderstanding we had. I hope there are no hard feelings." I smile a broad, friendly, *let's be friends* smile.

Then I kick the man in the testicles with all the force of my heavy combat boot, and he falls to his knees, grasping at his groin, bent over, moaning. A combat boot slammed into one's family jewels will take your mind off whatever else you were planning.

"Bitch," I add.

I spin around. The two men freeze. Their eyes turn to their fallen leader who is now rocking back and forth in a fetal position in the snow, whimpering. They turn and run as fast as they can.

Party's over.

The remaining thugs back away quickly. "Clean up this mess," I say. "We're not supposed to leave garbage when we're done with our games." I step away, allowing them to collect their comrade and carry him to safety. Lewis has disappeared.

Someone calls my name. "Marko Zorn. Stop where you are." It's a woman's voice. "Turn around. Slowly."

I do as directed. There's something authoritative about that voice that can't be ignored.

"You were brawling with other recruits. Fighting is not permitted at Camp Rockwell, Mr. Zorn." Mrs. Davenport smiles at me.

"It wasn't a brawl. It was more like an animated discussion."

"You violated orders."

"What business is that of yours?"

At this point, I sense movement. Two objects are creeping along the ground toward me. They must be Bruno and Ingrid. I hear their guttural growls.

"I make it my business," she says. "I'm in charge of

discipline at Camp Rockwell. And you are very much in need of discipline, dear boy."

"What if I say no?"

"Please don't make this more unpleasant than it needs to be." She turns and walks away. "Follow me."

"I thought we were all on the same side," I call out after her.

"Myland thinks so. He's a fool. I'm not yet convinced about you. You haven't passed my personal test."

I hesitate.

"Move right along, dear."

Bruno and Ingrid growl louder. So I follow her.

Mrs. Davenport leads me to one of the better-maintained buildings in the camp. We do not go to the front entrance. Instead, she takes me to the back of the building where we stop at a door with a sign that reads Official Use Only.

She fumbles in her coat pocket, withdraws a key ring, takes out a key, and unlocks the door.

"In you go, Tiger."

"Why should I do that?"

"Because I tell you to."

The door she opens is made of heavy oak several inches thick. Why such a massive door? *What the hell?* I think to myself. The two dogs growl.

I step into a small room about the size of a large walk-in closet. It's furnished with a single wooden bench. The walls are cedarwood; the place is lit by a single, low-wattage ceiling light bulb. A heating element is built into the wall.

"Is this your personal 'test?'" I ask.

"See you in an hour."

She winks at me and shuts the door, and I hear the sound

of a heavy lock being closed. The light goes out, and I'm in total darkness. I stand still for several minutes, hoping something good will happen. It doesn't. I reach blindly around the space and can touch all four walls from where I stand in the middle. I grope across the space and locate the door. There's no knob or handle on the inside. I fling myself against the door. It doesn't budge. I have some experience breaking through heavy doors, and I know when it's impossible.

One hour, she said. I can deal with that.

I take off my topcoat and lay it on the bench and sit down. Not exactly comfortable, but I'll manage. I wait patiently. A little red light on the wall heating element goes on, indicating someone has turned on heat.

I begin to feel warm. Then warmer. Sweat trickles down my face. The temperature in the space is rising rapidly. Soon, I'm sweating. I grope in the dark for the wall heater, guided only by the little red light, hoping to find an off switch. There isn't one. I realize that the heat is being controlled by someone outside the room.

I take off my boots and wool socks. That doesn't help. Then my fatigues. I lie flat on the bench and try not to move. I seem to remember that moving increases body temperature.

The room temperature continues to rise. I take off my underwear. That doesn't help. I'm soaked through as I lie motionless and naked on the bench in a pool of my warm sweat.

I lose track of time. How long have I been here? My head's beginning to ache. I try to think logically, but I can't make sense of anything. Where am I? And why am I here? *Where* is here? I think I remember meeting a strange woman. I try to sit up but feel dizzy and immediately lie down again. I try to take my pulse, but can't seem to find an artery. Thoughts flood my brain, but they're a jumble and make no sense.

Faces. Places I've visited. Scenes from movies. Some from movies I've never seen. I'm on a white beach somewhere. I'm in the Luxembourg Gardens in Paris. I don't remember seeing crocodiles here. Suddenly it's important that I remember the difference between alligators and crocodiles. I'm losing my mind between moments of lucidity. My tongue sticks to the roof of my mouth.

I'm passing out.

There's a sound at the door. The lock clicks, the door opens, and a blast of freezing air fills the room. I roll off the bench and stand up. I lean against one of the walls to keep from falling.

Standing at the door is Mrs. Davenport. "For heaven's sake, Zorn. Put some clothes on. You look ridiculous."

Chapter Twenty-Nine

I DRESS, SHIVERING. It's dark outside when I leave the hotbox. Mrs. Davenport and the two dogs are gone. I struggle through the snowdrifts back to my barracks, and once inside, I go to a sink in the shower room, turn on the cold water faucet at full blast and drink in great gulps, using my hands to scoop the water into my mouth. That helps some, and my head begins to clear. I lie on my bunk, shut my eyes, and try to make the world stop spinning.

I don't rest for long. Sergeant Porter orders the company to assemble for inspection. I pass with a minimum number of gigs, which infuriates Porter.

Before he moves on to his next victim, Porter punches me in the chest with his index finger. "I've been informed you were brawling this afternoon. That's strictly forbidden."

I take offense at being poked in the chest by somebody's finger. After my time in the hotbox, I have no margin of patience left. Porter must sense the danger and quickly withdraws his finger.

Porter takes out his frustrations on the other recruits, looking for evidence of incorrigible bed-wetting. One of the chief miscreants is Charlie Apple, who stands, red-faced and humiliated, at the foot of his bunk. Porter yells that bed-wetting, along with poor posture, is a sure sign of defective moral character and is in violation of Nazi ideals. Porter then moves on to Lewis and screams at him for several minutes, calling him a retard and a degenerate. Lewis argues back, always a serious mistake during an inspection. Losing all control, Porter yanks the mattress and blanket from Lewis's bunk and flings them to the floor.

After Lewis has reassembled his bed, Sergeant Porter leads us out of the barracks to the chow house, where I eat everything on my tin plate. Mrs. Davenport hasn't ruined my appetite, just my self-esteem.

Lights are turned out promptly at ten. In the dim emergency light, I carve another "X" into the wall calendar. My "X" is larger than the others. It's been a memorable day. I curl up on my bunk and cover my head with the thin pillow to muffle Howard's nightly tirade, and I fall into a fitful sleep.

It's still dark when I'm suddenly awakened. There's activity at one end of the barracks. A cluster of men is huddled near the front door, arguing. By now all the recruits are awake. Some of us gather at the front door to observe.

Several noncoms I don't recognize try to push us away, but we crowd in close.

The front door is wide open, and I slip by the cluster of officers and step outside. I'm only partially dressed, and the cold hits me like a physical blow that takes my breath away. The area is brightly lit by a floodlight above the barracks' door and by flashlights. Somebody, I don't know who, pushes me back inside the barracks with angry orders to stay away. I step back, but not before I see what's lying on the ground.

Lewis is sprawled out in a pool of blood and brains. He's been shot in the left eye.

Chapter Thirty

W E'RE AWAKENED BEFORE DAWN. We dress and march to the large building where, a few days ago, we took our oath of allegiance and learned to salute properly. We're joined by members of other companies, and the hall is packed. Standing along the walls are officers dressed in black. Our Commandant, in full SS uniform, appears. He looks stressed.

There is a heil salute from the assembled recruits, but it lacks conviction. The Commandant returns the salute with a flabby "heil."

Once the troops have settled down and it's quiet in the hall, the Commandant speaks. "Last night at approximately zero three thirty, a spy was exposed. We learned that this man was a newspaper reporter who had infiltrated our ranks." The Commandant's voice is raspy. I don't think he's slept recently. "Let this be a lesson to you all. Never forget. Spies will be executed." The Commandant taps his riding crop nervously against his shiny boot.

A deep hush falls over the crowd. No name is mentioned, but all of us in Bravo Company know that it was Lewis.

"The punishment for spying is death. There is no appeal." He scans his audience. "This man—this spy—has been seen talking to our troops. Questioning them. Trying to expose our plans—our secrets. If any of you have spoken with this spy, tell us now. We must know what kind of questions he was asking. What he wanted to know. Now is the time to speak." The Commandant searches the faces of those seated before him. He points at us with his riding crop. "Sergeant Porter has admitted to talking to the spy. Porter has been properly punished—stripped of his rank. Now is the time for you to speak up. Tomorrow will be too late."

There is frightened silence among the ranks.

The Commandant pauses, and then, he gives a halfhearted Heil salute. "Dismissed!"

We return to our barracks where the mood is somber. Nobody mentions what happened during the night, but it's on all our minds. There is no sign of Sergeant Porter. A couple of new noncoms I've never seen before have taken over, but they don't seem to know what they're doing. Everyone is scared. Even the noncoms. Is Porter being punished for what happened to Lewis? Or for talking to him? The recruits mill around the barracks nervously, whispering among themselves.

We spend the rest of the day at firing practice, once again with poor results. At the end of the day, we have our usual dinner, after which I wash pots and then abscond with two pieces of stew meat. At 11:30, a noncom escorts me to my guard duty post. It's outside the building I think is the command center.

As soon as I'm sure I'm not being watched, I move in close to examine the razor wire fence surrounding the building. The fence has been well installed, and the steel stanchions are sturdy and strong, deeply anchored in the frozen ground. The razor wire is heavy. Even in the dark, I know it would be impossible for me to get through or over the fence without special tools.

During the day, I've seen no movement near the building, but tonight, there is activity at the main gate, with military vehicles entering and leaving regularly. Most of them are trucks and personnel carriers. They arrive at the main gate, guards check the drivers' manifests, the gate is pulled open, and the vehicles enter. A second set of sentries opens the doors to the building, and the vehicles drive forward and disappear inside. The gates close behind them. I can see that the guards are sloppy. They're tired and cold and don't inspect the vehicles either coming or going. These are civilians playing soldier.

Over the sound of the truck engines, I hear another noise. It's close and ominous. The two damn dogs are creeping up on me. "Popcorn!" I call out, recalling the code word Mrs. Davenport used to call off the savage beasts. It doesn't have any effect. I repeat it, louder this time. That usually works with humans. It doesn't seem to work with dogs. It just seem to annoy them. Obviously, Mrs. Davenport has more authority than I have. I rummage around in my pockets, find the chunks of meat I stole from the kitchen, and toss them in the dogs' general direction. The growling stops and the dogs slink away.

Standing just outside the razor wire fence, I monitor the truck traffic, but I know I'm not going to learn anything useful standing here in the snow. I must get inside the building. If I can't get in the back way, I'll have to get in through the front.

Chapter Thirty-One

It's morning, and Bravo Company is trucked to the firing range.

I assume command of my team as the Commandant asked. The only badge of authority is the bayonet at my belt. I introduce the troops to firing-line safety and the rudiments of unit maneuvers. I also try to explain the basics of field medical care. My munchkins are hopeless.

Why do I care?

Do I really want to train these guys and make them into an effective fighting unit? In the end, who are they going to fight? Me? My friends? The US Army? On the other hand, I can't just go through the motions. The officers observing us would see through that, and I'd lose any chance to gain their trust and confidence, so I put on a good show.

At the end of the live-fire session, we return all remaining live rounds, then do some simple tactical squad training, moving through a nearby forest, pretending we're infiltrating an enemy position. Fortunately, I don't lose any of my men, although it comes close.

My men? I catch myself. *What the fuck am I thinking?*

Charlie Apple keeps dropping empty ammunition clips into the snow, and I have to help him find them.

"Thanks, sir." He never uses my name, not even the fake name I've been assigned.

"I want you to find a stone for me," I say to him.

"What kind of stone, sir?"

"A small one. Flat and smooth on one side."

"What's it for?"

"That's a military secret."

On our return to barracks, we march to the dining facility. As soon as I've done my kitchen duty, I slip a couple of pork chops into my pocket. Back in the barracks, I lie on my bed and try to rest. The new noncoms are nowhere in sight. Howard starts a rant about the Rothschilds. I don't care. I won't sleep tonight.

As soon as I'm sure Howard and the other recruits are asleep, I slip out of my bunk, put on my fatigues and combat boots, and leave the building. It's dark, and there's no one around. It's snowing lightly, which is a good thing as it will cover my tracks as I cross the camp, staying close to the buildings to make myself as invisible as possible.

Instead of approaching the command building from the side, as I did when on guard duty, I go to the road leading to the main gate, crawl into a drainage ditch by the roadside, hunker down, and wait. I'm well hidden in the dark. Within a few minutes, three heavy military trucks roll by.

As I wait, I become aware I have company. The two beasts have joined me in the ditch. Slowly, very cautiously, I toss the chops in their direction. They pounce and then approach me, crawling along the ditch, and stop a foot or so away. I reach out and tentatively pat the head of one of them. I think it's Ingrid. Then I pat the other. As soon as I've assured myself that neither plans to remove my hand and that we are all good friends now, I lie still and listen to the sounds of the trucks coming and going. I wait until a convoy of four trucks approaches.

Now's my chance.

I slip out of the ditch, tell Ingrid she's a good dog, dash across the road, and jump onto the rear fender of the last truck in the convoy, hauling myself up by grabbing a handle on the door. As the truck rumbles along the roadway, I press myself flat against the rear panel and hang on.

The truck slows and comes to a stop. We've arrived at the main gates. From my observation, I know the routines of the guards. Two guards will handle the outer gates, swinging them wide open to allow the truck convoy to pass through. A third guard will examine the driver's manifest. The second set of guards manages the inner doors so the trucks can enter the building. No one looks at the backs of any of the trucks.

Within minutes, the truck convoy is inside the building. If anybody looks, I'm totally exposed. I drop to the ground and hide behind a large personnel carrier until I'm sure no one is patrolling this end of the building. The convoy moves to the far end of the building, where it stops, and a dozen men begin loading crates onto the trucks.

I creep along the wall, careful to keep hidden behind rows of parked vehicles. I pass the door to the office where I had dinner with the Commandant and Mrs. Davenport. The room is empty, the lights out.

Every few minutes a new convoy of trucks arrives, and newly loaded trucks depart. I reach an area of the building with large storage bays stacked with crates. As I make my way along the back wall, I'm looking for the cylinders Brückner's agent photographed. There's nothing here like that.

Time to get out.

I move back toward the main entrance doors, preparing to hitch a ride on one of the departing trucks, staying in the shadows as I move.

I'm ready to leap onto the last truck in a departing convoy and make my escape when a voice shouts, "Jesus! Zorn. Don't you ever learn?"

Mrs. Davenport steps from behind a small truck. She's dressed in black military fatigues and wears large green sunglasses. "Wasn't the first time enough?"

"Are you planning on torturing me again?"

"I haven't decided yet." She leans against the truck fender and crosses her arms, regarding me through her sunglasses as if I were some exotic species of insect. "I'm of two minds about that."

"If you'll excuse me, ma'am, I should be getting back to my barracks. They'll miss me."

"You're not going anywhere until I tell you to. And then you'll go where I say."

The men working in the building must have heard our voices, and two armed guards show up and look questioningly at Mrs. Davenport. She waves them away dismissively with the back of her hand.

"Did you find what you were looking for, dear?" she asks. "Zyklon—I assume that's what you're after—is not here. This location is much too insecure. Zyklon is tucked away where you and your friends could never find it. It's cold here, don't you think? Let's go somewhere more comfortable."

Am I due for another visit to the hotbox?

She walks away without looking back. After a moment's hesitation, I follow. We walk out through the main gates of the building, which the guards hold open for us. They make the heil salute to Mrs. Davenport. They obviously know her and are deferential. She makes no effort to return their salute.

I follow her across the campgrounds and soon the dogs join us, loping along at our side. I'm a little anxious, as I have nothing more to offer them.

"What the hell have you done to Bruno and Ingrid?" Mrs. Davenport says. "They were trained to kill. Now you've turned them into fucking lap dogs. You've ruined them. You should be ashamed."

I follow her to one of the trailer homes parked near the command building. She unlocks the trailer door, and gestures for me to go inside.

Chapter Thirty-Two

A SMALL COUCH is tucked into one end of the trailer. Two chairs are set in front of it. In the center of the trailer is a kitchenette and, in back, a bed, covered with rumpled sheets and blankets. The place smells intensely of green jasmine, dense and musky and pungent.

Mrs. Davenport opens a cabinet door in the kitchenette and takes out a bottle of Four Roses bourbon and two glasses. She fills each glass halfway and passes one to me. Then she pulls off her snow boots and sits, barefoot, on the couch across from me. She sips her drink, looking at me over the rim of her glass.

"Why don't you join me here on the couch?"

"I'm fine where I am."

"You're a fugitive from justice, charged with murdering two fellow police officers and stealing top-secret files from the FBI. Someday, you must tell me how you managed that."

I'm silent.

"I'm told you served with the Rangers. General Grant speaks highly of you."

"As you know, Grant tried to have me court-martialed."

"I'm sure he had good reasons. What's important is that you have combat experience. That's what we need just now. That's why you're here at Camp Rockwell. It's the only reason you're still alive.

"What do you think of our troops?" she asks.

"Hopeless," I say.

"The fact that we need you does not mean you're free to snoop around the camp in the middle of the night. By all rights, you should be severely punished."

"Why are we here?"

"You're a policeman and have worked closely with government agencies, including with that witch, Carla Lowry. Is it true you're shagging her? Never mind. I wouldn't believe you whatever you said. My feet are cold. Come here, sit next to me, and rub my feet."

I remain where I am and don't answer.

"You know you want to. Don't be shy."

"Why do you bother to train these troops? For that matter, why do you need me? You have Zyklon."

"You don't know?" she asks, genuinely puzzled.

"Not a clue."

"Zyklon is just one piece of the plan. I certainly don't trust you enough to share our plans, although you may possibly have the opportunity to experience the events for yourself up close. Until then, you'll just have to be patient. You say our troops are hopeless. What would it take to turn them into an effective fighting force?"

"A miracle would help."

"I'm fresh out of miracles. What else?"

"Enough time for real military training."

"We don't have time. January 20 is Inauguration Day. It says so in the US Constitution—the Twentieth Amendment—look it up. What else do you need?"

"Military-grade weapons. Ones that actually work."

"Could you do the job with the right weapons?"

"I could make the troops better than they are now."

"The Commandant can get the weapons you need."

"Would he do that?"

"He'll do whatever I ask. If you cooperate. In the meantime, you still need to convince me you're on our side."

"I've been charged with the murder of two police officers, including my own partner. What more proof do you need that I've switched sides?"

"Not good enough. The murder charges against you are bogus."

"How can you be so sure?"

"Because I know for a fact that you did not kill those two people."

"And you know this how?"

She pauses. "Because I was the one who killed them."

For a moment I can't breathe. My heart is racing. "You killed Latasha?"

She smiles sweetly. "Was that her name? It was necessary. The young woman was snooping around, asking about that damn crossword puzzle."

"So was I. Why didn't you come after me?"

"Because I need you. I didn't need her."

I reach out and grab Mrs. Davenport by the throat. Her neck is slender. My thumb is pressed against her trachea. I can feel her blood pulsing through her left carotid artery. All I have to do is press hard.

Her eyes never leave mine. They show no fear. I release my grip slightly. She speaks.

"I know exactly what you're feeling, my love. You want to crush the life out of me. You want to watch me die in your hands. I can feel your anger coursing through every fiber of your body. I can feel that rage in your hand around my throat."

"But you're not afraid."

"Because I know you won't kill me."

"I wouldn't be so sure."

"Why are you incapable of killing?" she asks. "Do you even know? Maybe you're afraid of finding out. Maybe you're afraid of what you'd learn if you looked too closely into your own soul."

She's wrong. She doesn't know me as well as she thinks.

I take a deep breath and release my hand from around her throat. "I need to know what happened." My voice is shaky. "That moment you killed her." Almost a whisper. But I get the words out.

"Are you sure you really want to know? I advise against that. Don't make me tell you."

I swallow hard. "I must know how Latasha died."

Mrs. Davenport pats the settee next to her. "Come. Sit. Make yourself comfortable."

I don't move.

"I went to the apartment of Billy Collins, the man you tried to arrest. I knew that girl would be coming to investigate him. I stepped out of his apartment, I saw her—what did you say the girl's name was—Latasha? Such an attractive young thing. She was coming up the stairs toward me, accompanied by a uniformed police officer. I waited for them at the top of the stairs. She was no more than ten feet from where I stood. She looked up, and our eyes met. I think she knew in that last second that her life was at an end. I shot her in the head. And the other cop. It was that simple. Satisfied now? It's time we got to know each other better."

"If it's all the same to you, I'd prefer to spend the night in the hotbox."

"I'm not giving you that choice." She studies me with a

steady gaze. "We have a great deal in common, you and I. You probably don't want to hear that, but it's true. I think that's what Cosmo Hunter sees in you. And Myland, as well. That's why they sought you out. They recognize a kindred soul. Come. Sit next to me. Do you want Myland to trust you?"

"Do you mean the camp Commandant?"

"That's right. His name is Myland. And he can get you whatever equipment you need. I can arrange that. Come! Sit."

"Are we negotiating here?"

"Of course we are. Everything in life is transactional, my dear. Get used to it. You know what you have to do. Do we have a deal? God damn it, Zorn! We don't have all night."

Chapter Thirty-Three

It's two o'clock in the morning when I leave the trailer. On the way, I stop and throw up. Back in the barracks, I undress in the dark. I think I may have lost some bits and pieces of clothing somewhere, and I reek of expensive perfume and—what else? I take a long cold shower, scrubbing myself hard with soap until my skin is red. I'm stiff and sore in odd places, and I discover bruises and bite marks I don't remember getting.

Did I pass Mrs. Davenport's test?

No matter how hard I scrub, I can't get rid of her—or a sense of self-disgust. Mrs. Davenport is irresistible and repellent. I've just made violent love to the woman who murdered my partner. I will never forgive her for that. Or forgive myself. But I can't stop thinking about her. I throw up one more time, but I have no retch left.

For Mrs. Davenport, sex and death are two sides of the same coin. I don't think she makes much of a distinction between the two. Mrs. Davenport is obviously unhinged and a mortal threat to me—not to mention to Western civilization—but she's right about one thing. We have much in common, and that's deeply disturbing. The sooner I get away from her, the better. But for the moment, we need each other. We are locked in a demonic embrace.

I don't sleep well.

In the morning, a truck arrives at the firing range, and we unload crates packed with M-16 rifles, all in mint condition. We're also issued ammunition and five M-60 light machine guns. I'm now armed with equipment that actually functions. Maybe my troops will function as well.

The routines of the next few days blend into one another. Each morning, my team is up at daybreak, trucked to the range, and practices firing exercises with the M-16s and the machine guns. All I can think about is Mrs. Davenport.

I show the troops how the weapons are constructed, how they operate, and what they can do. I teach them to disassemble and reassemble the weapons blindfolded. In between, I teach weapons safety. I don't want them killing each other. Not just yet. There'll be time for that later.

We're losing more members of Bravo Company—the troublemakers, the misfits and screwups. I don't want to think about what happens to them. I have a sudden vision of Lewis, his brains staining the white snow crimson. The lost troops are replaced by new men from other companies. It appears Bravo Company has now become the center of training and is going to be the point of the spear in any future combat.

God help us all.

I'm training the new recruits how to kill people. Collectively, they look reasonably sharp on parade. Their range firing is not great but as they're only cannon fodder, it probably makes no difference.

Do I really give a damn?

Each night, after an intensive day of training, I collapse on my bunk bed, ready for sleep. I carve a fresh notch into my wall calendar. I'm running out of blank cells. I'm running out of time.

The rant from the lower bunk begins. At least that takes my mind off Mrs. Davenport.

"Our men aren't ready," Howard says loudly. "They don't know what they're doing."

"They're learning." I hope that shuts Howard up.

Fat chance.

"They're not morally strong enough to fight for our Leader."

Curiosity gets the better of me. I shouldn't encourage this lunatic conversation, but I can't help myself. "Who is this army we're supposed to fight?"

"The Negroes. They should never have been allowed to come to this country. The mud people and the Jews," Howard says. "You know that the story about the Holocaust is all fiction. The Jews invented those stories so we would feel sorry for them and give them all kinds of privileges. The hooked-nosed bankers run everything these days. They run Wall Street, the schools, Hollywood, and the TV. They control the weather. You think hurricanes and tornadoes just happen on their own?"

I pass out and have a nightmare about Mrs. Davenport. The Commandant called her the Bride of the Apocalypse and warned me to be careful.

A little late for that.

At the end of the third day of training with the new equipment, as we're about to board trucks to take us back to the main camp, Charlie Apple brings me a stone he's found. It's been cleaned of dirt and is smooth and flat. I hide the stone in my fatigue pockets and explain to Charlie that the stone must be our special secret.

After lights out that night, I sit on the rear steps of our barracks in the dark. I dribble a small amount of gun oil on the stone, then slide my bayonet blade back and forth over the surface. The blade does not glide easily, but I gradually manage to get something like an edge. I pay particular attention to the weapon's point. My bayonet will be of more use to me as a stabbing weapon than a cutting one. It's nowhere near perfect, but good enough. I hope I never have to take the weapon from its sheath.

When I close my eyes each night and try to sleep, nightmares race through my mind, featuring Mrs. Davenport. During these days, I see no sign of her. I find I'm looking for her everywhere, listening for the sound of her voice. Her trailer is still parked where it was, but there's no sign of activity. What does the Bride of the Apocalypse do on her days off?

And I'm no closer to Zyklon than I was on the day I arrived at Camp Rockwell. In the meantime, I'm training a bunch of yahoos how to use military-grade weapons. My team is nowhere near close to professional military standards, but I know how much damage a .50-caliber machine gun can do, even in the hands of an inexperienced gunner. I'm creating a dangerous force, and I'm dismayed to find that, in my heart, I want to see my troops do well. Shouldn't I be wishing they'd all screw up? Or desert?

What's happening to me?

My only solution is to find Zyklon and see that it's never used. That way, the combat units I'm training won't ever see action. Then my troops can go back to their dead-end jobs, their farms and sports bars, and their weed. Right now, that's my only hope. It's their only hope.

Chapter Thirty-Four

We've just finished a firing exercise when the lieutenant who escorted me to the dinner with the Commandant approaches. "You are to report to the Commandant. Immediately." I follow him, and we climb into a Jeep—no Mercedes for me today.

The lieutenant drives me to the command center building. Today, the front gates are wide open, the guards vanished. Inside, the building is deserted—the vehicles are gone, and the storage bays are empty. There's no one in sight except for the Commandant sitting at a small folding table in his office, smoking a cigarette. He dismisses the lieutenant. There is no sign of Mrs. Davenport. I'm relieved. And yet ... I'm also disappointed.

"Sit down," the Commandant orders.

I give him a Nazi salute—"Sieg." I still play the game, then take a seat at the table.

"Is Mrs. Davenport not joining us today?" I ask.

"She's barking mad. You realize that, don't you? She's not known as the Bride of the Apocalypse for nothing. Just a friendly warning. She's dangerous. She's a vindictive bitch who will fuck you over at the first opportunity. She eats men for snacks."

"I kind of figured that out."

He lights a new cigarette. "Are our troops ready?"

"That depends." I can't bring myself to say "sir." "Ready for what? It depends on the conditions we'll be operating in."

"If we encounter resistance, it will be at close quarters."

"What kind of terrain should I expect?"

"Forget terrain. Your men will be operating underground."

What the hell does "operating underground" mean?

"If we encounter resistance," I ask, "what kind of forces should I expect? Regular military units?"

"We might have to engage paramilitary force. Well-trained and well-armed. That's all you need to know." He opens a file. "There is one part of your background I need to clarify before we move on to your role in the final phase. You were court-martialed while in the US Army. Why was that?"

"I was charged with refusing to carry out a command from a superior officer."

"By what authority did you act? You were not the ranking man in your unit."

"By no authority. I just refused to do it."

"You disobeyed a direct order. You thought you knew better than your commanding officer?"

"I did know better. I was on the scene. My commanding officer was at a forward operating base miles away, nowhere near the action. Our mission was to destroy a building in a small village we were told was a command post for insurgents. As usual, we had bad intelligence. I determined the building was no command center. There were several families living there, including small children. I informed my commanding officer of the situation and told him I was aborting the mission."

"You had no authority to abort the mission."

"Somebody had to do something to prevent a serious crime. I did something."

"Your commanding officer ordered you to go ahead and carry out your orders and destroy the building and all those in it. Is that correct? He ordered you to use hand grenades to clear the area. You disobeyed that order. You refused to carry out a direct order from your superior officer."

"That's about right."

"With people like you in the Army, it's no wonder the United States lost the war. Who was your commanding officer?"

"General Robert Grant."

"That wasn't the end, was it? There was an incident in that village soon after you informed General Grant that you would not complete your mission. What happened?"

"I was patrolling the village with one of my team. We turned a corner and came face-to-face with an armed insurgent aiming a Kalashnikov at us. He was clearly the enemy—just not *my* enemy. He was probably just some local farmer, no more than twenty years old. What he saw were two infidels who'd invaded his country. He was terrified, and he hesitated. That was his mistake. The guy I was with took him out with a three-shot burst."

"Did you learn anything from that experience?"

"Never hesitate."

"You have a reputation for insubordination. You believe you know better than your superiors."

"I do."

"Do you believe you could carry out an order from a superior officer in our new army?"

"I will carry out orders from my superior officer."

"What's different this time?"

"I believe in the cause we're fighting for. I believe in our new Leader. I did not believe in the cause the US Army was fighting for. I did not believe in our leader."

Does he believe this bullshit? If he doesn't buy it, my entire mission is dead.

"What's wrong with you?" the Commandant demands. "Why couldn't you kill that man armed with a Kalashnikov? That's what you were paid to do."

"It's complicated."

"Your refusal to kill is borderline sentimentality. In the new order, there will be no place for compassion or pity. You must be strong. You must be ruthless."

"I'll make a note of that."

The Commandant shakes his head. "Before I decide to assign you to a key role in the critical stage of our conflict, I have one final question for you. Think carefully before you answer. You met with Cosmo Hunter. What did he want?"

"The same thing you want—he wanted to know the identity of Black Sun."

"Did he tell you to kill Black Sun?"

"Yes."

"Why you?"

"Because he's convinced I have a criminal mind."

"Don't you?"

"There are some things I do not do."

The Commandant takes a last drag on his cigarette, then crushes it under his boot. "You're in. Understand—there will be no turning back. Tomorrow begins our final stage, the first day of the end of the world. The true test of your loyalty to the cause. And to your Leader. There will be no day after tomorrow."

Chapter Thirty-Five

TODAY is the beginning of the end.

At just after six in the morning, a noncom shows up in Bravo Company barracks and announces that all routine activities are canceled for the day. He orders us to remain in barracks until further notice. The man distributes armbands, and we're instructed to wear them on our right arm, just above the elbow. The armbands are red with a black circle which, I must assume, is Black Sun. Sergeant Porter is back with us, now stripped of his sergeant's stripes, demoted to insect rank along with the rest of us.

"Keep these on at all times," the noncom directs. "Without your armband, you will be shot."

I sit on my bunk bed and study the calendar I carved on the wall. There's an "X" in all the empty cells except for today and tomorrow. I don't bother to inscribe anything in them. What would be the point? Two days until Inauguration Day. After that, it's end times.

The men in Bravo Company are delighted to stay indoors where it's warm and they can goof off. They shouldn't be delighted. Although I'm uncertain what it's a sign of, I know it's a bad sign.

At noon, the first buses arrive at the camp. They park in the large meadow just south of the main exercise field where they disgorge men who form ranks. All are heavily armed. They then board different buses or military-type vehicles and are taken away.

I'm watching a small army assemble.

Around noon, a second noncom, clutching a clipboard, arrives in our barracks. The recruits of Bravo Company stand at sloppy attention.

"Collect your gear. All personnel are to leave now," the noncom shouts. "You are to board bus number sixty-four, which is waiting at the exercise field. You will then be taken to your next assembly point."

The recruits shrug into their winter coats and boots and shuffle toward the front door.

"The following are to remain here." The noncom studies his clipboard. "Nelson! Howard! Porter! Apple! Front and center!" The four of us form a ragged line. "You are all assigned to a special detail. Until sixteen hundred hours, you are to remain here under the command of Recruit Nelson." He points to me. The other three stare at me in shock. I try to look modest.

"That's impossible!" Porter shouts. "I outrank Nelson. He can't be in charge. He's not an officer. There's some mistake." He glares at me.

The noncom jots something on his clipboard. "Those are your orders. There is no mistake. You will be picked up at sixteen hundred hours, at which time, transportation will take you to your next assignment."

He turns on his heel and leaves. The barracks are empty now except for the four of us.

We glance uneasily at each other. Charlie Apple looks bewildered. Porter is furious. Howard lies on his bunk and sulks. Charlie reads a Spider-Man comic book, then shuts his eyes and sleeps. Porter paces the floor, occasionally looking at me accusingly.

I stand on the front steps of Bravo Company barracks and survey the area. Camp Rockwell is deserted. There's no one in sight. No lights in any of the buildings. No traffic.

"Hey Lover, come to me." Mrs. Davenport stands across the road, wearing a heavy winter coat and knee-high boots. "It's time to say goodbye."

"I'm waiting for my transportation," I say, hoping she'll go away. But also wishing she'd stay.

"It won't leave without you. Trust me." She turns and walks across the empty campgrounds.

What the hell? I can't seem to say no to her. I follow, catching up not far from the command center building. I hope this is one of her good days.

We pass the lot where her trailer was once parked, now gone, and she takes me across the empty field to the blue Sikorsky helicopter.

"Are we going somewhere?" I ask.

"I'm going somewhere. You're staying here. At least until you're told to go somewhere else." She walks around the aircraft, inspecting the exterior and the engine cowlings as part of some kind of preflight check. Her actions are efficient and professional. She knows what she's doing.

"Aren't you going to join us for the big day, Mrs. Davenport? Are you going to miss all the fun and excitement?"

"I'll see that everything goes according to plan. Myland has decided to trust you. I'll be keeping my eye on you, dear. Don't disappoint me." She climbs into the helicopter cockpit. "One last piece of advice. Don't trust Myland. He's dangerous and devious."

"That's what he said about you."

"Did he indeed?" She shrugs. "Today the Commandant needs you. As soon as he stops needing you, he'll kill you. My advice: Kill him first."

Mrs. Davenport disappears into the cockpit, doing whatever pilots do before takeoff. After a moment, the engine kicks in, and the horizontal rotor blades begin to turn, slowly at first, then with increasing speed. The downdraft almost knocks me off my feet.

Mrs. Davenport leans out of the cockpit and waves. "Take care, Lover. I'll be watching you. Don't fuck up. I'll see you on the other side."

The other side of what? I wonder. Before I can ask, she closes the cockpit canopy. A moment later, the helicopter rises, hovers, and then pulls away until it disappears above the trees into the leaden gray sky.

I return to the barracks.

At 15:45, I rouse my troops and tell them to assemble outside the barrack's front door, and there we wait for our transportation. Camp Rockwell is a ghost town.

"Where are the others?" Porter asks.

"They've gone to war," Howard says.

"What war?" Charlie asks.

"The war we're in, idiot," Howard says. "The war to save America." He has obviously been paying attention in class.

A few minutes later, the headlights of a five-ton army truck glow through lightly falling snow and stop in front of us. An officer gets out of the passenger seat and orders us to climb into the back of the truck. There, we sit on wooden fold-down benches. Someone closes the back panels, and a moment later, we're on the move.

I have no idea in what direction we're going. The truck bumps and sways, so I figure we're on back country roads somewhere. I sense, but can't be sure, that we're going up, maybe driving further into the foothills.

We stop after about forty minutes, and someone opens the back panels. The officer orders us off the truck. We're in open country. There are no buildings in sight. No traffic. Not a single light. The wind is blowing out of the hills, swirling snow around us.

"Stay here," the officer says.

"How long?" I ask.

"Until somebody tells you to go somewhere else."

Without another word, he climbs back into the truck, and it drives off, leaving the four of us alone and cold in a snowstorm. I have no idea how long we stand there, stamping our feet to keep our toes from freezing. It's too cold to talk, even to complain. I seriously think of making a run for it. There's nobody to stop me. But where the hell would I run to? I'm in the middle of nowhere. Numb with cold. How far could I get? And what about Zyklon? And Black Sun? I still have a job to do.

After what seems like several hours but is probably no more than thirty minutes, new headlights approach through the snow. It's a panel truck with lettering on the side reading Mike's Plumbing and Heating. The truck is followed by a minibus filled with men. The truck pulls to a stop, and the Commandant steps out. He's quickly surrounded by a half dozen men armed with assault rifles, all wearing Black Sun armbands. The Commandant is wearing a full Nazi military uniform, a pistol in a holster at his waist.

He examines the four of us. "Into the truck. Now!"

A man carrying a submachine gun opens the rear doors of the panel truck, and we hurriedly climb in, grateful to be out of the wind. Inside there are benches on either side. And an iron rack containing cylinders lashed together with steel bands behind the driver's compartment.

I count twenty cylinders. Each is stenciled Zyklon C.

I've reached my goal. I've finally found Zyklon—so close, I can reach out and touch it. *Now what the hell do I do?*

Someone slams shut the truck's back doors, and we're almost immediately in motion. We sit in the dark with no idea where we are and where we're going. At least it's warm. For over an hour, I'd guess, we rock along rough country roads.

I think about escape. I could try to hijack the shipment and drive back to DC to deliver Zyklon in triumph. There are defects to my plan, though. For one, it won't work. At least someone on my team would fight me. Porter and Howard would probably refuse to cooperate. And I'd be shot to pieces by the escort guards. I need a better plan.

We're on smooth pavement—probably some county or state tributary road. We're moving faster on what feels like a highway surface. Then we're in stop-and-go slow mode. I assume we must now be in some urban environment. Maybe there's other traffic. Maybe we're in the outskirts of a city. We're probably encountering the occasional traffic light. We could be anywhere in any city. I've lost track of time and don't even know whether it's night or day.

We come to a complete stop. Outside the van, there is silence. Those of us in the back sit nervously waiting. I'm sure we all sense this is the end of one journey. The beginning of another. Nobody says a word.

After a few minutes, the rear doors open, and the Commandant orders us to get out. We're in an empty lot somewhere, surrounded by a few low-lying commercial buildings. It's almost dawn, and a dim light suffuses the winter sky. Artificial light from distant buildings and street-lights and early morning traffic creates its own dawn. The Washington Monument rises above the horizon.

We've arrived in Washington, DC.

The armed guards are deployed around the perimeter of the lot. In the pale morning light, I recognize some faces. They include recruits I trained. They are among the more competent ones. That gives me no comfort.

Two of the guards wheel up a handcart, and the Commandant orders me and my team to load the Zyklon cylinders onto the cart. We unlash the cylinders from their steel bands and cables, and one by one, we pass each cylinder across the truck bed to one another and then onto the handcart. The Commandant records the numbers written on each cylinder as we load and stack them.

Not far from where the truck is parked, there is a set of heavy iron doors lying flat on the ground, secured by a massive iron chain and several padlocks. The Commandant opens the locks, and two guards pull away the chains and heave open the doors. The Commandant takes a cell phone from the pocket of his topcoat and turns his back on us. It takes him less than twenty seconds to make the call. He's obviously letting someone know he's arrived at his destination. He and Zyklon.

The Commandant puts the phone back into his overcoat pocket, and we follow him down through the iron doors. Inside is a concrete ramp leading down into a dark interior. My detail pushes the handcart through the doors and down the ramp. It's a gentle slope, but I order my team to keep a careful hold on the cart, so it does not get away from us and roll down the slope on its own. I don't want to think about what would happen if one of the cylinders should crash and rupture.

The Commandant leads the way, holding a large flashlight in one hand. Guards armed with assault rifles surround us. Do they have any idea what the cylinders contain?

The doors behind us slam shut with a massive clang, and we're standing in the dark tunnel.

Dante's words come back to me: "Abandon all hope, ye who enter here."

Chapter Thirty-Six

T HE CITY OF WASHINGTON is a whited sepulcher—outside, bright and gleaming; inside, there is corruption and death.

Washington is two cities: the city of the rich and the city of the poor, the city of the powerful and of the wretched, of Black and white, the super educated and high-school dropouts. It's a city of public buildings and gleaming marble monuments, of bronze equestrian statues of past heroes, of parks and tree-lined streets, and it's the city of the homeless.

It's also divided in another way, though only a few see that. There's the city aboveground, but beneath lies a buried city. A city without sun whose permanent residents, except for a few maintenance crews and the occasional lost soul, are rats and cockroaches.

This is the underground world, a world of tunnels and passageways and hidden chambers, sewers, caverns, and corridors lined with cables, air ducts, conduits, pipes carrying water and gas and superheated steam to heat government buildings. And, among them, ancient rivers so old their names have been long forgotten.

Here, entombed beneath the city, are the arteries and the nervous system of a modern metropolis—cables carrying messages at the speed of light: emails, invitations to children's birthday parties, top-secret orders to U.S. Offutt Air

Force Base in Omaha. Television cables carrying reruns of *SpongeBob SquarePants*, game shows, breathless news reports of revolutions and natural disasters from around the world and the deaths of thousands, Major League Baseball and local crime reports. Water and gas lines and high-voltage cable power the city, and miles of telephone and computer cables weave through these dark caverns.

Here is also the city's digestive track, where waste is kept out of sight and disposed of along with the occasional dead body washed down from the storm drains. Rivers of sewage and waste flow through these tunnels beneath Washington's gleaming buildings and broad avenues.

This is a place where those who live in the sun and the fresh air are forbidden to venture. It's been sealed off by government agencies I've probably never heard of. Many of the maps of the tunnels and passages and hidden places are classified top secret; they trace the routes of old water mains and sewage tunnels and ancient rivers. Some maps are so old they're handwritten in fading ink on yellowing, crumbling paper.

No one lives in this underworld except the damned.

Black Sun has found a home here, and I'm entering its underworld through the gates of hell—or maybe a back door to hell. This is where I will confront the true Black Sun. This is where the final battle is about to begin.

The Commandant and I walk along the narrow tunnel for several hundred yards.

"We may run into some resistance," the Commandant tells me. He tries to act calm, but he's obviously nervous. "Nothing we can't handle, but I like to be prepared. There is nothing to be worried about."

Then why do I feel worried?

We stand just a few inches apart in the dark tunnel, only partially illuminated by his flashlight. "There's a dissident group in our ranks, led by a traitor. He may attempt to interfere with my plans."

"You mean there's someone who means to stop you?"

"I mean there's someone here who means to kill me."

"The Führer?"

"There is only one Führer. This man who threatens me is a pretender and a fraud. He is the false Führer. No more questions now. Do your duty, Mr. Zorn. Today we make world history. I hope I can depend on you to play your part. Don't disappoint me."

He turns and studies the map using his flashlight. I stand next to him and try to read the map over his shoulder, but I can't make out the details. All I see is that it is marked Defense Intelligence Agency and is classified top secret.

I gently reach into the Commandant's topcoat pocket. I haven't lost my touch. I'm relieved I can still do a decent dip. I remove the cell phone unnoticed from the pocket.

We're in a narrow, low-ceilinged tunnel that seems to be used for heavy electric cables, which are fastened to the walls with massive brackets. At an order from the Commandant, we move slowly forward. After a few hundred feet, we come to an intersection where two tunnels branch off. The Commandant stops to study his map, then turns to the right and leads us into a larger tunnel. We work our way along a concrete pathway ten feet wide, down a gentle slope. We're heading deeper beneath the city.

The Commandant walks ahead, looking for danger. Listening. It's clear we share these tunnels and caverns with something else. And not a friendly something. We turn into another narrow tunnel; the surface of cracked white ceramic tiles is grimy and damp with water and mold. Along the pavement walls are heavy iron pipes, which, I assume, carry water or gas. Thick bands of electric cables loop from the ceiling. I know we're deep beneath the city now, but I have no idea where.

The Commandant stops and nervously consults his map. I drop back, far enough so he can't observe or hear me. I take out the phone I removed from his coat pocket and quickly dial Carla's number at FBI headquarters. I get a signal on the screen telling me that the number I dialed is blocked. I punch in the number for Kelly Flynn at police headquarters. I get the same message. The Commandant is moving now, and I'm running out of time. I realize some kind of signal jamming system must be activated. That's why the Commandant made his call before entering the underworld. He knew there'd be no cell phone service.

We're in a communications dead zone.

Or are we? I punch in a number I think I remember. This time the call goes through. I get a standard voicemail recording. I have no idea whose. There's no identification. Just a string of numbers. I thank whatever cyber god there may be that there are people who have the technical expertise to override the anti-jamming system. Probably the same people who activated the system to begin with. All I know is that the man who gave me this private number long ago told me to use it. Did he guess then when and where I might do that?

I type a one-word text message. "Zyklon." I hit send, delete, and close the connection. I hope to God my message is read by a friend. Not that I have any friends in this hellscape.

The Commandant is moving again and leads us away from the broad tunnel into a narrow passageway. There's barely room for the handcart with its Zyklon cylinders. I take this opportunity to return the Commandant's cell phone to his coat pocket. At this point, I can only hope that I remembered the number correctly, that my text message was actually transmitted, and that somebody at the other end would know what it meant and how to trace the message back to our location. Whoever receives the text message better be one of the good guys. In this underworld, I should know better—there are no good guys down here. But at least I may have created confusion and chaos. That's something I'm good at.

We're moving in what I think is a southerly direction. I'd assumed we were heading toward the Capitol Building and the temporary reviewing stands constructed in front of it, where the inauguration is to take place later today. Now I sense we're taking a different course. I try to reconstruct the geography of the city in my mind, but I'm thoroughly disoriented. I can't tell where we are or imagine where we're going.

After a half hour stumbling through narrow, dank passages, I sense movement ahead of us. I'm pretty sure it's not sewer rats. I'm right behind the Commandant, and I grab his arm.

"Stop!" I whisper. "We've got company. Cut your light."

The Commandant switches off his flashlight and orders his guards to form a tight periphery around the handcart and its cargo.

There's a flash of light ahead.

"We're ambushed," I yell into his ear. "Hit the ground!"

"They've located us! How the hell did they find us?" the Commandant's voice shakes with panic. I don't tell him how the opposition might have found us.

There are muzzle flashes from further along the tunnel.

Two of Myland's armed escorts crumple to the ground. In the narrow tunnel, the sound of gunfire echoes like exploding mortar shells.

Somebody got my message. I'm not sure whether I should be relieved or terrified. Or both.

I hear more shots ahead in quick succession. One of the men hit in the first exchange of fire lies on the ground next to me, conscious and gasping for help. In the faint light, I recognize the young lieutenant who served dinner at the Commandant's office. The Commandant draws a Luger and fires, putting a bullet through the man's head.

We're in an impossible position, caught in a narrow space. I hope to hell the opposition is not armed with grenades. If they are, we're done for.

"Pull back," I yell. "We've got to get out of here fast. Back into the tunnel we just left. Get out of this space. They'll pick us off, one by one. Your men should take defensive positions here."

"We must save Zyklon. They must not get it."

"My detail will move Zyklon back and take cover." It's time for me to act before we're all killed. "Hold your position here," I order two of the remaining armed troops now lying just ahead of me. "Give us cover. Lay down heavy suppressing fire. Don't let them get past you. As soon as we've formed a defensive position, back down the tunnel and regroup."

The Commandant freezes.

The men sense somebody's taking charge. They'll do what I say until we're no longer under enemy fire.

I order my detail to move the handcart back along the narrow passage and into the wider, open tunnel behind us. We shove the handcart tight up against one wall and regroup at the entrance.

"Who attacked us?" I demand of the Commandant.

"They're traitors," he says, his whisper hoarse. "They're my enemy. And today, your enemy. They were waiting for us. How did they do that?"

The Commandant kneels on the floor beside me. "Is Zyklon safe?" His voice is tense.

I wonder whether a stray round may have hit one of the cylinders. What would that mean? We quickly inspect the cylinders in the dim light, running our hands over their surfaces, looking for ruptures or holes. Even dents. We find no damage.

"You have three choices," I tell the Commandant. "We can retreat back to the entrance to the tunnels where we came in and get the hell out of here. Forget about Zyklon."

"No retreat." The Commandant's voice is hoarse. "Never! We can't let the enemy get Zyklon. What is the second choice?"

"Stay here and die."

"The third?"

"Take some of your men and backtrack through the tunnels, circle around, and attack your enemy from behind. You have a map. Use it! The rest of your men stay here and hold the opposition down. I'll protect the cylinders."

The Commandant nods. He quickly gathers a dozen men, and they all disappear back through the tunnels behind us.

There's a sudden barrage of gunfire from up ahead. I hear a groan and feel the weight of one of the members of my team slump against me. I grab the man by the shoulders and lay him down on the wet concrete floor. In the dim light, I can just make out Sergeant Porter's features. He's breathing—a wet, sucking breath. Porter has a serious chest wound—a round has probably pierced a lung. There's nothing I can do for him. Even if I had light, even with some kind of first aid kit, he's lost.

I hate to lose one of my men. Even if the man is Sergeant Porter—a devoted Nazi, a man who, in another life, would be my enemy. But he's in my detail. For an hour or so, he was my responsibility.

Porter stops breathing. He's gone. My hands are sticky with his blood.

In the chaos and darkness, I could slip away, unnoticed. I could hide in this labyrinth of caves and secret passages for days, maybe weeks. But it would mean giving up Zyklon. Not to mention dying of starvation.

And it would mean deserting my men, most of whom I despise. But for now, they're my men, and I can't just leave them to die in these dark tunnels with the rats.

What the hell is wrong with me?

"Grab the handcart and go!" I order Howard and Charlie.

"What about the Commandant?" Howard demands angrily.

"He'll find us. Go!" The three of us grab the handcart and push it through the corridors, away from the fighting, leaving Porter behind.

We're now back in one of the sewage tunnels. I can't really see it, but I can smell it. Charlie and I are pulling the handcart as Howard pushes it from behind. The path is narrow and the footing slippery. We move along the edge of an open sewer, our feet inches from the brink. We're following a river of excrement.

I consider, for a moment, letting the Zyklon slip into the sewer. I imagine the cylinders sinking slowly below the surface. Then what happens? Would the cylinders corrode, eventually releasing Zyklon gas into the water system? Maybe into the air. Maybe killing thousands.

I wish I knew what the hell I was doing.

Just ahead is a small side shaft, and I tell my detail to move the handcart inside it and wait.

"Why are we stopping?" a voice behind me demands. It's Howard.

"Moving so close to the edge of the sewer is dangerous. A false step would be fatal."

"We must protect the Commandant." Howard stands inches away from me. "We can't be separated from our Leader."

"We stay here," I yell back. "I'm in charge of the detail."

"You're a traitor. I saw you sharpening your bayonet." Howard is losing control. "I've seen you carving things into the barracks wall. You college boys are traitors."

The tunnel is narrow, and there's no room for me to maneuver. I press myself hard against the shaft wall. Howard lunges at me. I feel his foot slip on the slimy stone floor. He tries to grab me but loses his grip.

I hear a strangled cry as Howard slips and falls away into the blackness. Then he's gone. I reach out to grab him, but he's already beyond reach, and he sinks slowly below the surface, swept by the current of excrement under a low arch.

Into what?

"Move," I yell at Charlie. "Grab the cart." We push the cart along the corridor, then come to an intersection with two tunnels branching off. I don't recognize either. I have no idea where we are.

"Don't stop!" I yell. Behind are voices. Gunshots. A muffled explosion. They do have grenades.

We're in the middle of a goddamn war.

We enter a wide corridor, dimly lit by overhead fixtures. The walls here are of wood. Signs read, "Authorized Personnel Only," "Command," and "Officer of the Day." There's a sign with a magenta trefoil on a yellow background.

"Are we gonna be okay?" Charlie Apple whispers in my ear. He's afraid. Why shouldn't he be?

"Stick close to me. We'll be fine." I'm lying, of course, but what's the point in telling the truth? I've never found it to be helpful.

I try the first door. It's firmly locked. The next door. Same thing.

The third door swings open, and Charlie and I quickly step into a dark room.

"Shall I kill them both now, sir?" a voice asks from the darkness.

Chapter Thirty-Seven

"I'VE BEEN WAITING for you, Detective Zorn."

Ceiling lights flicker on.

I'm standing in what looks like a regular business office. The walls are maple veneer. Two metal office desks fill the center of the room. On each desk, there's a purple blotter and a pencil holder, a telephone with a rotary dial, and a manual typewriter. There are steel filing cabinets and, on the walls, a poster labeled Emergency Evacuation Plan, a calendar showing the month of August 1953, and a photograph of President Dwight D. Eisenhower. A clock shows the time—8:23. The hands are motionless.

I'm in a fucking time warp.

This place must have been constructed as a bomb shelter sometime in the late forties or early fifties. It would have been abandoned long ago, useless against a nuclear attack on Washington. But it's still here—silent and empty—patiently waiting.

Sitting at one of the desks is Cosmo Hunter. Behind him stands Drago Escher—Cosmo's driver, guard dog, and shrink—holding a double-barreled shotgun pointed steadily at my head.

"It took you long enough to bring me my Zyklon," Cosmo murmurs.

"I ran into traffic."

"Bring Zyklon into the room, Mr. Zorn. Quietly. No sudden moves, please. Dr. Escher here is eager to cut your throat. Don't provoke him."

"I can dispose of them both right now, sir," Escher says.

"Not yet, Doctor. I must ask this man a question first. Then he's yours. When you do dispose of him, don't use that cannon you're carrying. The sound will draw the attention of Myland and his troops and bring them here. Use your knife."

"Don't hurt the boy," I say. "He's an innocent bystander."

"Nobody's an innocent bystander in this world. Bring the handcart into the room."

Charlie and I drag the handcart stacked with Zyklon cylinders through the door. Cosmo Hunter rises, closes the door, and gently caresses one of the cylinders, his fingers gliding along the metal surface.

"Have you figured out the identity of Black Sun?" Cosmo asks.

"I have."

"When?"

"The moment your brother, Myland, told me he was in Mexico City on June 12."

"Why was that relevant?"

"Because I know that Black Sun was in DC and Mexico City on that same day. There's only one way Black Sun could have been in two places at the same time. There are two Black Suns. You are one."

"Very good, Detective."

"Not good at all. It means there are two Hitlers ready to seize power after the overthrow of the United States Government. Two men who are now engaged in mortal combat. You and your twin brother, Myland, are both the Anointed One. You are both the Risen Hitler."

"I am Black Sun. I am the Führer. Myland is a fraud. I have always been and will always be Black Sun. That is my fate."

"I wouldn't depend on fate, if I were you. Fate betrayed Adolf Hitler once before. In 1945, in Berlin, when he lost the war."

"Fate didn't betray Adolf Hitler. Adolf Hitler betrayed fate. He hesitated at that last moment. He failed to use Zyklon against his enemies. He lost his nerve. That will not happen again. All that remains for me is to destroy Myland and allow destiny to take its course."

"You and Myland are identical twins. Am I right?"

Cosmo hesitates. "From a strictly biological point of view. For the first months of our existence, while still in our mother's womb, we were joined. We shared the same placenta and competed for oxygen and for nourishment. Even then, we struggled for survival. From the moment of our inception, we were competitors and enemies. When we were born, we were conjoined, and a surgeon had to separate us. As soon as I was old enough to hold a weapon, I left my mark on him."

"No more talk!" Dr. Escher shouts. "It is time for action."

I ignore Escher. "Is this your little hideaway, Cosmo? Is this where you spend your days planning the destruction of your brother, Myland? You, who own and direct the most modern communications technologies in the world? You write letters on a manual typewriter? You use a rotary phone? A little retro, don't you think?"

"I prefer the old ways. I don't trust microchips or computers or algorithms."

"But you yourself designed the most modern computer technology."

"That's why I don't trust it. Modern technology gets between me and the person I speak to."

"Now that you have possession of Zyklon, does that make you the true Black Sun?"

"I have always been the true Black Sun. I am the Anointed One."

"Your brother will try and stop you."

"He may try. Where is Myland now?"

"Somewhere in this warren of tunnels and passages. I expect he's hunting for you at this very moment."

"He's still fighting his pointless war? Still lost in his mad dream of world conquest, is he?"

"I thought dreams were supposed to be a good thing."

"Not Myland's dreams. His are fever dreams—nightmare fantasies. He lives his life playing soldier. I'll see that he dies playing soldier. Myland will never leave this underworld alive. Nor will you. Did you not get my warning?" Cosmo goes to the door. "I'm going to join my men now. I will find Myland and put an end to this farce. Doctor, you stay here. When I return, we'll move Zyklon to the target area. In the meantime, you can dispose of them both if you wish, although the little one is useless, and Zorn is no threat either. He's incapable of killing."

Cosmo leaves, and Escher and I study each other, anticipating the other's next move. But I have the advantage. I know he won't use the shotgun. He's afraid of Cosmo's disapproval.

But he's going to kill somebody. His bloodlust is up. I see it in his mad eyes. He yearns to kill. He's going to shift the shotgun to his left hand to free his right hand.

He's still too far away.

"Tell me something, Drago ..."

"It's Doctor."

"Okay, Doctor. Aren't you doctors supposed to help

people? Don't you guys take some kind of oath? Like, 'do no harm?'"

He laughs. "I must have skipped class that day." He steps toward me to study my face.

Just a little closer now.

"You're not afraid of me," I say. "Why aren't you?"

"Because I know you're not capable of killing me in cold blood. From a strictly clinical point of view, you're an intriguing mystery."

One step closer, Doctor.

"Are you speaking as a trained psychiatrist?"

He looks deep into my eyes.

What does he see there?

"I'd say you experienced a profound psychic trauma a long time ago. Probably when you were young. You did something that scarred you for life. You killed somebody. Is that it? You've experienced profound guilt ever since. That's your problem." He shifts the shotgun to his left hand. This is the end game. "Now is your chance to atone for your acts. Your last chance, Detective. You have one minute left to express regret. Then I will cure your problem. For good. No charge. Professional courtesy." Escher is holding his knife. "Okay, Charlie," Escher says under his breath. "If that's your name, come out here. Let's get this over with. Then your friend here ..." He gestures with his knife at me.

"Is that your diagnosis, Doctor? I suffer from some kind of guilt complex?"

"Very good, Zorn. We're close to resolving your problem. I believe you once killed someone, and you've felt guilty about it ever since. It's emasculated you. That's your problem right there."

"It's true, I did once kill a man in cold blood. But you're

wrong about one important thing. I never regretted what I did. And that's my real problem."

A bayonet is not a throwing knife. It's far too heavy, and the balance is all wrong. But when you've got nothing, nothing will have to do.

Escher's face contorts with rage and pain as he looks down at the bayonet now buried deep in his gut, just below the rib cage. He tries to shift the shotgun back to his right hand, but it's too late. He sinks to his knees. He mumbles something, but his mouth is filled with curses and blood, and it's hard for him to talk.

I kick the shotgun across the room, well out of his reach.

I've just killed a man. I don't know how I feel about that.

I pull open the office door, and Charlie and I push the handcart into the corridor. I take a last look at Dr. Escher, slumped on the floor, then switch off the lights.

This office and its occupant will have to wait a while longer for Armageddon.

Chapter Thirty-Eight

THE SOUNDS OF COMBAT reverberate through the passageways. Small-arms fire and the quick bursts of machine-gun fire are not far off. Here we're in an echo chamber of tunnels, and I can't tell how far away the shooting is and from what direction.

Charlie and I stumble through one tunnel after another, pushing the cart with the Zyklon cylinders, until we reach a passage maybe twenty feet wide and fifteen feet high, dimly lit by a few ceiling lights. Fastened to the walls are massive pipes, covered in heavy insulation, secured by steel bands. I'm pretty certain these are pipes bringing high-pressure steam from one of Washington's central heating plants.

The gunfire is moving closer.

I press my hand against the insulation covering the super-heated steam pipe. It's scorching hot, and I snatch my hand away.

I turn to speak to Charlie, and I'm suddenly face-to-face with a man in a Nazi uniform clutching an M16 assault rifle. He's just a kid—he can't be over sixteen or seventeen—and he stares at me, wide-eyed, scared out of his mind. Like that kid in the village years ago.

He's the enemy. Just not my enemy. In his panic, the kid hesitates. That's a mistake. I leap forward and hit him in the gut with my fist. He doubles over. I hit him again with a quick jab to the back of his head, and he's out. At the far end of the tunnel, a dozen armed men erupt from a side tunnel.

"Is he dead, sir?" Charlie asks. Breathless.

"He'll be okay."

The armed men are charging us.

"Charlie," I yell, "Run! As fast as you can. As far as you can. Run like hell! Now."

"Where to, sir?"

"Anywhere but here."

Charlie turns and disappears.

I snatch the M16 from the hands of the unconscious kid and fire, point-blank, into the steam pipe above my head, emptying the full clip. The insulation shreds. Some of the rounds pierce the pipe's metal casing. I spin away to avoid the superheated steam now erupting from the pipe. In seconds, scalding steam is filling the tunnel.

I grab hold of the handcart and push it forward, moving fast. I reach an opening to a narrow side passage. I glance quickly behind me and see the armed men who were charging me collapse, overwhelmed by the superheated steam.

I feel severe pain on my left shoulder and arm and parts of my neck. My tunic protected me some, but I know I have suffered bad burns. As I plunge through the dim tunnels and passages, the searing pain increases. I need a doctor. But I've just killed the only doctor in the house.

As I sprint through the tunnels, I keep having the sense I'm being watched—that I'm not alone in this underworld. Twice, I stop and look into the darkness. And listen. Nothing.

The gunfire has stopped.

I emerge at last into a wide, cavernous space. Somewhere

there's the sound of flowing water. I know there was once a river down here called Tiber Creek running from the base of the Capitol Building into the Potomac River, through what is today the National Mall. I must be near the old riverbed now. The river was buried underground long ago and forgotten. That means I must be somewhere beneath Constitution Avenue paralleling the National Mall, probably heading generally east, toward the Capitol Building. My worst fears are confirmed. I must be close to what Cosmo referred to as the target area.

I stumble forward, and suddenly I'm standing on the banks of a small stream—what was once Tiber Creek. Two hundred years ago, this grass-covered embankment was a swampy meadow where people came to fish for herring and perch.

I don't have time to contemplate what this place was like then. I have something more immediate to worry about.

Standing at the edge of Tiber Creek is the Commandant, who I now think of as Myland Hunter. He's holding Charlie Apple in his grip, his Luger pressed against Charlie's head.

Chapter Thirty-Nine

W E WALK QUICKLY through the tunnels, Charlie and I pushing the cart loaded with Zyklon cylinders, Myland Hunter close behind, his Luger pressed against the back of my head. We enter a gallery twenty feet wide, the ceiling above ten feet high. Two of Myland's guards, each holding an AK-47, are stationed at the entrance. They salute Myland with a Nazi salute, arms raised stiffly, as we enter.

We have arrived at our final destination.

A little sunlight streams through small gaps in the ceiling, forming a latticework on the concrete floor. We must be just below street level here. The daylight filters through a manhole cover above us. Judging by the bright sunlight streaming into the gallery, it's morning now. The snowstorm must have blown over, and it's a sunny day in Washington — a perfect day for an inauguration.

A stainless steel pipe rises from the floor to the ceiling, its top secured to the manhole cover on the street above us. A large tank sits on the floor, connected to the pipe by a heavy, flexible metal tubing attached to a round wheel, the rim attached to the hub by three iron spokes. It reminds me of the Wewelsburg Mosaic — a circle linked by spokes, connected in the center to a black hub. The symbol of Black Sun.

Along one wall is a shelf that holds radio and communications equipment. And a television set.

Myland aims his Luger at me. "Do you know what my men just found? Drago Escher, Cosmo's mad-dog drug supplier. With a bayonet stuck in him."

"Dead?"

"Very. What's more, the bayonet looks just like a standard US Army issue. Like the one I requisitioned for you. And you seem to be missing yours. The only way you could have gotten the drop on a professional killer like Drago Escher is if he'd let down his guard. He must have turned his back on you. I won't make that mistake. You've not been honest with me, Mr. Zorn. You led us to believe you don't kill in cold blood. Drago must have bought into your scam. That wasn't very sporting of you."

I say nothing. *What is there to say?*

"Where is Cosmo?" Myland demands. "I know he's down here somewhere. I sense him nearby, prowling these tunnels and sewers."

"The last time I saw Cosmo, he was searching for you. I think he means to kill you."

"Have you joined his side? Have you betrayed me and joined forces with Cosmo?"

"I don't have a dog in this fight. You and your brother Cosmo can both go to hell."

"I should kill you now, but I've lost most of my men, thanks to Cosmo. So, I need you and your little friend for one final task."

Charlie and I spend the next hour attaching hoses—very carefully—that link each Zyklon cylinder to the central tank. Charlie proves adept at securing the connections. Better than me.

"I was a plumber's apprentice," Charlie murmurs to me. "I know washers and valves."

When we're finished, the Zyklon cylinders are linked to street level. Black Sun is now armed and ready.

"Time's up, Detective."

"Your brother will find you. He will defeat you."

"My brother? When did you know?"

"When you told me you were in Washington on June 12. But Black Sun was in Mexico City that same day and at almost the same time. I realized that Black Sun had to be two people. Except, in a sense, you are one person, isn't that right?"

Myland's face flushes with rage. "Cosmo and I were once a single zygote. After conception, that zygote split into two embryos. Only then did we become two—me and Cosmo. Two distinct people." Myland touches the scar that disfigures his face.

"He carved that scar into your face to leave his personal mark. You and Cosmo are both Black Sun."

"Cosmo is not Black Sun." I can see the loathing in Myland's eyes. "I am. I have always been. I will always be Black Sun."

"Don't be so sure. Cosmo believes he's the Anointed One. It is he who will be the new Hitler."

"Cosmo is the false Hitler!"

"Cosmo and his men have eliminated most of your troops—swept the board of your pieces. What's to stop him from checkmating you and becoming the unchallenged Black Sun?"

"It's too late. Without Zyklon, Cosmo is helpless. Without Zyklon, he is nothing." Myland glances at his watch. "It's time. The president is on his way. It will soon be over." He switches on the TV resting on the shelf, and its screen glows to life.

A woman appears on the screen announcing that the new

president and the first lady are heading for the presidential limousine to take them to the White House.

"We're right on schedule," Myland says.

"But your target is miles away."

Myland doesn't answer, glancing instead at his watch.

I suddenly understand. "You're not going to the president. The president is coming to you."

"He's following a strict schedule established months ago. They must keep to it. After all, the motorcycle police serving as the honorary escort are already mounted on their bikes. Military units are in position. The Shriners are waiting impatiently. Hundreds of members of high-school marching bands from all over America are standing in the cold, waiting to march down Pennsylvania Avenue. We must not keep them waiting."

The announcer says: *"The president and first lady are boarding the presidential limousine."*

"You know your brother Cosmo is insane," I say. "He's a psychopath."

"Of course. Everyone knows that."

"I suppose it runs in the family."

"That's what they say. Being insane is no disqualification for being a world leader. Sanity creates doubt. That leads to hesitation. A true leader can never have doubts. He must never hesitate."

"What happens when the president arrives?" I ask.

"The president's limousine will stop at the Navy Memorial." Myland points to the ceiling above us. "That's just over our heads. Secret Service agents have been prepositioned at this location for hours. In just a few minutes, the president, flashing his brightest and most ingratiating smile, will emerge from the limousine, accompanied by the lovely first lady. They will wave to the spectators lining the parade route. The president will mix with the crowd. Of course, he is heavily protected. Secret Service agents surround him. Agents have been mixing with the happy crowd all morning. Snipers patrol from the roof of the National Archives building, just across Pennsylvania Avenue, scanning the crowd with high-powered binoculars. The area is patrolled by uniformed men and women from military units. DC police line the streets. Every eventuality has been thought of. The president is invulnerable."

"*The president's limousine is moving down Pennsylvania Avenue.*" The TV announcer is almost breathless.

Myland studies the screen. "The president will walk along the rope line, shaking hands with his adoring public. He is scheduled to remain at the Navy Memorial for exactly seven minutes. At 2:40, the president and the first lady will return to the limousine, to continue their trip to the White House. And to destiny."

"What role does Cosmo Hunter play in all this?"

"Cosmo plays no role. He ceased to exist years ago."

"Where is the vice president?" I say, getting ready to make my move.

"He's in his own limousine some distance from the president's cortege. He'll stay a safe distance away. We wouldn't want to take the spotlight from our new president, would we?"

"*The president is approaching the Navy Memorial,*" the announcer says reverently.

"What happens now?" I ask.

"When the president and first lady are about to return

to the limousine—at 2:40 Eastern Standard Time—I will turn this valve, and Zyklon will be released. I have insisted on reserving that honor for myself. That's in four and a half minutes. After a sleep of seventy years, Zyklon will awake and escape through the manhole cover above us to street level. It will spread over the surrounding area. This will kill everyone nearby, depending on the wind, of course. We estimate a minimum of two hundred people will die within minutes, including spectators, Secret Service agents, nearby military, and police personnel. And, of course, the president. There's enough Zyklon in these cylinders to kill a thousand people. But we figure a few hundred deaths will be an adequate demonstration."

The rumble of hundreds of police motorcycles overhead is getting closer.

I move so that I stand between Myland and the release valve.

"All this will be on national television," Myland goes on. "The death agony of the Leader of the free world. The death agony of democracy in America and all it stands for. This will be a moment when history begins again." He is staring intently at the screen.

"The murder of the president will just make people mad," I say.

"Of course, it will make people mad," Myland says, still watching the screen. "And afraid. That's the whole point. They will see the assassination of a popular American political figure as a further sign of the collapse of our society and our country—indeed the collapse of Western civilization. The public will search for enemies. And the internet will provide many. We have bots that are ready to go—illegal immigrants are responsible. Black militants did it. The Jews are behind the conspiracy. Arabs and Muslim extremists planned it all. Your choice. It will be all over the internet in minutes. Every conceivable conspiracy theory will be broadcast. There will be riots. The news will show men in the streets burning police cars. Black men looting liquor and grocery stores."

The sound of hundreds of police motorcycles vibrates the space. They're passing along the street right above us.

The president is coming.

"What if there are no riots? No looting?"

"We have plenty of stock footage. It's all theater. It doesn't have to be real. It will feel real, like the country is descending into chaos and anarchy. We will see that it does. We have deepfakes ready to be released showing the president's opponents taking credit for his murder. The people will demand that a strong man take charge and exact revenge. The president must die to make room for the new leader. This has been the way of power for thousands of years—the eternal return."

On the TV screen, the president, smiling broadly, is emerging from his limousine. He waves to the cheering crowd.

Something metal is tossed into the room.

"Secure the space!" Myland orders. The two armed guards move to block the entrance.

"Lie flat, as close to the floor as you can," I yell to Charlie Apple. "Hands over your head. Cover your ears." I duck behind the large tank that sits on the floor.

There's a blinding flash and a deafening sound I feel in my bones. When I open my eyes, the lights in the room have been blown out. The blast destroyed the two guards at the entrance. The tank I'm hiding behind has been deeply dented but has suffered no serious damage. Myland Hunter has been thrown back against the far wall and is struggling to his feet, holding his Luger.

A flashlight beam sweeps over the two dead guards. A figure stands at the entrance, his face lit by the light from the manhole cover above us. "Myland," Cosmo calls out. "You're supposed to be fucking dead. Be a good boy and die."

My ears are ringing, and I can't make out what the TV announcer is saying.

Myland recovers his balance. He's been wounded and is bleeding from his arms and chest. There's a large cut on his forehead. He aims his Luger shakily at his brother Cosmo.

The two men stand in the dim light streaming down through the manhole cover above us. Cosmo and Myland are identical. Except Myland's face is disfigured by his vivid scar.

"Myland, you've ruined everything," Cosmo screams.

"See you in hell!" Myland fires his Luger.

Cosmo jerks back but is still standing, bleeding from a wound in his left shoulder. Myland steps closer for another shot. They're barely two feet apart now. He fires. Nothing happens. The clip is empty.

"The president and first lady leave the limousine and wave to the cheering crowd."

"Don't interfere." Myland Hunter's voice shakes. *Fear? Rage?* "This is my time."

"Never!" Cosmo lurches forward and grabs Myland by the throat. For a moment, they struggle in each other's arms. Cosmo breaks away from the embrace. He's badly wounded, his shirt soaked with his blood. He stumbles backward.

There's cheering from the street.

Cosmo reaches down and snatches an AK-47 from the hand of one of the dead guards.

He fires, and Myland Hunter collapses.

Cheers from the street.

Cosmo points the gun at me. "You! Open the valve."

I thrust my arm through the spokes of the release valve. Now it can't be moved unless I disentangle my arm from the wheel. Cosmo will have to go through me—dead or alive—and remove my arm to release Zyklon. "No."

"Now! Open the valve!"

"No."

Cosmo takes a step closer to me. "Let go of the valve!"

"Fuck you!"

"Have it your way. Your funeral." He slips his finger around the trigger. "Bye-bye."

Cosmo Hunter's head explodes.

Chapter Forty

CHARLIE APPLE holds the AK-47 in both shaking hands. His face is white. He stares in horror at what's left of Cosmo Hunter. At what he's just done.

"Did I do wrong?" Charlie's voice is almost a whisper.

"No, Charlie. You did right," I say as I disentangle my arm from the wheel spokes.

I snatch the AK-47 from Charlie's trembling hands, wipe off his prints, and toss the gun away.

Above us, from the street, I hear cheering. The president has left the scene to continue his journey to the White House. I take the secret map from Myland's pocket.

You saved American democracy, I think, but I don't say that. Explaining this to Charlie would be too much for him to bear. He's better off not knowing.

Above us I can hear the sound of a marching band approaching. They're playing "Stars and Stripes Forever."

"What just happened?" Charlie gasps, pointing at Cosmo and Myland Hunter, both crumpled on the floor.

"Nothing, Charlie." I grab him by the arm and pull him quickly out of the chamber. "Forget everything that happened here today, Charlie."

Of course he can't forget.

"Never tell anyone about what you saw," I say, "or what

you did here. Not one single word. Not to your family. Nobody. Do you understand?"

He nods in silent, shocked agreement.

"Let's go, Charlie," I say.

Following the map, Charlie and I eventually find our way to an outlet from hell, and we emerge from the Washington underworld, blinking into the sun. We're on the far north side of the National Mall. Most of the crowd, gathered to witness the inauguration, has dissipated. There are distant sounds of marching bands on Pennsylvania Avenue.

We walk quickly to a nearby bus station where we find a group of teenagers hanging out in the food court. I sell them the arm bands we were issued, telling them they were a special insignia for an elite SS unit. I use the money to buy a ticket and put Charlie on a Greyhound bus to take him home. I don't expect to see Charlie Apple ever again.

I make my way across the Mall to police headquarters, where Kelly Flynn sees to it that I'm not shot on sight. I spend the next six hours in a series of interrogation rooms, where an army of bureaucrats questions me and I sign multiple forms, all marked Top Secret. I'm only fitfully truthful about what happened at Camp Rockwell and in the sewers and tunnels beneath the city. I never mention the name Charlie Apple.

When my interrogators finally finish with me, and I've signed all their forms that I fail to read, I'm escorted to Kelly Flynn's office. Waiting for me there are Kelly, Carla Lowry, and Walter Brückner.

I'm offered some much-needed coffee and a dried-up cheese sandwich and proceed to tell them what happened, trying not to contradict what I told my interrogators earlier today. I skip over some details.

Carla tells us that technicians from the US Army's Chemical Biological Center have removed Zyklon from beneath Pennsylvania Avenue and have taken the cylinders to their secure laboratory in Edgewood, Maryland.

"I suppose that puts an end to the assassination plot. The revolution will have to wait," Carla says. She studies me closely, expecting me to agree. I am silent.

"You left quite a mess down there," Carla says. "Among other things, the brothers Myland and Cosmo Hunter, the two richest men in the world, were found dead. We also found a man who we think was Cosmo Hunter's assistant. He was killed by an Army bayonet. Marko, please tell me you had nothing to do with any of this."

"Me? Certainly not. I was hiding in a small tunnel the whole time."

"What can you tell us about Bobby Grant?" Carla asks, diving right into the heart of the matter. "Can I charge him with treason?"

"My guess is Grant knew what was going on. But he's not smart enough to have planned any of this himself and was probably not trusted enough to be involved in the details at any stage."

Kelly sighs. "Then we have nothing on Grant."

"I wouldn't worry about Bobby Grant," I say. "If he knew about the plot to kill the president, that means he knows far too much about Black Sun. It's only a matter of time before Black Sun comes for him. Some morning, he'll be found dead in the White House Rose Garden. Do you think Grant will get a state funeral?"

"Not my department, thank God," Carla says.

"What happened at the end with the Hunter brothers?" Kelly says.

"They killed each other," I say, without elaboration.

"Good," Kelly says. "Less of a problem for me. I don't understand why the brothers recruited you, Marko, to find Black Sun. They each knew from day one who Black Sun was."

"They were each competing with the other to seize control of the Black Sun organization. They both dreamed of becoming the new Hitler—creating a Nazi Reich in America. Each used his vast economic resources to finance a neo-Nazi network in order to seize power as the reincarnated Hitler. They didn't know the other brother's plans, so each independently recruited me. They knew I didn't belong to either camp. They thought I knew or could find out what the other brother was up to."

"Now that two of the richest men on the planet are dead, who gets the world?" Brückner asks. No one has an answer.

"What did Myland and Cosmo Hunter plan to achieve?" Kelly asks.

I don't say these words: *They planned, each in his own way, to buy America. We came close to a fire sale.*

"What about that woman you spoke about in your debriefing today?" Carla asks. "You referred to her as Mrs. Davenport. The lady does not appear to exist. I've had my people do a deep search for her. No such person has ever been issued a birth certificate, a Social Security number, or a passport from any country. She's never voted in an election, paid taxes, or applied for a credit card."

"I wouldn't worry about it," Kelly says. "Mrs. Davenport exists only in Marko's fever dreams."

Carla gets to her feet before I can argue. "I've got to get back to my office."

I don't think Carla wants to hear details about the Bride of the Apocalypse—delusional or, worse, real.

"Me too," Brückner adds. "Berlin is getting frantic." He probably feels the same way about Mrs. Davenport.

Kelly and I are left alone.

"One moment, before you go," Kelly says to me. "I've arranged to have all charges for the murders of Latasha and Sergeant Findley quashed. I'm afraid we will never learn who the true killer was. Carla has done the same on the Federal espionage charges. You're no longer the country's most wanted criminal."

"Do I get a raise?"

"There's one more thing." She reaches into a desk drawer and removes an object wrapped in tissue. "Carla's people did a search of your home while you were away, and guess what they found?"

It's my cigarette lighter.

"It was in my goddamned safe," I say. "They had no business searching my safe."

Kelly picks up the lighter and examines it. "I didn't think you smoked."

"I don't."

"Why do you carry this around?"

"It suits me."

"There's a name engraved on the lighter. It says 'Carla.' I thought you might want it back."

There's an awkward silence. I know Kelly wants to ask me about Carla. And about Mrs. Davenport. But she doesn't. Now is not the time. The others think Mrs. Davenport is an illusion. Kelly isn't so sure.

I know she's real. I have the wounds, scratches, and bite marks to prove it.

I get to my feet and go to the door. I should go before Kelly changes her mind and gives me a third-degree interrogation about what happened with Mrs. Davenport. And I have things to do.

When a man's partner is killed, he's supposed to do something about it.

Mrs. Davenport and I have unfinished business.

THE END

Acknowledgments

My heartfelt thanks to my agent, Judith Ehrlich, for her encouragement and guidance in the jungle of writing and marketing fiction; to Laura Apgar, Dr. Audrey Farley, and Wyn Cooper for their careful reviews of the manuscript, thoughtful editing, and creative advice; to Amy Cecil Holm for final copy editing; to my Project Manager Meg Gilbert for her invaluable help. And a special word of thanks to Ludovica Villar-Hauser and her company Parity Productions. Ludovica not only produced and directed two of my plays in New York and London but has provided advice and encouragement throughout the writing of this book. *Black Sun Rising* would not be possible without creative support from my publisher Meridian Editions and the promotion team at Meryl Moss Media Group.

And thanks most of all to Therese, my wife, who has to put up with me.

About the Author

OTHO ESKIN is a graduate of Bowdoin College in Bruns-
wick, Maine, and The George Washington University Law
School in Washington, DC, where he received a Juris Doctor
law degree. After serving in the Army, he joined the United
States Foreign Service. During a career of over twenty years,
he was stationed in Washington, DC, and in Damascus,
Syria, Belgrade (then capital of Yugoslavia), Reykjavik,
Iceland, and Berlin (at the time the capital of the German
Democratic Republic [East Germany]). He had special as-
signments to New York, Geneva, Switzerland, and Caracas,
Venezuela. He was vice chairman of the United States del-
egation to the United Nations Conference on the Law of the
Sea. He participated in the negotiations on the International
Space Station, was the principal US negotiator of several
international agreements on seabed mining, and served as
US representative to the United Nations Committee on the
Peaceful Uses of Outer Space.

He speaks French, German, and Serbo-Croatian. He was
a frequent speaker at conferences and testified before the
US Congress.

Otho's career in the Foreign Service helped prepare him
for thriller writing. In several of his foreign assignments, he
served in countries governed by hostile, sometimes unstable,
regimes. While stationed in East Berlin during the Cold War,
for example, the East German Intelligence Service (Stasi),
operating on behalf of their Soviet masters, tried to target

him as a spy. They listed him in a book entitled *Who's Who in CIA*, suggesting that Otho was a US intelligence agent. He was not.

At another post, one of Otho's casual contacts was arrested, charged by the regime with espionage, and publicly executed by hanging in a public square. Otho observed this horrific event in person—and it haunts him to this day. It is a constant reminder that espionage and black operations, the source of thriller stories that entertain readers, have real-world life and death consequences.

On retirement from the Foreign Service, Otho took up writing plays and thriller novels. His first thriller, *The Reflecting Pool*, introduced Marko Zorn, a maverick Washington, DC, homicide detective—dangerous and unpredictable, a bit louche, and a cynical troublemaker and hustler who refuses to play by other people's rules but has a strong moral center. Marko hates guns, preferring instead to use his wits to get out of trouble when threatened by his opponents.

Otho's plays have been produced in Washington, New York, London, and elsewhere in Europe.

Otho is married to writer Therese Keane, and they live in Maryland.

www.OthoEskin.com